AHSOKA

E. K. JOHNSTON

DISNEP

LUCASFILM
PRESS

LOS ANGELES · NEW YORK

SUSTAINABLE
FORESTRY
INITIATIVE
Certified Chain of Custody
Promoting Sustainable Forestry
www.sfiprogram.org
SFI-01054
The SFI label applies to the text stock

To the Royal Handmaiden Society.
We are brave, Your Highness.

MANDALORE BURNED.

Not all of it, of course, but enough that the smoke filled the air around her. Ahsoka Tano breathed it in. She knew what she had to do, but she wasn't sure it would work. Worse, she wasn't sure how long it would work, even if it did. But she was out of options, and this was the only chance she had left. She was there with an army and a mission, as she might have done when she was still Anakin Skywalker's Padawan. It probably would have gone better if Anakin were with her.

"Be careful, Ahsoka," he'd told her, before handing over her lightsabers and running off to save the Chancellor. "Maul is tricky. And he has no mercy in him at all."

"I remember," she'd replied, trying to scrape up some of the brashness that had earned her the nickname Snips the first time they'd met. She didn't think the effort was tremendously successful, but he smiled anyway.

"I know." He rolled his shoulders, already thinking of his own fight. "But you know how I worry."

"What could happen?" Acting more like her old self was easier the second time, and then she found that she was smiling, too.

Now, the weight of her lightsabers in her hands was reassuring, but she would have traded them both for Anakin's presence in a heartbeat.

She could see Maul, not far from her now. Smoke wreathed his black-and-red face, though it didn't seem to bother him. He'd already put aside his cloak; battle-readiness oozing from his stance. He was in one of the plazas that wasn't burning yet, pacing while he waited for her. If she hadn't known that his legs were artificial, she never would have guessed they weren't the limbs he'd been born with. The prosthetics didn't slow him down at all. She walked toward him, determined. After all, she knew something she was pretty sure he didn't.

"Where's your army, Lady Tano?" he called as soon as she was within earshot.

"Busy defeating yours," she replied, hoping it was true. She wasn't going to give him the pleasure of seeing how much his calling her Lady Tano hurt. She wasn't a commander anymore, even though the battalion still treated her with the same courtesy they always had, because of her reputation.

"It was so nice of your former masters to send you out alone and spare me the exertion of a proper fight," Maul said. "You're not even a real Jedi."

Malice dripped from his every word, and he bared his teeth at her. His was the kind of anger that Master Yoda warned the younglings about, the sort that ate a person whole and twisted every part of them until they were unrecognizable. Ahsoka shuddered to think what Maul must have suffered to become this way. Still, she was smart enough to use it to her benefit: she needed him angry enough to think he had the upper hand.

"It'll be a fair fight then," she retorted, looking him up and down. "You're only half a Sith."

That was rude for no reason, the type of thing that

would've had Master Kenobi rolling his eyes, but Ahsoka couldn't bring herself to regret it. Taunting one's enemy was customary, and Ahsoka was going to use all the cards she was dealt, even if it wasn't polite. He was right, after all: she was no Jedi.

Maul was stalking sideways with a dark feline grace that was oddly hypnotic and twirling the hilt of the lightsaber in his hand. Ahsoka tightened her grip on her own lightsabers and then forced herself to relax. She needed him to come closer. It was a bit like meditation, this waiting. She knew it had worked against Maul before, on Naboo when Obi-Wan beat him the first time. She reached out to the Force and found it waiting for her, a comfort and a source of power. She opened her mind to it and listened with every part of her that could. Then she moved, mirroring Maul across the plaza and taking one step back for every step he took toward her.

"No Jedi, but still a coward," he said. "Or did Skywalker forget to teach you how to stand your ground before he threw you aside?"

"I left under my own power," she told him. In the

moment, the words felt like the truth despite the pain that lay underneath them. She ignored the hurt and refocused on her sense of balance, on Maul.

"Of course. And I volunteered for that garbage pile, and those first monstrous legs," Maul said mockingly. She felt his rage swell within him, almost to the breaking point but not quite yet.

He activated the lightsaber and quickened his steps. It was easy for her to pretend he'd caught her off guard, to stumble backward, away from his vengeful charge.

"I'll bet you volunteered for this, too, Lady Tano," he crowed. That much was correct, but he could perceive only her weakness. His anger blinded him to all else. "One last attempt at glory to impress a master who has no further use for you."

"That's not true!" she shouted. Just a little farther now. He was almost ensnared.

He bore down on her, cruel laughter scraping out of his throat, and still she waited. Then, just before she was in his reach, she sprang the trap.

The familiar hum sang as she activated her lightsabers

and moved to engage, one last feint. Maul lunged forward and Ahsoka took a quick step back, drawing him past the point of no return. He swung down, directly at her head, and she responded with all her strength. Her weapons locked with his, holding him exactly where she wanted him to be.

"Now!" she commanded her unseen allies.

The response was fast, too fast for Maul's distracted defense. Ahsoka threw herself clear just in time.

The ray shield came to life, trapping her prey with his lightsaber still raised against her.

01

SHE WAS ALONE, something she was never meant to be. Her people were tribal, blood and bond, and her ability to use the Force gave her a galaxy of brethren from all species. Even after she left the Jedi Temple, she could feel the others when she wanted to—the ebb and flow of them in the Force around her.

Until, of course, she couldn't.

Now she almost preferred the solitude. If she was alone, she didn't have to make choices that affected anyone other than herself. Fix a malfunctioning motivator or not, eat or not, sleep or not—dream or not.

She tried to dream as little as possible, but that day in particular wasn't good for it. Empire Day. Across the galaxy, from the Core to the Outer Rim—though somewhat less enthusiastically in the latter—there would be festivities commemorating the establishment of order and government by Emperor Palpatine. It was the first such celebration. The new Empire was only a year old, but the idea of celebrating the day at all nauseated her. She remembered it for entirely different reasons than peace.

Mandalore had burned, and even though she, Rex, and the others had managed to save most of it, their victory had been immediately undone with such violence that Ahsoka could hardly bear to think about it. So she didn't.

"Ashla!" The voice was loud and cheerful, wrenching her from her memories. "Ashla, you'll miss the parade!"

Living in the Outer Rim had its benefits. The planetary populations were small and not highly organized, making it easier to live under an assumed name. She could also easily stay far away from any of the major hyperspace lanes. Most of the planets in the Outer Rim didn't have anything interesting enough to attract Imperial attention anyway, and the last thing Ahsoka wanted to do was attract attention.

What she hadn't accounted for was the attention of her neighbors, the Fardis, a local family who seemed to have their fingers in every bit of business that happened on Thabeska. They took her under their wing—as much as they could with Ahsoka maintaining her distance. She was still grieving, in her own way, and it helped if she told herself that she didn't want new ties, new friends.

Thabeska suited her. It was dusty and quiet, yet there were enough newcomers that she didn't stick out. The planet did a brisk trade in water and tech, but nothing on a large scale. Even the smuggling operations—luxury goods and off-world food for the most part—catered to a relatively small number of people. No self-respecting pirate of Ahsoka's acquaintance would stoop so low. It was as good as any new place for "Ashla" to call home.

"Ashla, are you in there?" the girl outside shouted again. Too cheerful, Ahsoka thought with a shake of her head. Empire Day wasn't that exciting, even if you believed in the propaganda. The girls were up to something, and they wanted her to know it.

Ahsoka considered her options. She was known for wandering out onto the flats alone. There wasn't anything dangerous there, and certainly nothing that would be dangerous to her. So she could sit quietly, pretending she wasn't home, and if anyone asked later, she'd just say she'd gone for a walk.

She stood and crossed the floor of her tiny house. It wasn't fancy enough to have rooms, or even room dividers, but one of the things growing up in the Jedi Temple prepared a person for was austerity. If Ahsoka didn't own things, she had less to carry with her when it was time to go. She tried very hard not to think about the empty weapon belt she had kept, though she didn't wear it.

She had heard the warning in the girls' show of cheerfulness as they called to her, but she needed more details. The only way to get them was to open the door.

"I'm coming, I'm coming!" she said, hoping she sounded enthusiastic.

Ahsoka had met the Fardi clan at the shipyards when she'd arrived on the planet. They ran most of the shipping from there, legal and otherwise. Ahsoka would have avoided them entirely, except the younger ones followed her about like ducklings and she hadn't worked up the bile to discourage them yet. She opened the door and found four of them staring up at her, with a couple of the older girls behind them. The older ones didn't look as carefree as the little ones did. Ahsoka tensed and then forced herself to relax. She reached out with her senses, very carefully, but if there was something to feel it was still too far away.

"Ashla, you have to come right now," said the eldest. There were so many Fardi children that Ahsoka struggled to remember which name belonged to whom. She looked down at them and had a nagging feeling that she was forgetting something.

"Yeah!" said one of the gaggle of children. "Dad's got fancy guests asking to meet any new people, and you're new, so you should come! You can sit with us for the parade and flyby."

A year's residency still qualified Ahsoka as new, even though it was the longest she had stayed on a single planet since she'd become Anakin Skywalker's Padawan.

"There are a lot of ships in the yard right now," the eldest one said carefully, as though someone might be listening to her every word. "For the flyby. From all over the place. Security's a disaster as they try to log everything."

Out here, fancy guests meant clean clothes. Even the well-off Fardis were always coated with the dust that blew in off the flats. Ahsoka imagined the crisp lines and dull colors of Imperial uniforms. They would make an impression on Thabeska.

Ahsoka knew what the Fardis would do. They had their legitimate businesses to consider, not to mention all the family members. They would tell the Imperials anything they wanted to know, and Ahsoka couldn't hold it against them. She had apparently made a good enough impression to warrant the visit and the hint about the shipyard. It was as much as Ahsoka could expect.

"Why don't you guys go on ahead?" she said, and nodded solemnly to the older girls. She didn't know if their parents knew they were here, but she wanted to let them know she appreciated the risk they were taking. "You can save me a seat while I clean up. I slept in a bit this morning, and I can't go to the Empire Day parade like this."

She gestured down at her clothes. They were the only ones she owned, and everyone knew it, but it was enough of an excuse to get the job done.

The little ones chorused entreaties that she hurry up but promised to save a place for her. The older two stayed quiet and herded their siblings back toward the center of town. Ahsoka didn't watch them go. As soon as they turned around, she shut the door and took a moment to gather herself.

She didn't have a lot to pack. Her single room was bare except for the bed and thick floor mat where she might have entertained guests, had she ever received any. She rolled the mat aside and uncovered the compartment where she kept a little currency and her blaster. She threw everything in a bag and put on a short cowl that would cover her face. She was going to have to get a new one soon: her head had grown again, and her montrals were almost too tall for the hood.

As she shut the door of her house for the final time, the air was split by an all-too-familiar whine. The flyby had started, and it seemed that the Empire was showing off the maneuverability of its latest fighters.

The streets were deserted. Ahsoka could hear the music, raucous and martial at the same time, as the parade passed along the main avenue several blocks over. She couldn't figure out why there were so many Imperials all of a sudden. Surely Empire Day wasn't the only reason. But the planet didn't have much besides dust and the Fardis. And a survivor of Order 66.

Two armored Imperials rounded the corner. Ahsoka held her breath and reached out. There was nothing familiar about them. They weren't clones. They were the newer recruits, the stormtroopers. Nothing much to worry about then.

"What are you doing here?" They raised their guns. "Why aren't you at the festivities?"

"I'm on my way," Ahsoka said, careful to keep her face

pointed at the ground. "I was out on the flats this morning, hunting, and lost track of the time."

"Move along," said the stormtrooper, though he didn't lower his gun. The other one said something into his comm that Ahsoka couldn't hear.

"Happy Empire Day," she said, and turned down an alley in the direction of the music.

She didn't wait to see if they would follow her. She jumped to a first-story window and climbed up the building until she reached the roof. So close to the main Fardi compound, the houses were nicer than her little shack. They were taller and had flat roofs. More important, they were built very close together, to save on construction costs. It wasn't a perfect traveling path, but for someone with Ahsoka's abilities, it was passable enough.

Hoping that no one could see her, she ran along the tops of the houses. Even with the danger, it felt better than anything Ahsoka had done in a long time. She didn't use the Force to run—there was no point in taking unnecessary risks—but she did use it to make sure each jump across the streets below was safe. Every time she looked down, she saw more stormtroopers patrolling. They didn't appear to be searching for a specific target, though. The pair she'd talked to must not have raised any alarm.

Ahsoka reached the edge of the row of tall houses and crouched, looking down over the shipyard. There were two under the Fardis' control, and this was the smaller one. The bigger one would have had a larger selection and possibly more holes in its security system, but the smaller one had a roof approach, so Ahsoka decided to take her chances here.

The ships were mostly Imperial, and therefore not good targets. They would have been registered and tagged, and probably had some kind of tracking device. Ahsoka looked at the troop carrier with some regret. Of all the ships docked there, it was the one with which she was most familiar, but she couldn't take the risk. Instead, she focused on a small freighter tucked in at the very back of the yard.

It was a Fardi ship, one of the legal ones, but Ahsoka knew it could be made less legal very quickly. The Fardis paid her to tinker. She was a good mechanic, and she'd earned their trust through diligent work. The ship was also unguarded. Ahsoka didn't know if it was an invitation or not, but she wasn't about to let the opportunity pass her by.

There were maybe twenty stormtroopers in the yard.

Before, when she could openly use the Force, that would have been no trouble at all. Now, with just her blaster, Ahsoka took a moment to consider her options.

Anakin would have crashed right through, regardless of personal risk. Even without his lightsaber, he'd have been fast enough and strong enough to make it. It would have been very noticeable, though. Explosions had tended to follow close behind her old master. She missed the excitement, but this was not the time for it. Master Obi-Wan would have tried to charm himself through and would invariably have ended up making as much noise as Anakin anyway.

"When are you going to admit you're on your own?" Ahsoka muttered. "They're gone. They're dead, and now it's just you."

As motivational speeches went, it was not her best, but it did spur her into action. She risked a jump from the rooftop to the alley below, prioritizing speed over anything else. She pulled the blaster out of her bag. Quickly, she unseated the overload dowels in the ammo pack and set the blaster on the ground. Now she had to move. She ran down the alley and leapt over a short wall into a family garden. A few steps and another jump took her to a different alley, and she raced toward the shipyard.

She reached the open area just as the blaster exploded. The stormtroopers reacted immediately, falling into neat lines and running toward the noise with admirable dedication. They didn't completely desert the yard, but it was good enough for Ahsoka's purposes.

Ahsoka stuck to corners where she could hide and behind crates to block the remaining Imperials' sight lines. She reached the ramp of the Fardi ship and was aboard before anyone was the wiser.

"I hope I'm not stealing anything you need," she said to her absent benefactors. "But thanks for the ship."

The engine hummed to life just as the other stormtroopers returned to the yard, but by then it was too late. Ahsoka was in the air before they could set up the heavy weaponry and out of range before they could fire. She was away, on the run again, and she had no idea where in the galaxy she was going to go next.

02

FROM ORBIT, Raada didn't look like much. The readout from the navicomputer wasn't particularly enthralling, either, but that was part of Ahsoka's reason for choosing the moon. It was small, and out of the way even by Outer Rim standards, with only one resource. Ahsoka could be unremarkable here. She didn't like to make the same mistake twice, and she had made a big one on Thabeska, getting involved with one of the planet's most prominent families.

Ahsoka set the ship down in what could barely be called a

spaceport and secured it against theft as best she could. While in transit, Ahsoka had made some modifications to the vessel, hoping to conceal where she'd gotten it from, and discovered that a fairly sophisticated ground-lock system was already in place. Recoding it had been relatively straightforward, even without an astromech droid like R2-D2 to help. She did one final check, her eyes drawn to a pair of metal rings that demarcated a pressure valve on the power console. The rings had no purpose beyond making the panel look clean and tidy. Ahsoka pried them loose and pocketed them without much more thought. That done, she shouldered her bag and walked down the ramp.

On the ground, Raada had a distinctive, though not altogether unpleasant, odor. There was life on the moon's surface that the computer didn't account for: green and growing. Ahsoka could sense it without effort and drew in a deep breath. After a year of either space or Thabeska's dust, it was a welcome change. Perhaps when Ahsoka meditated here, she would find something between her and the yawning gulf that had haunted her since Order 66.

A few people were in the spaceport, loading crates onto a large freighter, but they ignored Ahsoka as she made her way past them. If there was someone she was supposed to pay for a berth, Ahsoka didn't find them, so she decided to worry about that later. A place like Raada had even less of a legitimate government than Thabeska or a Hutt-controlled world, but Ahsoka could handle any local toughs who thought she might be easy pickings. What she needed now was a place to stay, and she knew where she wanted to start looking.

Raada had only the one major settlement, and Ahsoka would not go so far as to call it a city. By Coruscant standards, the settlement barely existed at all, and even the Fardis would have turned their noses up at it. There were no tall houses, no rooftop highways, and only one market near the dilapidated administration buildings in the center of town. Ahsoka headed straight for the outskirts, where she hoped there would be an abandoned house she could borrow. If not, she'd have to start looking outside of the town.

As she walked, Ahsoka took note of her new surroundings. Though the architecture was monotonous and mostly prefabricated, there was enough decorative embellishment that she knew the people who lived in the houses cared about them. They weren't transient workers: they were on Raada to stay. Moreover, judging by the variation in style, Ahsoka could tell that the people who lived on Raada had come from all over the Outer Rim. That made the moon an even better place for her to hide, because her Togruta features would be unremarkable.

After a few blocks, Ahsoka found herself in a neighborhood with smaller houses that had been cobbled together with no sense of aesthetic. This suited her, and she set to looking for one that was uninhabited. The first one she found had no roof. The second was right next to a cantina—quiet enough in the middle of the day but presumably loud and obnoxious at night. The third, a couple of streets over from the cantina and right on the edge of the town, looked promising. Ahsoka stood in front of it, weighing her options.

"There's no one in it," said someone behind her. Ahsoka's hands tightened on lightsaber hilts that were no longer there as she turned.

It was a girl about Ahsoka's age, but with more lines around her eyes. Ahsoka had spent her life on starships or in the Jedi Temple, for the most part. This girl looked like she worked outside all the time and had weathered skin to show for it. Her eyes were sharp but not vicious. She was lighter than Master Windu but darker than Rex, and she had more hair than both of them combined—not that that was difficult—braided into brown lines neatly out of her way and secured behind her head.

"Why is it abandoned?" Ahsoka asked.

"Cietra got married, moved out," was the reply. "There's nothing wrong with it, if you're looking for a place."

"Do I have to buy it?" Ahsoka asked. She had some credits but preferred to save them as long as she possibly could.

"Cietra didn't," said the girl. "I don't see why you should."

"Well, then I suppose it suits me," Ahsoka said. She paused, not entirely sure what came next. She didn't want to volunteer a lot of personal information, but she had a decent story prepared if anyone asked.

"I'm Kaeden," said the girl. "Kaeden Larte. Are you here for the harvest? That's why most people come here, but we're almost done. I'd be out there myself, except I lost an argument with one of the threshers yesterday."

"No," said Ahsoka. "I'm not much of a farmer. I'm just looking for a quiet place to set up shop."

Kaeden shot her a piercing look, and Ahsoka realized she was going to have to be more clear or she'd stick out in spite of herself. She sighed.

"I repair droids and other mechanicals," she said. She

wasn't as good as Anakin had been, but she was good enough. Away from the Temple and the war, Ahsoka had discovered that the galaxy was full of people who were merely good at things, not prodigious. It was taking her a while to readjust her way of thinking.

"We can always use that," Kaeden said. "Is that all your stuff?"

"Yes," Ahsoka said shortly, hoping to discourage further questions. It worked, because Kaeden took half a step back and looked embarrassed.

"I'll let a few people know you're setting up when they get in from the fields tonight," she said, before the pause grew uncomfortably long. "They'll be along tomorrow with work for you. In a few days, it'll be like you've never lived anywhere else."

"I doubt that," Ahsoka said, too low for Kaeden to hear. She cleared her throat and spoke louder. "That will be fine."

"Welcome to Raada." Kaeden's tone was sardonic, a forced smile on her face, but Ahsoka smiled back anyway.

"Thanks," she said.

Kaeden walked back up the street, favoring her left leg as she went. The limp was not pronounced, but Ahsoka could tell that the injury was painful. That meant medical treatment on Raada was either expensive or unavailable. She shook her head and ducked through the door of her new house.

Cietra, whoever she was, was clearly no housekeeper. Ahsoka had expected some mustiness, given the abandoned state of the house, but what she found was actual dirt. The floors and the single table were coated with it, and she was a little worried what she might find on the bed. Ahsoka ran a finger across the tabletop and discovered that the dirt was mixed with some kind of engine grease, which made it sticky.

"The things Jedi training doesn't prepare you for," she mused, and then bit her tongue. Even alone, she shouldn't say that word. It felt like betrayal, to deny where she'd come from, but it wasn't safe and she couldn't afford to slip up in public.

Ahsoka found a cupboard that had cleaning supplies in it and set to work. It was an easy job, if tedious, and strangely satisfying to see the dirt disappear. The cleaner wasn't a droid, but it was efficient. As it hummed around the room, Ahsoka was able to find the best place in the house to hide her things.

The panel under the crude shower came off and revealed a compartment just large enough for her stash of credits. Everything else went under the bed, once Ahsoka finished disinfecting it. Then she sat cross-legged on the mattress and listened to the cleaner circumnavigate the room. Its hum reminded her of the training spheres she'd used as a youngling. She closed her eyes and felt her body ready itself for the energy bolt, though she was pretty sure the cleaner wasn't going to shoot her.

From there, it was easy to fall into her meditation. For a moment she hesitated, afraid of what she'd seen—*not* seen—since the Jedi purge, but then she let herself go. Meditation was one of the things she missed most, and one of the few things that wasn't likely to get her caught, even if someone saw her doing it.

The Force felt different now, and Ahsoka wasn't sure how much of the difference was her. By walking away from the Temple, from the Jedi, she had given up her right to the Force—or at least that's what she told herself sometimes. She knew it was a lie. The Force was always going to be a part of her, whether she was trained or not, the way it was part of everything. She couldn't remove the parts of her that were sensitive to it any more than she could breathe on the wrong side of an airlock. Her authority was gone; her power remained.

But there was a darkness to her meditations now that she

didn't like. It was as if a shroud had been wrapped around her perceptions, dulling her vision. She knew there was something there, but it was hard to make out, and she wasn't entirely sure she wanted to. The familiar presence of Anakin was gone, like a disrupted conduit that no longer channeled power the way it was meant to. Ahsoka couldn't feel him anymore, or any of the others. Even the sense of the Jedi as a whole was gone, and she'd been able to feel that since she was too small to articulate what it was that she felt. The feeling had saved her life once, when she was very young and a false Jedi came to Shili to enslave her. She missed it like she would have missed a limb.

The cleaner ran into the bed platform twice, stubbornly refusing to alter its course. Ahsoka leaned down and turned it in the other direction. She watched it for a few moments before she retreated back into her meditation, this time not quite so far. She wanted to get a sense of Raada, something more than her initial response could tell her, and this was as good a time as any to do it.

The moon stretched out around her. She was facing the center of town, so she reached behind where she sat. There were the fields, mostly harvested as Kaeden had said and ready for the next season's planting. There was stone, rocky hills and caves where nothing useful could grow. There were large animals, though whether they were for labor or food, Ahsoka couldn't tell. And there were boots, dozens of them, walking toward her.

Ahsoka shook herself out of her trance and found that the cleaner was cheerfully butting itself against the door to the shower. She got up to turn it off, and the new sound reached her ears: talking, laughing, and stamping feet. Her new neighbors were home from their day's work in the fields.

CHAPTER

03

KAEDEN SHOWED UP on Ahsoka's doorstep bright and early the following morning with two ration packs and a—

"What is that?" Ahsoka asked, staring at the mangled bits of scrap Kaeden held under her arm.

"Your first patient, if you're interested," Kaeden replied cheerfully.

"I can't fix it if I don't know what it was supposed to do in the first place," Ahsoka protested, but held out her hands anyway.

Kaeden took this as an invitation to enter. She deposited the broken pieces into Ahsoka's hands and then sat on the bed, putting the rations down beside her.

"It's the thresher I lost a fight with," Kaeden said. If she felt strange about sitting on the place where Ahsoka slept, she gave no sign. Then again, the bed was Ahsoka's only furniture, besides the low table.

Ahsoka spread the pieces on the table and sat down on the floor to look at them more closely. She supposed that the contraption might have been a thresher. But it could have also been a protocol droid, for all the mess it was in.

"I'd hate to see what happens when you *win* fights," Ahsoka said.

"It was not my fault." Kaeden said it with the air of a person who has made the argument, unsuccessfully, several times before. "One moment we were cruising along, set to make quota and everything, and the next thing I knew, disaster."

"How's the leg?" Ahsoka asked. Her fingers moved across the table, rearranging parts and trying to figure out if anything was salvageable.

"It'll be well enough to go back to work tomorrow," Kaeden said. "I'll keep my harvest bonus, particularly if I don't have to pay to replace the thresher."

Ahsoka gave her a long look.

"I'll pay you instead, I mean," Kaeden said quickly. "Starting with breakfast. Dig in."

She tossed Ahsoka a ration pack. Ahsoka didn't recognize the label, except that it wasn't Imperial or Republic.

"No place like home," Kaeden said, ripping her own pack open. "There's not much point in living on a farm planet if you have to import food. These just make it easier to keep track of who gets what."

"I guess that makes sense," Ahsoka said. She tore the packaging open and took a sniff. She had definitely eaten worse.

"Anyway, can you fix my thresher?" Kaeden asked.

"Why don't you tell me what went wrong with it, and I'll see what I can do," Ahsoka said.

She turned back to the table and continued to move the parts around while Kaeden told her about the mishap. Ahsoka was used to the way clones told war stories, but Kaeden could have given them a run for their credits. To hear her tell it, the thresher had suddenly developed sentience and objected to its lot as a farming implement, and only Kaeden's quick thinking—and heavy boots—had prevented it from taking over the galaxy.

"And when it finally stopped moving," Kaeden said,

winding up, "my sister pointed out that I was bleeding. I said it was only fair, since the thresher was bleeding oil, but then I passed out a little bit, so I guess it was worse than I thought. I woke up in medical with this fancy bandage and the stupid machine in a tray beside my cot."

Ahsoka laughed, surprising herself, and held up a bent piece of what had once been the thresher's coolant system.

"Here's the problem," she said. "Well, I mean, part of your problem. If you can replace this, I can rebuild the thresher."

"Replace it?" Kaeden's smile died. "Do you think you can just, I don't know, unbend it somehow?"

Ahsoka looked down. This wasn't like the Temple, or even her field experience commanding troops. There were no supply lines and no backup, not without cost. Replacement was a last resort.

"I can give it a shot," she said. "Now tell me more about how things work around here."

The previous night, Kaeden had not been overly curious about Ahsoka's reasons for coming to Raada. As the girl chattered on about work rotations and crop cycles, it occurred to Ahsoka that having reasons might not be important. As Kaeden described it, Raada was a good place to lead an unmomentous life: hard work, ample food, and just enough official enforcement that local freelancing was discouraged. No one asked too many questions, and as long as you met your work quotas, your presence was unremarkable. Ahsoka Tano wouldn't do very well here, but Ashla would do just fine.

Ahsoka looked for something heavy she could use to hit the metal. If she was going to fix things professionally, she was going to have to invest in some tools. She mentally counted her credits and tried to figure out how many of them she could spare against an unknown future. She would have to make an investment at some point, and tools would help sell her cover story.

She ended up using the heel of her boot and hitting the piece against the floor to avoid breaking the table. It wasn't top quality when she was finished, but the part would no longer let coolant leak out. She set to reassembling the thresher around it.

"I've left my ship at the spaceport," Ahsoka said. "Do I have to register it with anyone?"

"No," Kaeden said. "Just make sure you lock it up tight. There are more than a few opportunists around here."

She meant thieves, Ahsoka understood. Nowhere was

perfect. "That's why I left most of my gear on board," she lied. "It's more secure than this house is."

"We can help you with that," Kaeden said. "My sister and I, I mean. She's good at making locks, and I'm good at convincing people to leave you alone."

"When you're not losing fights with machinery, I assume?" Ahsoka said.

"Most people lose arms and legs when things go badly," Kaeden said in her own defense. "I'm too good for that."

Kaeden rolled off the bed and walked over to take a look at what Ahsoka was doing. She hummed approvingly and then pointed to the random pieces still on the table.

"What are those for?" she asked.

"I have no idea," Ahsoka replied. "But they didn't seem to have a place in the machine, so I left them aside. I think it should work, once you refill the coolant and refuel the lines."

"I can do that when I reattach the blade," Kaeden said.

She flipped a switch and the repulsors fired up, lifting the thresher off the table about a meter. She turned it off just as quickly.

"Excellent," she said. "I'll test the steering and the other parts when I'm outside, but the repulsors were the part I was worried about. It's not much good if it can't fly."

Ahsoka wasn't sure how much good it would be if it wouldn't steer, but she was also not the expert, so she let it pass.

"You're welcome," she said. She pulled the rest of the food out of the ration pack and ate it quickly. Kaeden watched her eat.

"I'll pay you in food, then?" the girl asked. "I mean, it's a good way to start, and later we can work out other arrangements."

"Can I trade rations for tools?" Ahsoka asked.

"No," Kaeden said. "I mean, food rations aren't worth much to those of us who have been here a while."

Ahsoka considered her options. She hadn't had time to take a full inventory of the ship, and it was possible that the tools she needed were there. And she did need to eat.

"Just this once," she said, hoping she sounded like someone who was experienced at driving a hard bargain. "Next time we're going to negotiate before I do any repairs."

Kaeden picked up the thresher and smiled. She still seemed a little guarded, which suited Ahsoka just fine. She was, she reminded herself, not trying to make friends, particularly not friends who were at perfect ease sitting on her bed. That sort of thing bespoke a level of intimacy in most cultures. The Jedi

Temple was not a place where such things were encouraged, and Ahsoka never felt motivated strongly enough to go around the rules the way that certain others had.

"I left the crate outside," Kaeden said. "You can come and get it."

Ahsoka followed her out the door and saw the promised payment—food enough for a month, probably, and maybe longer if she was careful with it. Kaeden was right: food was only worthwhile to trade if you were new. Clearly, shortage was not an issue. She dragged the crate inside as Kaeden made her way down the street, her limp much less noticeable than it had been the day before. Alone again, Ahsoka lifted the crate onto the table, and fought off the childish impulse to do the work with her mind instead of her arms. The Force wasn't meant to be used so lightly, and it wasn't as though throwing boxes around was real training. Her focus needed to be elsewhere.

Using the Force was a natural extension of herself. Not using it all the time was strange. She would have to practice, really practice with proper meditation, or someday she would need her abilities and be unable to respond in time. She'd been lucky to escape Order 66, and her escape had not been without terrible cost. The other Jedi, the ones who had died, hadn't been able to save themselves, powerful or otherwise.

She felt the familiar tightness in her throat, the same strangling grief that came every time she imagined what had happened when the clone troopers turned. How many of her friends had been shot down by men they'd served with for years? How many of the younglings had been murdered by a man wearing a face they implicitly trusted? And how did the clones feel after it was done? She knew the Temple had burned; she had received the warning not to return. But she didn't know where any of her friends had been during the disaster. She knew only that she couldn't find them afterward, that her sense of them was gone, as if they had ceased to exist.

Ahsoka felt herself spiraling down through her grief and reached out to grasp something, anything, to remind her of the light. She found the green fields of Raada, fields she hadn't even seen with her own eyes yet. For a few moments, she let herself get lost in the rhythm of growing things that needed only the sun and some water to live. That simplicity was heartening, even if at that particular moment she couldn't remember exactly what Master Yoda had said about plants and the Force.

The extra pieces of Kaeden's thresher were still on the table. Ahsoka leaned down and picked them up, absently weighing them in her hands before she put them in her pocket. There, they jingled against the rings she'd taken off the ship console the day before. If she kept accumulating tech at this rate, she was going to need bigger pockets.

Thinking about what she needed reminded Ahsoka that she really ought to check her ship for tools and other useful items. She looked around the house quickly: the crate was on the table, but it was nondescript, and the panel over her credits in the shower was secure. It didn't look like anything that would appeal to a thief, but Ahsoka was uneasy as she shut the door behind her.

"I hope Kaeden needs something else fixed soon," she said under her breath to a nonexistent R2-D2. "I'd feel better if I had a lock."

One of the problems with spending a lot of time with an astromech droid was that one tended to continue talking to it even when it was no longer there to talk to.

Ahsoka walked up the street, toward the center of town and the spaceport. She paid more attention to her surroundings this time, noticing the little shops perched on corners, waiting for customers. Most of them sold the same goods and sundries, and Ahsoka needed none of them. The larger houses in the center of town no longer looked intimidating now that Ahsoka had a place of her own to retreat to. Two places if she counted the ship, which was still parked in the spaceport, exactly as Ahsoka had left it. She opened the hatch and went inside.

It would draw too much attention if she did a flyover of the hills near her house. If she wanted to scout out the caves, she was going to have to do it with her feet. The house and the ship were a good start, but it would be nice to have a place she could go in an emergency.

"Food, tools, safe place in case I need to run," she said out loud. She really should stop that. She missed R2-D2.

It wasn't much of a plan, but it was better than nothing.

04

KAEDEN DIDN'T COME BACK the next day, which Ahsoka took as a sign that the girl had healed enough to return to work. In the daylight, the Raada settlement was mostly deserted. Nearly everyone who lived on the moon worked in the fields. Those who didn't—food vendors and the like— usually followed the field workers out of town in the morning. It made sense to go where the money was.

This meant that Ahsoka had her days to herself, or at least she would until Kaeden made good on her promise to tell the others that Ahsoka could fix things for them. When the quiet got too much for Ahsoka to bear, she tucked a ration pack into her bag, filled a canteen with water, and headed toward the hills.

It was warm enough that she didn't need her cloak, though she knew that when the sun went down, the heat would drain off quickly. Ahsoka was used to fluctuating temperatures. When she'd been a Padawan, she'd only occasionally known what sort of planet she might end up on, and that was good training when it came to learning how to adapt. At least it didn't get cold enough on the moon that she'd need a parka.

There didn't seem to be much in the way of wildlife on Raada. Ahsoka had seen a few avians clustered around the water sources when she flew in. There must have been pollinators of some kind, but when it came to big things—predators or creatures worth hunting for meat—Raada didn't offer much in the way of variation.

The place would've driven Anakin to distraction, unless he somehow managed to arrange for podraces. No real technology to fiddle with, nothing dangerous to protect hapless villagers from—just work and home, work and home. He never said as much, but Ahsoka knew her master had gotten enough of that growing up on Tatooine. Master Obi-Wan would have said Raada was a good place to relax and then somehow stumbled on a nest of pirates or a ring of smugglers or a conspiracy of Sith. Ahsoka—Ashla—was hoping for something in the middle: home and work, and just enough excitement to keep her from climbing the walls.

In the meantime, climbing the hills would do. Ahsoka had left the plains and was walking over rolling hills, each covered with rocks and whispering grasses that concealed all manner of dells, hollows, and caves. Though the settlement itself was indefensible, the surrounding area would be a more than adequate place to stage an insurgency if needed. There were good vantage points of the spaceport, and the caves would provide cover from aerial assault. The only trouble was water, but if the farmers had tech like portable threshers, they must have portable water sources, too.

Ahsoka stopped on a hilltop and shook her head ruefully. She could not stop thinking like a tactician. The clones— before they would have tried to kill her—would have said that was a good thing. Anakin would have agreed with them. But Ahsoka still remembered, vaguely, Jedi training before the war. They hadn't focused so much on tactics then, and Ahsoka had still been interested in what she was learning. Surely, now that she had nothing left to fight for, she could go back to that.

"Not until you're safe," she whispered. "Not until you know for sure that you are safe."

Even as she said the words, she knew it would never come to pass. She would never be safe again. She would have to stay ready to fight. She guessed the Empire wouldn't visit Raada anytime soon, as there was nothing on the moon they needed, but she knew how Palpatine worked. Even when he was the Chancellor, he liked control. As the Emperor, as a Sith Lord, he'd be even more of an autocrat. With people like Governor Tarkin to help him, every part of the galaxy would feel the Imperial touch.

But Raada was clear of it for now, at least. Ahsoka left the hilltop and ventured into one of the caves. She was pleased to discover that it was dry enough that she could store food there if she needed to, and tall enough that she could stand up without the tops of her montrals brushing the ceiling. She wouldn't want to live here permanently, but in a pinch it wouldn't be so bad.

Toward the back of the cave was a natural low shelf where a piece of rock had broken off and left a flat surface. Part of the shelf had cracked and fallen onto the cave floor. Ahsoka picked it up, noting that the edges of the cracked piece matched up with the solid shelf. She set the piece down where it had broken off, and it fit neatly into place, with only a thin seam revealing the break. Ahsoka picked up the shard of rock again and fished in her pocket for the metal pieces she kept there. She set them down, under where the broken rock would go, and put the slab back on top. It still fit.

It wasn't much of a hiding place, but Ahsoka didn't have much of anything to hide yet. It was more of a promise, a possibility, like how she'd judged the tactical value of the settlement and surrounding hills. If she needed to, she could cut into the rock underneath to make a larger compartment.

Ahsoka stood up, leaving the metal pieces under the stone. She could return for them if she needed. She suspected that this wouldn't be the only cave she set up, but it would be the one to which she gave the most attention. It was the closest to the settlement, the first one she could reach if she was running.

Yes, it would do for a start.

◆ ◆ ◆

Kaeden's repaired thresher was doing a fabulous job. Once she'd refueled it and added more coolant, the machine worked better than it ever had. This did not go unnoticed.

"Hey, Larte," Tibbola said at lunch break. "Where'd you

get that? It looks like your old beast, but it moves like a new one."

Tibbola was one of the oldest farmers, unmarried and mean when he was drunk. Kaeden avoided him as much as possible, but the man had a sharp eye for changes, and a faster thresher would be more than enough to catch his attention.

"I had it fixed after it sliced me up," Kaeden said.

"Who did it?"

"You know, I didn't get a name," Kaeden realized. That was strange. She and the Togruta newcomer had talked for a while both times, and Kaeden had introduced herself. She'd even been inside her house. "She just moved into Cietra's old place."

"Clearly she's good at what she does," said Miara, Kaeden's sister. The younger girl sat down on the ground beside her and held out her hands for Kaeden's canteen.

"Get your own," Kaeden said.

"I'll refill them both on our way back out," Miara promised. Kaeden rolled her eyes and passed the container.

At fourteen, three years younger than Kaeden, Miara shouldn't have been working a full shift allotment, even though she was as capable as Kaeden had been at that age. Necessity was a harsh, if effective, teacher, and Kaeden regretted that the same pressures that had driven her to the fields at a young age had pushed Miara after her, though the younger girl never complained. As a result, Kaeden had a hard time denying her anything. Thankfully, Miara was wise enough not to press the advantage too far.

"If she can fix your old clanker like that, maybe I'll ask her to look at mine." Tibbola was cheap, and his thresher had been patched so many times Kaeden wasn't sure there was an original part on it.

"You're not going to be able to put one over on her," Kaeden warned him. "She's smart."

"Maybe I'm more charming than you are," Tibbola said with a leer. He got up and left.

"Not with breath like that," Miara said, giggling. Kaeden couldn't help laughing, too. "We'll warn her. Where's she from?"

"She didn't say that, either," Kaeden admitted. "Mostly we talked about Raada."

"You can't blame her for being cautious if she's new to the moon, and on her own," Miara pointed out. "You're right about her being smart. She probably wants to know what it's like in town before she opens up."

"Who's opening up?" Four bodies thumped to the ground around them—the rest of their threshing crew joining them for lunch.

"Kaeden made a friend!" Miara said teasingly.

"Did she now?" Vartan, their crew lead, waggled his dark eyebrows at her. It would have had more impact if his eyebrows hadn't been the only hair on his head.

"She's a mechanic, of sorts," Kaeden said, ignoring his tone. It took more than mechanical aptitude to turn her head, though maybe she was going to have to reevaluate that. There was a lot to be said for cleverness. "I didn't get her name, but she fixed the thresher so well it's better now than when I bought it."

"I thought it seemed less murderous today," Malat said, digging into her food with long delicate fingers.

"We'll go and get her after shift and take her to Selda's," Miara declared, referring to the cantina where they went nearly every night. She got up and went to refill the canteens.

"What if she doesn't want to come out?" Kaeden asked.

"What else is she going to do?" Hoban asked. He had finished eating and was lying back on the ground with his hat over his face to shield his pale skin from the sun. "Sit at home by herself in the dark?"

"Maybe she likes that sort of thing," suggested Neera, Hoban's long-suffering twin.

"If Tibbola's going to introduce himself to her, we should make sure she meets other people," Vartan said. "Or she'll be so put off by him, she'll jump on the first ship out of here."

It was on the tip of Kaeden's tongue to mention that her new friend had a ship of her own, but something stopped her. No name, no history . . . she probably wouldn't want Kaeden spilling her secrets. Kaeden could understand that. There were plenty of things she didn't like sharing with her sister, let alone her crew, and she'd known her crew for years.

"All right," she said, finally. "After we're done for the day and cleaned up a bit, I'll go and ask her if she wants to come out with us. But you won't pressure her, and you won't bug her if she doesn't want to be bugged."

"Yes, ma'am," said Vartan, saluting.

The others laughed, and Kaeden was gracious enough to join in. The horn sounded, so she threw her head back and tipped the last crumbs of her lunch out of the package and into her mouth. Miara handed her a full canteen of water with a smile, and then it was back to work.

05

SELDA'S WAS A SMALL CANTINA, but it still produced an astonishing level of noise. Ahsoka was very glad she hadn't taken the house next to it, or she might never have gotten a good night's sleep again. There was live music, of course, but the place was also crammed full of people, none of whom seemed able to speak below a dull roar.

"Come on!" Kaeden yelled. "We'll sit in a corner and that will make it easier to talk."

Ahsoka had her doubts about that. Frankly, she had her

doubts about going out with Kaeden at all. The girl had shown up just as Ahsoka was agreeing to do a small repair for a truly odious man named Tibbola, and she had invited Ahsoka out for some real food. Ahsoka had tried to protest, but her heart hadn't been in it, and it wasn't until she and Kaeden were through the door of the cantina that Ahsoka wished she'd resisted a little harder.

"Are you sure about this?" she asked. "Isn't there some-place quieter?"

"What?" said Kaeden.

Ahsoka repeated herself directly into Kaeden's ear. How did anyone in this place hear anything? How could they order drinks?

"No," Kaeden replied. "Selda has the best food. It'll be a bit quieter in the back."

Ahsoka gave up and followed Kaeden through the crowd. The girl had broad shoulders and was not afraid to use them to clear a path. When they got through the main crush, Kaeden turned left and led Ahsoka to a table that was already occupied.

"My sister, Miara," Kaeden said, indicating the dark-skinned girl already seated at the table. Unlike Kaeden, whose dark brown hair was still tightly braided, Miara's hair was loose. It was very, very curly and surrounded her head like a cloud. Ahsoka liked it, though she had no idea how Miara kept it out of her way when she was working.

"Hi!" said Ahsoka. "I'm Ashla." She slid into the seat beside Kaeden and called Ashla's persona to the front of her mind.

Other introductions were made, and before long Ahsoka had shaken hands with Kaeden's entire crew. They were all human but one. Vartan was the oldest, a weathered man in his forties. At first Ahsoka thought his baldness was an affectation, like what some of the clones had done to keep their heads cooler in their helmets, but when she looked more closely, she realized that he didn't have any regrowth at all. She didn't really understand how hair worked, not having any herself, but she knew men were often sensitive about that sort of thing, so even though she was curious, she didn't ask.

Malat, a Sullustan woman in her early thirties, had to leave right after introductions were made. Her husband worked a different shift than she did, and she had to go home to feed the children. She reminded Ahsoka a bit of Master Plo, who had always thought of others even when he was busy or tired.

The twins, Hoban and Neera, were only a few years older than Ahsoka. They were very white compared with the others, and their matching blue eyes missed very few details. They were also much blunter than Kaeden had been when it came to asking Ashla questions about her past. Ahsoka knew that a little information would go a long way, so she offered up what she could.

"I'm a mechanic, or at least I can fix things," she said.

"It's good to meet you then," Hoban said. "Especially if you repair our threshers like you did Kaeden's."

"Did yours break, too?" Ahsoka asked.

"No," said Miara, "but they're all old and junky. Kaeden's works better now than it ever did, even when she first bought it."

"I'm happy to take a look," Ahsoka said. "You can't be worse than my last customer."

They all looked at Kaeden in surprise. She grimaced.

"Tibbola got to her before I did," she said.

"Well, at least he didn't scare her off completely," Hoban said. "And he doesn't drink here very often."

"Why not?" Ahsoka asked. "Kaeden said this place is the best."

Hoban and Neera exchanged looks, and Neera leaned forward.

"Tibbola is a mean drunk," she said. "And a stupid one.

Sober, he can control his tongue, but when he's had a few, he starts to say unpleasant things about people."

Ahsoka digested that. She wasn't used to unbridled emotions. She'd spent most of her life around people who felt deeply, but who managed, for the most part, to keep those feelings under control. It was one of the reasons that Barriss Offee's betrayal had stung her so deeply. Barriss had been angry with the Jedi Order and had sought to win Ahsoka's sympathies, if not her outright alliance, but she'd done so in the cruelest way imaginable: by tampering with Ahsoka's own choices. To have a person she considered a friend use her to unleash such deep anger and channel it at the Order had changed every part of Ahsoka's outlook. Although it wasn't exactly the same thing, Ahsoka was glad she wouldn't have to deal with the abusive mutterings of the local drunk. Ever since Barriss had poked all those holes in her certainty about the Jedi path, Ahsoka had worked hard to regain the control she'd once possessed. She wasn't in a hurry to give a new bully the opportunity to get under her skin.

"We don't like it," Miara said. "And neither does Selda, obviously, though he can't always turn away a paying customer."

Ahsoka followed Miara's gesture and saw a tall Togruta

male standing behind the bar. His skin was the same color as hers. His left lekku was mostly gone, though, cut off at the shoulder, and there was scar tissue where the injury had been sustained.

"Farming accident," Vartan said. "A long time ago. They can give you prosthetic hands and feet, but they can't do much about your lekku."

Selda caught Ahsoka's gaze—she really hoped he didn't think she was staring—and nodded formally. She waved, and he smiled. Then he went back to drying glasses, and she could see his prosthesis as he worked. It went all the way up to his left elbow and made him hold the glasses at a strange angle, but it didn't seem to slow him down.

"Now that he's seen you, I bet we get the best service," Hoban said.

"Idiot," said his sister, and cuffed him on the back of the head. His drink spilled as she jostled him. "Do you think all Togruta know each other?"

"Of course not," Hoban protested. He didn't even try to mop up the mess. "I just meant he'll be curious because she's new."

"You'll have to forgive my brother," Neera said. "He never thinks before he speaks."

"You're forgiven," said Ahsoka.

"I didn't—" Hoban started, but then gave up. "Where's the food? I'm starving."

Every cantina Ahsoka had been in before had been full of transients. Even on Coruscant, the bars were populated by people who were on their way somewhere else, even if it was only to a concert or another party. It was strange to be somewhere where everyone was local. On Raada, she was the stranger, and she got the distinct impression that if she'd walked through the doors alone, the music and the talking would have stopped and she'd have been the center of attention. Even shielded by Kaeden and her friends, Ahsoka was the focus of quite a few covert stares as people tried to figure her out.

"They'll get used to you soon enough," said Vartan. He stood up and prepared to push his way back to the bar for refills. "Do you want to order anything special? Tonight the drinks are on us."

"He's being ridiculous," Miara said. "Selda only has one kind of alcohol. Just get another round, Vartan."

He saluted her, a mocking gesture that Ahsoka found uncomfortably familiar, and went on his way. Miara and Kaeden started arguing with the twins about something, and

Ahsoka let herself half listen while she looked around the cantina. It was a habit, assessing her surroundings, but now would be a good time to find out if anyone was too interested in her. She mostly saw tired people who just seemed to want a hot meal at the end of the day. If it weren't for the music, she would have thought this was a commissary or mess hall.

"That's why Selda keeps it so loud," Kaeden said, when Ahsoka told her what she was thinking. "You eat in a lot of mess halls back wherever you're from?"

"Sometimes," Ahsoka said. "More often it was eating what we could where we could."

"You moved around a lot?" Kaeden said with some sympathy. "Even when you were little?"

"Not when I was little," Ahsoka said. "But for the last few years, yes."

"My parents settled us here when I was four and Miara was one," Kaeden said. "They died in the accident that cut up Selda so bad, but I was fourteen by then and just old enough to draw a wage. Vartan took me on because of my circumstances, even though everyone else thought I was too young. Then he took Miara on, too. Did you travel with your parents?"

The question shouldn't have caught Ahsoka off guard, but it did. She said the first thing that popped into her head.

"No, I don't remember my parents very well."

"Who'd you travel with then?" Kaeden asked.

"I'm, uh—dopted," Ahsoka stuttered, and hoped the noise of the cantina was enough to cover her hesitation. "Sort of." She went through her days trying not to think about her loss, lest her grief incapacitate her, but that just meant that every time it came up, it hurt like new.

Whatever question Kaeden had next was interrupted by the return of Vartan carrying a tray of drinks, Selda trailing behind him with a tray of food. Once everything was passed out, Selda took the seat beside Ahsoka and leaned in so only she would hear him.

"Are you set up okay here?" he asked.

"Yes," she replied, surprised at his kindness.

"There's been a bunch of new people, coming out from the Core worlds," Selda said. "Nonhumans."

Ahsoka had heard the rumors. The Empire was highly selective in who it admitted to positions of power. Palpatine wasn't afraid to step on his old allies, even on his home planet.

"I'm not running from anything that specific," Ahsoka said. Ashla's lies came easier every time. "I just wanted to be somewhere quiet."

The cantina band began what must have been a popular

song, because most of the people in the room started clapping and singing along with it. Ahsoka winced, and Selda laughed.

"I know what you mean," he shouted over the increased noise. "But if something changes, let me know. Or tell Vartan. He's closemouthed, but he knows which way is up."

Selda clapped her on the shoulder, the familiarity of the gesture surprising her again, and got up to return to the bar. Ahsoka watched him walk away. She could see the lines in his tunic and trousers where his body stopped and his prosthetics began. It must have been a terrible accident.

"What did he want?" Kaeden asked as Ahsoka turned to the plate in front of her and began to eat.

"Just saying hello," Ahsoka said. "It's good business for him to know people, isn't it?"

Kaeden nodded and let her eat.

The star chart was the only source of light in the room. Outside, the black of space was pricked by distant stars, and inside, all the consoles were dimmed as much as they could be. Jenneth Pilar believed in using only what was necessary and excelled in finding necessary things to use. Before the Empire he had been a broker, linking goods to buyers, using whatever merchant or smuggler he could find. Now he found other,

AHSOKA

more Imperial, channels for his talents. The Empire had great demand for every variety of commodity, and Jenneth knew the pathways of supply. Before, he had to balance negotiations among multiple parties. Now he just pointed the might of the Imperial military at a planet and it took what it wanted. He still got paid, and paid very well, so he didn't mind the destruction, and his hands were clean, so he didn't mind the blood.

This new assignment was a challenge, and Jenneth appreciated it. The Empire wanted a planet it could use for food production, preferably one with a small population that no one would miss. It was the second part that had stymied Jenneth at first, but after a few days of careful analysis, he had found the solution. All he had to do now was transmit the information to his Imperial contact and wait for the credits to show up in his account.

It was, perhaps, all a bit more official than Jenneth might have liked, but working for the Empire had undeniable benefits. His position was a lot more stable than it had been as a freelancer, and as long as he followed the directives he was given, he was mostly left alone. He would have preferred more outright power within the Imperial hierarchy, but it was still early in the business relationship. He could afford patience.

Born to be a cog in a machine, Jenneth had found the

perfect one. It was straightforward, quiet, brutally efficient, and profitable. The Empire didn't care what happened after it had what it wanted, and Jenneth didn't, either.

"Raada," he said, before he closed the star chart and sat alone in the dark. It was overly dramatic, but he was fond of the effect. "I hope no one is keeping anything important on you."

◆ ◆ ◆

Later that night, alone in her house, Ahsoka couldn't stop thinking about what Selda had said. In the noise of the cantina, it had been possible to ignore the warning, but in the quiet of her room, it wasn't so easy. The Empire was implacable, she knew, and heartless when it came to death and suffering, but surely the fastest way to incite resistance would be to target particular species. The Senate was still functioning, and someone in it had to have the power to protest.

But they wouldn't, Ahsoka realized. They would be too busy protecting their own planets. That was why Kashyyyk was besieged and why no one had interceded when some of the planet's Wookiees were dispersed to various mines and work camps throughout the galaxy. No one could help them. Most could barely help themselves. That was the Jedi's job, and the Jedi were gone.

Gone.

The Jedi were gone. Ahsoka thought it mercilessly, over and over again—still too afraid to say the words out loud—until she could take the final step: the Jedi were dead. All of them. The warriors, the scholars, the diplomats, the generals. The old and the young. The students and the teachers. They were dead, and there was nothing Ahsoka could do.

Why had it been her? She'd had that thought a hundred times since Order 66. Why had *she* survived? She wasn't the most powerful; she wasn't even a Jedi Knight, and yet she was still alive when so many others had died. She asked the question so often because she knew the answer. She just hated facing it, as painful as it was. She'd survived because she had left. She had walked away.

She'd walked away from the Jedi and she'd walked away from Thabeska, and because of that she was alive, whether she deserved to be or not.

She dried her eyes, picked up Tibbola's thresher, and went back to work.

AHSOKA LOOKED DOWN *at the grave, her heart a stone in her chest.*

She thought about all the clone troopers she had ever served with. They had been so quick to accept her, even when she first became Anakin's Padawan. Sure, part of that was their genetic code, but that only went so far. They respected her. They listened to her. They taught her everything they knew. And when she made mistakes, when she got some of them killed, they forgave her, and they stood beside her again when it was time to return to battle. The Jedi were gone, but what happened to the clones was almost worse. Their identities, their free will, removed with a simple voice command and the activation of a chip.

If she hadn't seen it for herself, she wouldn't have believed it was possible.

She felt completely alone in the Force, except for the dark nothingness that stared back at her every time she tried to connect with Anakin or any of the others. More than anything, she wanted a ship to appear, for Anakin to track her down or one of the other Jedi to find her. She wanted to know where they were, if they were safe, but there was no way to do that without compromising her own position. All she could do was what she had decided to do: go to ground.

She should have been at the Temple. She should have been with Anakin. She should have helped. Instead, she'd been on Mandalore, almost entirely alone, surrounded by clones and confusion and blaster fire. Maul had escaped, of course. She'd had the opportunity to kill him, but had chosen to save Rex instead. She didn't regret that, couldn't regret it, but the mischief and worse that Maul might wreak in a galaxy with no Jedi to protect it gnawed at her.

Now, there was the grave. Everything about it was false, from the name listed on it to the name of the person who'd killed him. It looked very real, though. And you couldn't tell clones apart when they were dead, especially not if they were buried in another's set of armor.

Ahsoka held her lightsabers, her last physical connection to the Jedi and to her service in the Clone Wars. It was so hard to give them up, even though she knew she had to. It was the only way to sell the con of the false burial, and it would buy her a modicum of safety, because whoever found them would assume she was dead, too.

But Anakin had given them to her. She'd walked away from the Jedi Temple with nothing but the clothes on her back and had struggled for a long time to find a new place in the galaxy. When she had found a mission, when she had reached out to her former master for help, he had reached back and given her the Jedi weapons to do the job. He'd accepted her return, and it felt like a failure to leave the lightsabers behind a second time.

She turned them on and told herself that it was their incandescent blue glow in the dark night that made her eyes water. How many Jedi were buried with their lightsabers today? How many weren't buried at all but left behind like so much garbage, their weapons taken as trophies? The younglings, had they known what to do? Who could they ask once their teachers had been cut down? Surely, there had been some mercy for—

She knelt, extinguishing the energy, and planted the hilts of both her weapons in the freshly turned dirt.

She stood quickly and resisted the urge to call the lightsabers back into her hands. They must be left there, memorializing the man they were recorded as having killed, a trophy for the coming Imperials to find.

And they were coming. Ahsoka could feel it in her bones. She had a ship, unremarkable and well built. Rex was already gone, his false death inscribed on the marker in front of her and the false report of her death at his hands credited there as well. When they were digging the grave, they had agreed to separate and head for the Outer Rim. It was chaotic there, but it was the sort of chaos where a person could get lost. The chaos on the Core worlds was motivated by Palpatine's new peace, and if Ahsoka tried to hide herself there, it would be only a matter of time until she was found.

She placed a hand on the grave marker and allowed herself one more moment to think about the man who was buried there and about the man who wasn't. She thought about her master, whom she could no longer sense, and the other Jedi, whose absence was like an open airlock in her lungs. With determination, she shut it. She stopped looking for Anakin through the connection they shared. She stopped remembering the clones, alive and dead.

She turned and walked to her ship. She wondered what she would say when she got to a new planet and someone asked her who she was. She knew her name was on a list of supposed criminals. She couldn't safely use it anymore. She couldn't say she was a Jedi, not that she ever could have said that in good conscience anyway. She'd given up that right. Now she paid the price, doubly, for her abandonment. At least the pilot's seat made sense. She knew what to do when she was sitting in it.

The ship hummed to life around her, and she focused on the things she knew for certain: she was Ahsoka Tano, at least for a little bit longer, and it was time to go.

06

AFTER THAT FIRST NIGHT at Selda's, Ahsoka settled into the rhythms of life on Raada without incident. Her acceptance by Kaeden and, more important, by Selda made everyone else treat her like she'd always lived there. The farmers brought her broken threshers and other pieces of equipment to fix, and the vendors and shopkeepers acted like she was one of their own. In the Core, Ahsoka had seen guilds and crime syndicates protect their members, but this was different. There was none of the fear or manipulation—except in the case of

Tibbola, whom nobody really liked. But even he paid on time and did his job.

It was kind of nice—when it wasn't excruciatingly boring.

"It's a family," said Miara. She had stopped by to install the lock on Ahsoka's door.

"But we're not family," Ahsoka protested.

Miara looked at her, an expression on her face that was almost hurt. Ahsoka had seen families before. She had saved families before. But it had been a while since she'd had one. It wasn't the Jedi way. She had been deeply loved on her home planet, but that was so long ago that all she could remember was the feeling of it, not the practical results.

"There's two kinds of family," Miara said after a moment. "There's the kind like me and Kaeden, where you get born in the right place to the right people and you're stuck with one another. If you're lucky, it turns out okay. The other kind of family is the kind you find."

Ahsoka thought about how the clones, even ones who had never met, defaulted to calling each other "brother." She had thought it was because of their genetics and military connection, but maybe it was something else.

"Kaeden and me, we were alone," Miara continued. "But

then Vartan hired Kaeden. He didn't have to. He didn't have to pay her full wage, either. But he did. All sorts of bad things could have happened to us when our parents died, but instead we got a new family."

Ahsoka considered this.

"Now, I don't expect you to tell me who died," Miara went on. "But clearly someone did. Kaeden said you were adopted, which means you lost family twice. So now you get us."

The younger girl was so determined that Ahsoka couldn't bring herself to correct her. She wasn't looking for a family, but Master Yoda had taught her that sometimes you found things you weren't expecting, and it only made sense to use them when you did. The people on Raada protected their own, with none of the violence or cruelty or cold-blooded calculation Ahsoka had seen at work in the Core. Maybe it was a good idea to take advantage of it, even though thinking about using her new friends on those terms made her a little uncomfortable. She looked at Miara, who was installing the final part of the lock.

"Isn't that sort of, I don't know, unfair?" Ahsoka asked, with exaggerated care. They didn't even know her real name, after all. "I mean, I just show up and you guys take me on?"

"Well," Miara said, "it's not like you aren't useful to have around. Everyone's tech works better after you finish with it, and that keeps Hoban's head from getting too big."

Ahsoka laughed. She supposed that was true.

In the distance, the horn sounded. Miara started to pack up her things.

"I've got to run," she said. "We're on the evening shift this week, so you're on your own for dinner for a bit. The lock's ready though. You just need to set the key. Tap your finger here."

Ahsoka did as she was told, and the lock turned green.

"Excellent," said Miara. "I mean, it won't keep out anyone who is really determined, but you'll know someone broke in, and they'll get quite the shock when they do." Miara's locks, it turned out, could be a little vindictive.

"Thanks," Ahsoka said.

Miara finished packing up and went on her way, leaving Ahsoka alone with a new lock and a host of new thoughts to tumble around in her head. She looked at the vaporator she was supposed to fix that afternoon and decided that she had spent too much time indoors during the past week. The tedium of an agricultural community was starting to wear on her. Oh, the Jedi had their rituals and obscure traditions, too, but Ahsoka was accustomed to those. Raada was a new kind of boredom, and Ahsoka never did well when she was bored. It was time to check on her cave and see what else she might find in the area.

She packed everything she would need for the day in the new bag Neera had given her when Ahsoka fixed the caf maker in the house Neera shared with her brother. She put in a ration pack, even though she had fresh food, too, and attached her water canteen to her hip, right beside where one of her lightsabers used to hang. She wrapped up all the metal pieces she'd collected since the last time she went out to the cave and put them in the bag, as well, then hoisted it onto her shoulders. It was much more comfortable than her last bag. Neera had altered it so it wouldn't rub against her lekku.

As Ahsoka made her way out of town, she passed quite a few farmers on their way to the fields. Several of them greeted her with Ashla's name, and she waved back with a smile that wasn't forced at all. She walked past all the houses and the few little gardens that lined the edge of town. Why farmers would want to garden in their spare time was beyond Ahsoka, but she had strange hobbies, too—except that hers were secret.

Whatever Miara might say, Ahsoka didn't think that families and secrets went well together, and she was much better practiced in the latter than she was in the former. Kaeden had already begun to ask leading questions, hinting that she'd like to know more about where Ashla had come from and what she did when she disappeared from town. Ahsoka did her best to change the subject. The hard part was that Ahsoka found she actually wanted to talk to Kaeden and tell her all sorts of things. They didn't have any life experiences in common, but Kaeden was a good listener, even though neither of them could solve the other's problems. Moreover, talking to someone who was mostly untroubled by the largeness of the galaxy helped Ahsoka focus, and she was having trouble with that sort of thing these days, even when she tried to meditate.

She was unbalanced, Ahsoka decided, pulled in too many directions by her new feelings and her old grief. What she needed was to recenter herself, and meditation was the best way to do that. She'd avoided those kinds of exercises for a while now, because she didn't like what she saw when she did them, but if she was going to regain control of her life, she was going to have to regain control of her meditations, as well. She could use that focus to make sure she didn't wander into a vision or memory, and in her regular life, it would help her keep her thoughts in order, not to mention keeping her tuned to the Force.

She felt calmer almost the moment she passed the last house, when the noise of feet and machinery was replaced by the whispering grass and the promise of solitude. A few clouds dotted the sky, and it was windy but still mild enough for Ahsoka not to feel the weather bite at her. It was, she decided, a good day for a run.

She tightened the straps on the pack Neera had made for her and then threw back her head and took off. The wind whistled past her as she picked up speed, and she felt like, if she could go fast enough, she might be able to fly clear off the moon's surface. She laughed, half in exhilaration and half at her own silliness: if she wanted to fly, she could just take her ship and fly. And anyway, she couldn't run as fast as she was capable, because she couldn't use the Force in the open. Even without the Force, it took much less time than before for her to reach the hills, and she slowed to a walk so she wouldn't miss the signs that led her to her cave.

Ahsoka retraced her steps, noticing more places where caves were cut into the stone. She wondered if any of them were connected. Hers wasn't, which was one of the reasons she liked it; but it might be useful to have more of a network, and those caves were more likely to have natural water sources that didn't rely on technology.

"Who exactly do you think is going to need these caves?" she asked herself.

She ignored her own question and ducked through the entrance to her hiding spot.

Everything was exactly as she'd left it, from the stone slab concealing her small pieces of tech to the footprints on the floor. She added the new pieces to the collection, her hand hovering over them as if she could build something, and then replaced the cover. Then she went to the middle of the cave and sat on the floor, her legs tucked under her.

She breathed in and out slowly, the way Master Plo had shown her all those years before when they had first met. She had been so confused back then, and more than a little scared. The slaver who had intercepted her village's signal to the Jedi and come to take her had been frightening, but the instant Ahsoka had laid eyes on Jedi Master Plo Koon, she had known she could trust him. Training with the Jedi as a youngling had fully restored her self-confidence, but at the same time it made her reckless and brash. It wasn't until she became a Padawan to Anakin Skywalker, and had to leave the Temple again, that she finally understood that the galaxy could be calm and tempestuous, safe and dangerous at the same time. The key, as always, was finding balance.

She did her best to think about that balance right now. She focused on her breathing and the moon she sat on. She reached out through its grasses and felt the sun, encouraging her to grow. She found the little gardens, each plant given special attention to ensure good health, and understood the farmers who tended them a little better. And she spread out across the fields, feeling the order in straight-ploughed furrows and organized harvesting. The bare fields were being turned again for new seed as the growing season shifted. Soon the threshing would be done and the crews would move to other work.

Raada's small wealth was on the ground, so Ahsoka didn't think to look up until the stones around her began to shake. If she hadn't been meditating, she wouldn't have noticed, but so deeply connected to the planet, she felt it more keenly then she felt her own body. There was something in the air.

Ahsoka's consciousness raced back across the grasslands to where she was sitting and found the cave walls and floor trembling. It wasn't the dangerous sort of shake, only the warning kind, and Ahsoka was glad for the advance knowledge. She stood slowly to work out the kinks in her neck and knees and stretched her hands above her head. Her fingers touched the roof of the cave, and she felt immediately grounded in her body and the physical awareness of her surroundings. Something was terribly wrong.

She left the cave, and as much as she wanted to race to the hilltop, she made herself be cautious. Standing on top of her own hiding place would be rash and she needed to be careful. She walked for several minutes, the shaking in her bones getting more and more pronounced, and then climbed to the top of another hill.

As Ahsoka looked toward the settlement, her heart sank. Hovering over the houses, dwarfing them in every way, was an Imperial Star Destroyer. She could see smaller ships emerging from its hangars and making for the surface of the moon. She knew they carried troops and weapons and all kinds of other dangers.

She thought she had gone far enough. She thought she had more time. But she was trapped again, and she would need to figure out what to do next.

The Empire had arrived.

07

HER FIRST INSTINCT WAS TO RUN. She was a good fighter, but she also knew when she was overmatched. Raada was remote; there was no need for an Imperial presence, especially one so heavy, unless the Empire had a good reason. A living Jedi—however inaccurate that designation—would certainly give the Empire cause. Even as she mentally calculated how long it would take to get to her ship, Ahsoka forced herself to slow down, to think—*focus*—before she reacted.

The Empire had no reason to suspect she was on Raada. Officially, Ahsoka Tano was dead, or at least presumed so.

Even if someone had traced her to Thabeska, no one there had known her true name or her destination when she left. The modifications she'd made to the ship she'd stolen from the Fardis would have rendered it almost impossible to track. There was no need for her to act rashly. She'd leapt at the chance to leave Thabeska and in doing so had left something important undone. She didn't want to make the same mistake again.

The walk back to town was long, and Ahsoka felt exposed the whole way. She watched as more and more Imperial ships landed, cutting off her escape, but she refused to panic. She would make calculated decisions this time, and to do that, she needed information. She didn't bother going home first, as it was already late afternoon. Instead, she went to Selda's, where she knew she was most likely to hear something useful.

The cantina was nearly empty when she arrived, as the crews were still making their way back into town after their shift. Ahsoka was going to head for her friends' usual table in the back but paused when Selda waved her into a seat at the bar. She trusted the older Togruta, knew it the same way she'd known to trust Master Plo, so she sat.

Ahsoka spent most of the early evening perched on one

of the barstools. Though this meant her back was to the door, it had its advantages: when you don't look at people, they assume you can't hear them. She overheard several conversations about Imperial theories that were not intended for her ears. Selda, from his place behind the bar, kept watch under the guise of his usual work. The system functioned pretty well.

They hadn't even talked about it, which was the strangest part. Ahsoka had just parked on the stool, Selda had nodded, and they'd begun. It was the sort of thing she might have done with Anakin, though espionage with Anakin Skywalker always ended with explosions, and Ahsoka had no intention of going that far. When two armored troopers and two uniformed officers walked in, she decided it was time to retreat somewhere less conspicuous. She needed only to learn as much as possible about what was going on, not get involved in any messes.

The cantina door opened again, and Kaeden came in, the rest of her crew behind her. It gave Ahsoka the excuse she needed to move. Selda had kept some food hot for the workers and carried it to their usual spot in the back as soon as he saw them enter.

"Hey, Ashla," Kaeden said quietly as she passed, and Ahsoka fell into step beside her.

"How was your day?" Ahsoka asked as they all sat down around the table.

"Tense," Vartan said, nodding in the direction of the Imperials. "Lot of new people come to watch."

"Hoban, get the crokin board," Neera ordered.

It was a testament to the seriousness of the situation that Hoban did as he was told without protest. As he returned with the enormous hexagonal board, Ahsoka saw the cleverness of Neera's idea: the board was shaped in such a way that the players moved around it. They would have reasons to put their heads together and talk, and it would look like they were only lining up the next shot. Hoban spilled the little round discs onto the board and sorted them by color. They began to play.

"How many new friends did you make today, Kaeden?" Ahsoka asked.

"None," Kaeden grumbled. "The troopers don't talk very much, and the officers seem to think we're beneath them."

She flicked a disc, and it lodged behind one of the pegs that protruded from the board. Neera huffed. It would be difficult to hit the piece. Hoban lined up a shot.

"They wouldn't talk to any of the crew leads, either," Vartan said. "We went to collect payroll and they were there, but whatever they want, it doesn't involve us at all."

"Oh," said Hoban, "it'll involve us, all right."

He flicked his disc. It bounced off one of the pegs and settled without hitting Kaeden's piece first, so he cleared it off the board. Malat lined up her shot and sunk the disc in the center of the board with little visible effort. Her points registered on the scoreboard and the celebratory song played. She fiddled with a wire until the sound cut out.

"I heard them at the fueling station," Miara said. Her shot missed Kaeden's piece, too, so she removed her disc. "They were asking about how fast things grow and how much we can plant at a time."

"Even Imperials have to eat," Neera said. "Do you think troopers grow on trees?"

A shudder ran down Ahsoka's spine.

"Are the troopers clones?" she asked, hoping she sounded casual enough. They were being aged out of the Imperial army, she knew, but it had only been a little more than a year, so it was possible that some of the newer ones were still active.

"I don't think so," Vartan said. "They didn't take off their helmets, so I can't be sure, but I heard them talking among themselves and they all sounded different."

Ahsoka always thought the clones sounded different, but Yoda said that was because she took the time to really listen to them. Still, if Vartan could tell them apart, that was probably a good sign for her own security. It was her turn, so she lined up a shot, aiming the same way Malat had. It occurred to her that it would be very easy to cheat at crokin if she used the Force, but now was not the time for experimentation.

Her shot went long, skimming over the center of the board and landing on the opponents' side. Hoban gloated. Now his team had something much easier to aim for. Neera took Ahsoka's piece with no problem and ricocheted her own piece behind a peg. Now it was up to Kaeden to make the hard shot.

Ahsoka had never played crokin before she arrived on Raada, though everyone claimed it was a very popular game. She found it oddly comforting. It could be played in teams or with just a pair, and the goals were twofold: get your own pieces on the board, but stay aware of your opponent, and knock any of your opponent's pieces off it. It was a good strategy game, and she thought Obi-Wan would have liked it. He was the more patient of her teachers.

"How long have those Imperials been here?" Vartan asked. He wasn't playing and instead just sat at their table, looking every bit the indulgent crew lead letting his people relax after a good day's work.

"They got here just a moment before you did," Ahsoka said. "They're still on their first round, and they haven't spoken to anyone since they gave Selda their order. The stormtroopers haven't sat down, and the officers just watch."

"Not exactly subtle," said Miara. Kaeden had missed her shot, and now Hoban was trying again.

"I don't think the Empire goes for subtle," Neera said.

"But why here?" Kaeden said. "I mean, there are better planets for food than Raada. We're tiny. We don't produce that much for export."

There was a very heavy silence. Malat's long fingers hesitated on her shot, and Ahsoka knew she was thinking of her children. Even though Ahsoka's concern for her own safety was no longer immediate, she had a bad feeling about this.

"I think it might be smart to start accumulating ration packs," Ahsoka said. She tried to sound knowledgeable but not expert. She wanted them to listen to her, not follow her orders. "If the Imperials start to dip into the food you grow to eat here, there isn't going to be a lot you can do to stop them."

"That's a good idea," Vartan said. "I'll let Selda know." His eyes flicked past the place where the Imperial officers were sitting. "Later."

Ahsoka nodded and took her turn at the crokin board. She missed the shot, as well. Neera's piece was just too well protected behind the peg. They did another full round, Ahsoka's side trying to dislodge Neera's piece and Hoban's team trying to dislodge Kaeden's. No one had any success, except that it was nice to focus on the frustrations of the game instead of the presence of the Imperials.

Neera was about to take the final shot of the game when there was a disturbance at the front of the cantina. The two officers had been joined by a third, a superior judging by his insignia. The officers stood and saluted. The stormtroopers remained motionless. The new officer leaned forward to confer with his fellows but spoke too quietly for Ahsoka to hear what he said. Then he marched to the doorway and fastened a notice to the wall. He looked around the cantina with some measure of scorn for the occupants before leaving. The other Imperials followed him out without looking back.

Selda walked slowly across the cantina toward the notice. Ahsoka wondered if he would tear it down, but he only read it quietly, his shoulders slumping more with every line.

"The thing about crokin," said Vartan, taking the last disc from Neera's grasp, "is that you don't have to hit the opponent's piece head-on. You can wing it, if you want, and hope for a good ricochet."

He lined up the shot and flicked the disc at Kaeden's. He clipped the edge, and both pieces went flying off the board.

"Sometimes you don't get it," he said. "But you still get points."

Neera's piece was the only one remaining on the board. Her points showed up on the scoreboard a moment later, once the board realized that all the pieces had been played and the game was over.

"We still win," Kaeden said. "We have Malat's points from the beginning."

"That's the other thing about crokin," Vartan added. "You have to remember every piece that's been played, even the ones removed from the board, because some of them might count against you in the end."

His words made Ahsoka uncomfortable. She didn't like the way she automatically began to think about tactics. She got up from the table and went to read the notice board. It was, as she suspected, a list of rules. There was a curfew in place now, which would, among other things, make it nearly impossible for anyone working the late shift to eat out when they were done. They'd have to eat at home. There were rules forbidding group meetings of more than a certain number. The Imperials weren't closing the cantinas, but they were shortening the hours and restricting the food and alcohol available. With the lost business, it would be only a matter of time before the cantinas closed on their own.

It was everything you'd do to keep the locals from communicating with each other and getting organized. It was everything you'd do to soften them up before the hammer fell. It was everything Ahsoka didn't think the farmers on Raada would be able to counter. Scenarios ran through her mind, ideas for insurgency and defense. Reluctantly, this time she let them.

She turned away from the notice and made space for the others who wanted to read it. She pushed her way back through the strange and crowded silence to where her friends were sitting, and when she sat down, she relayed what she'd read. She didn't tell them any of her conclusions about what the new rules meant. They would figure it out, or they wouldn't, but she would have to be careful to conceal her military experience now. There was no guessing how it might be used against her if the Imperials found out. She had to keep her secrets for as long as she could.

Ahsoka looked at the crokin board, at the single piece that remained despite the efforts of both sides. They'd traded shots, and even Ahsoka's mistake, which provided an easier target, hadn't been enough to change the game's outcome. Neera's piece hadn't been enough to make a difference in the end. The game had been settled on the third move, long before any of them was aware of it.

Ahsoka had no idea what points the Empire might have stowed away already, but she knew it was one of the tactics the Imperials used. Order 66 had been part of a very long game, and there was no reason to think that Palpatine had gotten any less foresighted since gaining full power. She was also aware that Raada didn't have much to fight with, if it came to a fight. No real ships for air support, no heavy artillery. But maybe it wouldn't go that far. Maybe they would be lucky. Maybe the Empire would take what it wanted and go.

Maybe it would, she thought. But what would it leave behind?

08

TWO STORMTROOPERS stopped at Ahsoka's house the next morning. She'd locked the door, setting Miara's device for security before she went to sleep. It was a small defense, but at least it would be a warning if she needed it. Now it prevented the stormtroopers from simply barging in.

The troopers hammered on the door, and Ahsoka considered her options. Resisting would be stupid at this point. For all she knew, they just needed directions or wanted a count of the number of people who lived in town. Ahsoka could handle two troopers, even if they turned out to be clones, but it wouldn't be quiet. Better to be Ashla for as long as she could. She took a deep breath, remembered to look at the ground, and opened the door.

"Can I help you, sirs?" she asked.

"Why aren't you at work?" one of them snapped. Vartan was right. They weren't clones. Ahsoka relaxed, just a little bit.

"I am at work," she said. "I mean, I'm not a farmer. I fix the equipment when it's broken, see?"

She gestured behind her, where the pieces of the broken vaporator were still spread out on the table. It was an easy fix, but the previous day had been a little distracting.

"We'll need your information," said the other trooper. "You may be reassigned to field work if it becomes necessary."

Ahsoka paused. She did not want to be exposed out in the fields. She didn't have a lot of freedom, but in town she could almost always find an excuse to leave and go into the hills. It was important she maintain that. She raised her eyes and looked directly at the stormtroopers' helmets, where their eyes were concealed behind lenses.

"You don't need to reassign me," she said, and leaned on them with the Force. "The work I do is important for food production."

It hung there for a moment, and Ahsoka wondered if she'd pushed too far. But then they looked at each other.

"We don't need to reassign her," said the first one.

"The work she does is important for food production," the second agreed.

Ahsoka smiled. "So glad we could have this little chat. Is there anything else I can help you with?"

The stormtroopers looked at her, confused for a moment. She could imagine their blinking eyes and perplexed expressions, except she didn't know what their faces looked like. She refused to imagine them with Rex's face. They shook their heads, lowering their blasters and taking half a step back.

"Make sure you follow the new rules," the second trooper said. "They are posted in several places around the town. Familiarize yourself with them."

"I will," she said. "Have a good day!"

She shut the door before they could say anything else. She liked how flummoxed they seemed by basic manners, though her intrusion into their minds was likely part of their befuddlement. She activated the lock with a quick press of her finger and it glowed green as it sealed the door.

"Remind me to ask Miara what happens if you get triggered," she said to the lock, absently running her hand across the control pad. Miara had said it would be shocking to any-one who broke in, and Ahsoka hadn't asked for specifics at the time. Now, though, it was probably a good idea to be aware of what everyone around her was capable of.

The Imperials were still setting up their base. The Star Destroyer was gone, or at least out of sight, but it had left behind the building blocks for a good-sized administrative building and barracks that could house several dozen storm-troopers. They hadn't had time to lock down the spaceport yet, and Ahsoka wanted to get her ship out of there before they did. The only problem was that she had no other place to put it.

She looked at the vaporator parts. They could wait another day.

She emptied the crate of ration packs—Kaeden's payment for the very first repair job—into her bag. Almost all of them fit, but after a moment's thought, Ahsoka took ten out and put them back in the crate. She would need some food on hand, after all. She added the latest package of metal pieces to the top of the bag and filled her water canteen. After a moment's thought, she added a cutting tool to the bag as well, then picked up the shredded cloths that the vaporator had been wrapped in when its owner dropped it off. She twisted them until they looked like a hunting sling and hung it from her belt, hoping that any Imperials she ran into didn't know that hunting on this moon was next to pointless. Then she went to the door and looked up and down the street.

There was no sign of the stormtroopers. They couldn't harass her neighbors, because most of them were at work, so they must have moved on. Ahsoka walked out onto the street and then made for the edge of town as quickly as she could. When she reached the last house, she looked around, and up, for any newly installed methods of Imperial surveillance but found nothing. Then she squared her shoulders and set out toward the hills as if it were any other day. There was a time for stealth, but when stealth was impossible, the only other option was to walk like she was meant to be there.

It was nerve-wracking. She had no indication that anyone was watching her, but she still felt uncomfortably exposed. At least it was less oppressive than it had been the day before, now that the Imperial ships were grounded. She didn't look back, but she wanted to, and it was all she could do to maintain an even pace as she walked. At last she reached the first line of hills and disappeared from view of the town.

Ahsoka went first to her cave, where she removed the stone slab. She used the cutter to slice away at the shelf until she'd hollowed out the hidden compartment she'd first imagined the day she found the cave. The tool was not made for stone, but it got the job done eventually. She hid the extra ration packs, along with the metal pieces. As she set them down, she thought she saw a familiar pattern to them that she hadn't noticed before. There were connections, wires, between the pieces that could still conduct power. Casually, she waved her hand over them and they moved to fall in line as she saw them in her mind's eye.

"No," she said, letting her hand drop. The pieces rolled across the stone, and she scooped them up. She had other things to do.

With everything secure again, Ahsoka left the cave. She paused at the entrance, wondering if there was something else she could do to conceal it from view, but she couldn't think of anything. The best she could do was make sure the inside of the cave looked entirely natural. She ducked back inside and cleaned up all her footprints.

Her pack significantly lighter, she continued into the hills. Now she was looking for something particular: a hill big enough that any cave inside it might be able to fit her ship. The freighter wasn't huge, but it was too large to stash in a hollow and hope no Imperials ever flew over it. She needed a cave, or perhaps a canyon where she could add her own cover.

She kept a close eye on the sky as she rambled through the hills, both in case she had company and to keep track of the time. She couldn't afford to have her disappearance remarked on, and even though Kaeden and the others wouldn't turn her in intentionally, all it took to raise suspicion was one overheard remark at a place like Selda's. Just when she was thinking she would have to head back to town and try again the following morning, she saw a dip in the ground ahead of her. It looked almost like an optical illusion, but when she got close to the edge, she saw that it was actually a small gully. The ship would only fit in sideways, which she knew it wouldn't like, but she could make it work.

"Well," she said, "that was the easy part. Now all I have to do is get the ship out here."

She really, really missed R2-D2. The little droid was always good at this sort of thing. She decided that stealing her own ship would be much the same as walking out to the hills had been. Stealth was impossible, so she would just have to do it.

Ahsoka went back into town. Again, she met no one and saw no signs that her movements had been observed. When she got near the Imperial base, she saw immediately why that was. It looked like every stormtrooper brought to occupy Raada was engaged patrolling the locals who had been press-ganged into construction. Ahsoka scoffed. Rex would never have been so lax with security. Even if it made the building process difficult, he would have insisted that some of his men patrol the streets.

It occurred to Ahsoka that the stormtroopers were not necessarily the strongest soldiers yet and none of the officers assigned to Raada had much experience. That was useful information.

She made it all the way to the spaceport before she met anyone. A very junior-looking Imperial officer was making a list of all the ships docked there. She considered using the Force to convince him to let her take her ship. She could pretend she was under orders from one of the overseers, who appeared to be the only people the Imperials would talk to. It would be easy to play the overwhelmed hired hand and then nudge the officer a bit when he was distracted.

At the same time, he might have been trained to recognize Jedi powers when they were used on him. The stormtroopers had been risky enough. Ahsoka couldn't take the same chance on an officer.

She could go home and fake up some credentials, but then she wouldn't be able to move the ship until the next day. Every moment she waited was another moment one of the Imperials might remember that they were occupying a planet and they should act like it. Ahsoka couldn't afford to wait. She walked out into the yard. She would have to play her way through this by getting more creative. Or, rather, Ashla would.

"You, stop right there," said the officer. Ahsoka was pretty sure he was trying to make his voice deeper than it was. "What are you doing?"

"I've come for my ship," said Ahsoka. "All these new security measures are making me nervous. I want to keep my property where only I have access to it."

"I assure you, the Imperial garrison stationed here will maintain a high level of security at this spaceport," the young officer blustered. "Your ship will be safe."

Slowly, and with considerable scorn, she looked him up and down.

"Are you high-level security?" she asked. "Because you don't inspire a lot of confidence."

His chest puffed out, and his face turned red. As she'd

hoped, she hadn't made him angry. She'd embarrassed him.

"I'm in charge of all the ships here," he told her. "It is my specific job and specific training to ensure that the spaceport runs smoothly and securely."

"I was able to walk right in here without anyone stopping me," Ahsoka said. "I hardly call that secure!"

"We're still getting set up," the officer said defensively.

"Well, that settles it," Ahsoka said. "I'll take my ship until you're done *getting set up*, and then I'll bring it back when I know everything is safe."

"I really don't think—" began the officer, but Ahsoka had already blown past him.

She was in the pilot's seat and preparing to take off before he mustered any kind of protest, and by then the engines were too loud for her to hear him. She took off and flew in the opposite direction of the hills. It wouldn't take much time to fly around the moon the long way, and it would help cover her tracks before she concealed the ship in the ravine.

As she flew, it occurred to her that she could just keep flying. She could leave Raada, run from the Empire again, and try to set up somewhere it hadn't reached yet. She could find a cave in some isolated mountain range, or an oasis in the middle of a desert. She could go far away and abandon everyone again. Not again. Not again.

She looked down at the fields of Raada, spread out below her, and knew it was a dream, anyway. There was nowhere she could go where the Empire wouldn't find her eventually. No matter how far she went, it would be behind her, nipping at her heels. She might as well face them here, where she was relatively anonymous and moderately prepared.

She set the ship down in the gully, wedging it in backward so that the nose of the vessel pointed straight at the sky. As she'd suspected, the landing struts were very unhappy with her, but the rocky sides of the ravine supported most of the ship's weight. She stayed on the bridge, lying back against the chair and looking up, her mind filled with too many thoughts. She didn't get out of the pilot's seat for a long time.

09

AHSOKA WAS LATE getting back to town, even running the whole way, but her ship was hidden and she was relatively sure no one had detected her as she was hiding it. She stayed in her house only long enough to throw the mostly empty bag on the bed and kick the crate with the ration packs in it under the table before heading to Selda's. She hoped Kaeden and the others hadn't been too vocal in wondering where she was.

There were even fewer people in the cantina that night, as most of them had headed home well in advance of the curfew. Ahsoka had seen this sort of thing before, when she was on Separatist-occupied worlds during the Clone Wars. For the first few days, the locals would observe the rules very closely and see what the reaction to breaking them was. Then they would begin to push back. If the Imperials reacted violently, the pushback could be extreme.

With the thinner crowd, she spotted Kaeden and the others immediately. Malat was gone already, presumably home to her children, but the others were crammed around the crokin board. They were playing a variation Ahsoka hadn't seen before. Instead of all the pieces being shot onto the board one by one, about half of them were carefully placed. In fact, it looked a lot like the Imperial—

Ahsoka sat down and brushed her hand across the board, scattering the pieces.

"Hey!" Hoban said. "We were working on that."

"Could you possibly yell more loudly?" Ahsoka gritted out between clenched teeth. "I don't think they heard you on Alderaan."

Hoban had the sense to look abashed.

"Ashla is right," Vartan said. "We should be more careful discussing things out in the open."

"Where's Malat?" Ahsoka asked.

"Packing," Neera said. "Her husband's family found them work on Sullust. The Empire's there, too, of course, but it's more established. We have no idea what's going to happen here, and they decided it wasn't safe, with the kids and all."

"It's a good idea, if you can manage it," Ahsoka said. "But there's going to be lots who can't."

"You have a ship," Kaeden said. "You can leave whenever you want."

"My ship has been stolen," Ahsoka said, and winked. "Who knows where I might find it."

"I'm glad you're staying," Kaeden said. "I don't know why, but I get the sense you're useful in situations like this."

Ahsoka smiled at her and turned to look at Kaeden's sister. "Miara, I have a question about your locks," she said. "You told me that if anyone broke in, they'd get a shock. What did you mean by that?"

"I set a small electric charge inside the lock mechanism," Miara said. "If it's not disarmed correctly, it delivers a shock that's strong enough to make a person think twice before stealing your gear. Also, there's a dye pack rigged to explode when the charge is delivered, so whoever tries it will stand out in a crowd. Why do you ask?"

Neera was looking at Miara speculatively. Kaeden appeared slightly ill.

"Could you do it with something other than dye?" Vartan asked. "And could it be a bigger charge?"

"Of course," said Miara. "Only then someone might really get hurt instead of . . . oh."

"Let's hold off on that for now," Ahsoka said. "We have other things to worry about."

"Why wait?" Hoban said. "If we can set explosives, why don't we just get rid of the Imperials now?"

"Hoban, keep your voice down." This time it was Neera who admonished him.

"All that would do is bring more Imperials, and they'd crack down harder," Ahsoka told him. "We can't dislodge them entirely. What we need to do is figure out how to survive while they're here."

"We better work quickly," Kaeden said.

There was a commotion at the door, and several uniformed Imperials came in. They glared their way to the bar, where they waited pointedly for the stools to empty. Then they took them over, effectively cutting off Selda from his clientele. The scarred Togruta continued to wipe glasses and arrange them on shelves as if nothing were out of the ordinary. Ahsoka marveled at his apparent nerves of steel.

"Why do you say that?" Ahsoka asked Kaeden.

"I heard the overseers talking today," she said. "They're going to add two hours to every shift, to get as much work out of us as they can."

"There won't be anything to harvest," Hoban said, finally keeping his voice down. "We're almost done, and then we have to wait until the new crops grow."

"The Imperials have something to speed that along," Kaeden said. "They'll use it, and we'll be harvesting again before we know it."

"I've seen them bringing in their own seed," Miara said. "Whatever we're planting, it won't be something we get to keep or sell."

"They'll buy off the overseers," Ahsoka said. "They'll give them enough money to go off-world, and then work the rest of us to the bone. I've seen things like this before."

"Where did you come from?" Neera asked.

"It's not important," Ahsoka said. "You just have to trust me."

"We have to blow things up," said Hoban. "Before they get too organized."

"No," said Ahsoka. "I know it's going to be hard, but we have to wait."

"Why?" Hoban demanded, but before Ahsoka could answer him, there was another disturbance at the front of the bar.

Tibbola was drunk, even though his shift had ended at the same time as Kaeden's. Ahsoka hadn't seen him in weeks, as the laborer made his rounds of the various cantinas and watering holes Raada had to offer. Now, when there were Imperial officers at the bar, he was present, and he was at his worst. Tibbola was cunning enough when he was sober, but this inebriated he was a mess. He'd been glaring at the Imperials ever since they cut him off from the bar. When they blocked his attempt to order another round, he lost what little control he had remaining and tried to muscle his way past them. His blows were clumsy, but he was strong, and enough of his hits landed that the Imperials responded in force. One of them pushed Tibbola back, hard, and Ahsoka knew it was only the opening salvo. The Empire didn't really do warning shots.

"You Imperials." Tibbola's words were slurred as he stumbled back. Somehow he managed to keep his feet. "Coming to my moon and messing with me. You have no idea what you're in for."

An officer casually punched Tibbola in the gut. It was a hard blow, hard enough that Tibbola went to his knees and vomited everything he'd had to drink but not hard enough to keep him down.

Tibbola roared insensibly and charged the officer. Ahsoka lunged quickly and blocked Hoban, who would have gone to help, until Neera could pull him back into his chair. Kaeden and Miara watched, horrified, as the officer deflected Tibbola's attack again. Then, calmly, the officer called out to the stormtroopers who'd been waiting in the street while their superiors drank. They came inside and put their hands on Tibbola's shoulders, keeping him down for good.

"The Empire will not tolerate disobedience," said the officer, more to the others in the cantina than to Tibbola himself.

Tibbola, in a moment of sobriety, seemed to realize what he'd done. His eyes filled with panic as he cast them around the room, looking for someone to help him. No one moved.

"No," he said. "I'm sorry, please!"

But it was no use. The officer gestured to the stormtrooper who stood closest to the door, and the trooper raised his blaster.

"Don't look," Ahsoka whispered into Kaeden's ear, and Kaeden pulled her sister's face down on the table, blocking both their views.

But it didn't block the sound of a blaster in close quarters, or the smell of charred flesh. At least it was fast; Tibbola didn't scream.

The Imperials stepped over the smoking body and exited the cantina. There was no noise for several moments after they left, except the sounds Miara made as she vomited beside the table.

"That's why we have to be careful," Ahsoka said, looking directly at Hoban when she spoke. His eyes were wide, and she knew he'd listen to her now.

"Come on, Hoban," said Vartan. His voice was gray, but determined. "We'll have to bury him tonight."

They picked up the body and carried it out. Neera trailed after them. She looked like she was going to be sick. Ahsoka suspected she'd rather be anywhere else but was reluctant to let her brother out of her sight. Ahsoka didn't blame her. Once they were gone, she looked back at Kaeden and Miara.

"Are you all right?" she asked.

There was a short pause, and then Miara leaned sharply forward, vomiting again into her empty bowl. Kaeden rubbed her sister's shoulders, even though her face was as wan as Ahsoka had ever seen it. Selda came over with water for them and some bread so that Miara could get the taste out of her mouth.

"How can you be so calm?" Miara demanded, her voice high. Ahsoka suspected that the bread was a bit stale and that focusing on chewing it was keeping the girl from full-on hysterics. "Where are you from?"

"Don't bug her," Kaeden said. Her voice was shaky. "Finish that, and we'll go home."

Kaeden wrestled the crokin board back onto the table. While Miara chewed obediently, Kaeden started firing pieces slowly, hitting the center target over and over again, even though that wasn't how the game went. Ahsoka figured it gave her something to focus on.

"You have to take a piece if it's there," Ahsoka mused, looking at the board.

"What?" Kaeden said.

"In crokin," Ahsoka clarified. "You don't just get to take the shots you want. You have to shoot at your opponent's pieces. So let's do that."

"Shoot with what?" Miara asked, her mouth full. "We don't have a lot of blasters."

"No," Ahsoka said. "Not like that. The Imperials want a fast crop. So what you do is slow it down."

"How?" Kaeden said. Both sisters looked better now. Ahsoka had successfully distracted them.

"I have no idea," Ahsoka said. "I'm not a farmer. But Vartan will know, or one of the other crew leads. You still talk to each other in the fields, right? And it's more difficult for the Imperials to overhear you there. You can organize yourselves that way. The crew leads will meet to discuss information and then pass it off to their crews."

"That's very smart," Kaeden said. "And it doesn't even break the rules. We're allowed to meet with our crews."

"I know. That's what makes it such a good plan," Ahsoka said with a wink.

"What are you going to do?" Miara asked. She swallowed the last mouthful of bread. "There's a space in our crew if you want it, because Malat's gone."

Ahsoka considered it—she'd be a terrible farmer, and that would surely slow them down plenty—but then she had a better idea.

"No," she said. "I'm going to stay a mechanic for now, but I'm going to stop being such a good one. If equipment can't be fixed, that will only slow you down more."

"We have to get moving," Kaeden said. "It's almost curfew and we have a bit of a walk."

It wasn't quite that late yet, but Ahsoka hardly needed to press the issue.

"Be safe," Ahsoka told them. "I'll see you tomorrow. Be careful when you tell Vartan my suggestion, but let him run with it if he agrees."

The sisters nodded and headed for the door. Miara took the long way around the cantina floor to avoid stepping on the place where Tibbola had fallen, and Ahsoka watched as Kaeden let her. Then Ahsoka made her way to the bar. She should be going, too, but she wanted to have a word with Selda before she did. She sat on one of the stools before realizing she didn't even know what she wanted to talk to him about.

"That was quick thinking, making sure the girls didn't see," Selda said. "I have a feeling you've seen too much, yourself."

"No argument there," Ahsoka told him wearily.

"Be careful, little one," he said. Ahsoka started to protest, but he raised his real hand and she stopped. "Even if you're not so little, you're littler than me."

She gave him a smile. It felt absurdly nice to be taken care of. Maybe that was what she needed, even if she didn't need it very often. Before, when she'd faced death, she'd had Anakin to talk it over with afterward. She'd handled it on her own since then, of course, but that didn't mean she liked it.

Selda poured all the leftovers into a container and passed it to her. The seal wasn't as good as the one on the ration packs, but the food would still keep for several days. Ahsoka walked home quickly, calculating how much food she could lay her hands on and how long it would last, depending on whom she shared it with. She was still doing variations of the equation when she fell asleep.

10

ONE WEEK BECAME TWO, and the crops grew slowly. The new Imperial overseers extended the shifts again so the farmers were in the fields for nearly the entirety of Raada's daylight. They did not increase the food rations or the number of breaks, though they did allow for more water intake. Imperial efficiency at its finest.

Ahsoka spent her days smuggling food, medical supplies, and water recyclers out to the caves. She had found a networked set in the hills between her original base and where she'd hidden her ship. Selda was her chief supplier in town, though she knew other vendors must have been pitching in, too. She didn't need to know all the details. She just had to do her part.

It had taken Vartan and the other experienced hands a while to identify what they were growing. They'd stalled the planting for as long as they possibly could. The plows all broke, and the mechanic was nowhere to be found, but then the Imperials had withheld food altogether and the farmers had gone back to work. The seeds were planted and watered, and now shoots could be seen sticking up from the soil. It was then that Vartan figured out what they were growing.

"It's not even real food," he said, his voice a disgusted whisper as they huddled around the crokin board at Selda's. "It's for their wretched nutritional supplements, you know, those things they make the military eat because they're tasteless and bland but have all the things you need to live in them."

"I don't see why you find that so offensive," Neera said. "Why do you care what Imperials eat?"

"Because this particular plant leeches everything from the soil it grows in," Vartan said. "By the time we harvest, the fields will all be useless dirt. Nothing will grow for seasons, and it's not like they're going to pay us anything we can use to buy fertilizer with. The whole moon will be ruined."

Kaeden and Miara exchanged worried glances. Raada was the only home they'd ever known, and they had no one else in the galaxy to look out for them. They had nowhere else to go.

"Are there other fields?" Ahsoka asked, her voice as low and calm as she could make it.

"No," Vartan said. "The whole of Raada is nearly useless to begin with. That's why there was never a Hutt presence or anything like that. We just had the overseers, and they were mostly reasonable, but I think the Empire scared them and they abandoned us."

"I can understand that," Neera said. Hoban glared at her. "I'm not saying I like it, but I understand it. Most of them have families, like Malat. Do you hate her for leaving?"

Hoban said nothing for a moment, and Ahsoka knew he was trying to stay angry, because the only other option he saw was hopelessness.

"Can we blow things up yet?" he asked, at last.

"Did you have something particular in mind?" Ahsoka asked.

"Do you?" Hoban demanded.

Ahsoka sighed, and decided it was time to lay all her cards on the table. Or at least most of her cards. If she kept holding out, it was only a matter of time before Hoban did something stupid, and that might put Kaeden and Miara in harm's way.

"There are caves out in the hills," she said. She took a crokin disc off the top of the pile and flicked it toward the center of the board. It landed neatly behind one of the pegs, blocking it from an opponent's shot.

"Everyone knows that," Hoban said. "There are too many to map effectively, and nothing grows out there, so no one goes there."

"I go there," Ahsoka said. "And I take all kinds of interesting things with me."

"You've been setting up camps?" Kaeden said. "Without telling anyone?"

"Selda knows," Neera said. Ahsoka raised an eyebrow and Neera shrugged. "Selda knows everything, and he's the one who'd be supplying your food, I imagine."

"Yes," Ahsoka said. "But it's not just food. There are several water recyclers and whatever medical supplies I could scrounge. There's also a lot of junked-up equipment. You know, sharp blades and circuits you have to be careful not to overload, because they might blow up on you."

"But you still want us to wait," Hoban said. "While our home dies underneath us."

"I want you to *think*," Ahsoka said.

"Lay off, Hoban. She's right," Neera said. She turned to the board and tried firing a crokin disc. It missed, bouncing off the peg that concealed Ahsoka's piece.

"What do you want us to do?" Vartan asked. "We can't slow down in the fields much more than we already are. The Imperials will notice and start withholding food again."

"Can you spare Miara and Kaeden for a few days?" Ahsoka asked. "I'd like to take them with me. Miara can start building those bigger *locks* you talked about, and Kaeden and I can organize the rest of our potential gear. I can fix a machine well enough, but Kaeden's more familiar with the local geography. She can help me decide where to put it."

Vartan looked at the girls and nodded.

"We'll tell the Imperials you're sick, if they ask," he said. "And we'll mysteriously forget where you live so they can't check on you themselves. It's not much of a cover story, but it's the best we can do."

"It'll be fine," Ahsoka said. "We only need a few days to get organized, and then we'll be able to check in with you again. In the meantime, keep your heads down. We're all in enough danger as it is."

Miara's gaze turned to the spot on the floor where Tibbola had been gunned down, but Hoban only glared at Ahsoka. If he had any protests to make, he didn't voice them. Instead, Selda arrived at the table with what passed for a hot dinner under the new Imperial restrictions, and soon everyone was too busy eating to talk.

◆ ◆ ◆

Jenneth Pilar sat in his new temporary office and scrolled through the numbers. It was therapeutic, seeing his calculations add up the way he wanted them to, over and over and over again. He was encouraged by the scarcity of errors and the smallness of the margins. He had everything figured out perfectly. Here, in this bare little room on this soon-to-be-bare world, he had calculated life and death and gotten paid for it. Not bad work, all things considered, though the food was terrible.

Raada was a tedious little place, but it would serve its purpose. The Empire would get what it wanted and then be on its way. The farmers would have their freedom again, for all the good it would do them. They really should have thought of the risks before they became farmers. Jenneth turned a blind eye to his part in their incipient suffering, a privilege that came with never really having suffered.

He looked out the window at the ordered rows in the fields and then the grasslands beyond them, where nothing useful could grow. Beyond that were the low-lying hills that made up the rest of the moon's surface—rocky, useless, and probably cold once the sun went down. But something about them niggled at Jenneth's sense of order. He hadn't included the hills in his calculations, because the planetary scans he'd studied had assured him they were barren. At the same time, their mere existence should merit their inclusion in his formula. He hated unbalanced equations.

In the morning he would commandeer a ship and take a closer look. He couldn't go now, as much as he suddenly wished to, because it was too late in the day. It was nearly curfew, with the sun setting and the last poor ragged souls stumbling home after a hard day of near slavery in service of the Empire. If only they knew what awaited them.

Jenneth looked with great distaste at his dinner, a tube of pure nutrition that left his insides feeling somehow cheated, and counted the days until he was away from this moon. It couldn't come soon enough. He pulled up his calculations again and let the running tally of labor, production, yield, and destruction wash over him. Not bad work, the jobs he did, and he was going to make sure he kept doing well enough that the Empire would keep paying him to do it. He had no intention of ending up like the benighted souls who called Raada home: destitute and marooned on a lifeless rock.

They talked in the fields. The Imperials couldn't hear what they plotted there, and neither could the girl who called herself Ashla.

"I don't think this is a good idea," Kaeden said. "Ashla wants us to wait."

"Ashla isn't from here," Hoban said. "She got to Raada only just before the Imperials did, and she wouldn't even tell you her *name* at first. We don't know anything about her. For all we know, she's with them."

"That's ridiculous," Kaeden said, but even Miara looked hesitant.

Kaeden bristled. She didn't like it when other people speculated about her feelings, especially when they were right. Neera held up a hand.

"Look, Kaeden, I know you like her, but think about it," Neera said. "Ashla said it herself. She doesn't understand farming. She doesn't really understand what we lose every day this blasted plant is in the ground. She has a ship. She can go whenever she wants."

"But she hasn't!" Kaeden said.

"Anyone with any sense has left," Neera said. "Anyone who can. And yet she stays. Why do you think that is?"

"Maybe she likes us," Kaeden said.

"Oh, Kaeden," Neera said. It was almost kind but edged too far into pity to be pleasant to hear.

"Don't treat me like a child, Neera," Kaeden said, and hated how petulant she sounded. "And don't you dare involve my sister in anything dangerous."

"I'll do what I want," Miara said. Kaeden looked sharply at her. They were almost the same height now. When had *that* happened?

"All we're saying is that when Miara builds things for Ashla's stores, she also builds things for us," Hoban said. "It makes sense to have our supplies split up. That way if something happens to Ashla, we're not strung out on our own."

Kaeden hesitated. She wanted to trust Ashla, but what

Hoban was saying made sense. Ashla had said a lot of it herself, or at least implied it. She'd worked with Selda without telling any of them, and she'd stolen her own ship. It couldn't do much harm for Kaeden to help her own crew make their own plans.

"Okay," she said. "I'm in. Tomorrow Miara and I will go with Ashla and learn as much as we can. And we'll share it with you."

"Good," Hoban said. He looked up and saw that Vartan was heading back toward them, so he turned away from the girls and focused on his job.

◆ ◆ ◆

Hoban was watering today. The work didn't take a lot of his concentration but required strong shoulder muscles, which he had in plenty. Miara was too little to be more than a runner, so she'd been carrying messages. Hoban's shoulders ached under the weight. He didn't mind hard work, but this was extreme, and it was only a matter of time before he got too weak to work on the rations he was given. And if he was feeling it, the others were, too.

The girls would crumple first, he knew. They were strong, but they weren't indestructible. Miara was already attracting too much attention from the Imperials as they questioned her abilities in the field. If they sent her off, she'd lose what small rations she was still getting. Hoban was helping them, even if Ashla couldn't see it. She just didn't understand farming like he did, but she would, and then she'd realize that they were all in this together.

AHSOKA GOT A *terrible bargain for the ship, but she didn't care. It was money she hadn't had before she made the trade, and the ship was too noticeable, too easy to trace. She was better off without it, even though she was now much less mobile. She cleared every trace of herself from the cockpit and hold, and handed over the launch codes with only a moment's hesitation.*

The man who bought the ship had brown skin and black hair and said his name was Fardi, even though Ahsoka hadn't asked. His daughters, or maybe nieces—Ahsoka wasn't entirely clear on their relationship—had been the ones to meet her at the landing pad. They had the same coloring as Fardi, only their glossy black hair was long enough to sit on and completely straight. They'd chattered about the city, about where Ahsoka could find food and a place to stay, so Ahsoka had asked if they knew of anyone who might buy her ship for a decent price.

Or at least a nearly decent price. But the trade had made her a friend, and it wasn't like she had bought the ship with her own credits in the first place.

The Fardi girls—it turned out Fardi was their family name—took Ahsoka under their wing, even though she was at least three years older than the eldest of them. It was they who showed her the vacant house she would buy and they who told her which shops had the best prices. Once they found out Ahsoka could fix droids, her place was secure in what she was coming to realize was a neat little smuggling operation. Sure, several of the Fardi businesses were legitimate, but they mostly served to cover for the less legitimate ones. Ashla didn't ask questions, so they liked to have her around. In return, Ahsoka made a bit of money and didn't have to answer any questions about where she'd come from, which she thought was a fair deal.

For several months, Ahsoka had slipped into a sort of functional comatose state. She refused to feel anything and didn't talk to anyone much, but she was able to go about the business of daily life as though nothing was wrong. Someone who knew her wouldn't have been fooled for an instant, but no one knew her anymore, so the deception held. She was even mostly able to deceive herself and believe that Ashla was a real person after all. She liked being useful and being a part of something, and the Fardis dealt in money, not blood, so she was able to sleep at night.

Two months before the first anniversary of Palpatine's ascension to Emperor, Ahsoka saw something that nearly changed everything. She was at the shipyard, tinkering with one of the bigger droids that wasn't easy to take off-site. Several of the youngest Fardi kids were playing in the yard, which they weren't supposed to do, because it was dangerous. Ahsoka was about to shoo them out when a stack of crates that a couple of the kids were playing on wobbled and started to fall.

Afterward, when she was able to think about it, Ahsoka

was glad to know that she'd responded instantly, reaching out with the Force. The numbness she had worked so hard to maintain since Order 66 remained intact, but she hadn't watched mutely as the crates fell, the children screaming as they fell, too. She'd acted.

And then the screaming stopped. The crates settled gently on the ground, and the children settled just as gently on top of them. The other kids stared, unable to figure out what had happened, but Ahsoka knew. She got ready to run. She looked around and saw little Hedala Fardi, too small to be included in the game, standing just clear of the crates with a fascinated look on her face.

"You know you're not supposed to play out here," Ahsoka said, hoping to head off any awkward questions the kids might have had. "You were almost crushed by falling crates. That's no way for a Fardi to go out!"

She was right to appeal to their pride and fear of the trouble they'd be in if they got caught. They made Ahsoka swear not to give them up—for her silence, she exacted from them a fair amount of sweets, the only currency they had—and then they all ran off. They never mentioned *it again, and Ahsoka was fairly certain they hadn't even noticed their brush with physical impossibility.*

She watched Hedala closely after that. She was certain that the child was the only one who'd fully seen and understood what Ahsoka had done. Three days later, she watched with some horror as Hedala, left alone by the older kids, casually moved a small stone from one side of a doorway to the other without laying so much as a finger on it.

She should have done something. She should have told the girl's family and helped get her off-world. But she had no idea how to hide a Force-sensitive child from the Empire. She could barely hide herself. So she did nothing instead. She told herself she would think of a plan, but she didn't, or at least she didn't try very hard.

And then it was Empire Day and the Imperials came in greater numbers. Ahsoka could have stood her ground, could have fought them, but she couldn't take on the whole Empire herself. When the Fardi girls warned her and offered her a way out, she took it without a second thought. She didn't remember Hedala Fardi until she was in orbit, and then it was too late.

11

KAEDEN SAT CROSS-LEGGED on top of a crate, with a map of Raada spread out in her lap, and watched her sister. Miara was working on a series of explosives, all with higher yields than any of the stingers she put in her locks, and Kaeden was a little sickened by how easy it was for Miara to build them. Ashla had gone out for an hour or so, to fetch something, she'd said, and Miara had taken advantage of the time to build bombs that were more to Hoban's specifications than the ones Ashla had suggested.

"It's a good combination, I think," Miara said as she worked. She was oblivious to her sister's distaste, or else she was willfully ignoring it. "Ashla's bombs are good for the joints of Imperial walkers or blowing doors open. Hoban's will clear our path wherever we need to go."

"What if there are people where you're clearing?" Kaeden asked. "It's like turning your thresher loose, only it's people who get cut up instead of crops."

For the first time Miara hesitated. Then her expression hardened.

"It's us or them," she said. She didn't sound fourteen any-more. "Kaeden, we don't have a choice."

Kaeden didn't say anything. She'd spent a couple of hours the day before, after their shift was over, trying to talk Miara out of Hoban's plan, but it hadn't done any good. Every time she tried, Miara countered with an example of a time some-one on Raada had helped them before they were old enough to help themselves. Kaeden felt each one of those debts like a weight around her neck. Before she was old enough to work full shifts, it had been kindness and generosity that kept her and her sister fed and let them keep their family house, the one their parents had built when they'd decided to settle on

Raada. It wasn't much, but Kaeden liked making breakfast on the stove her father had used, and she liked fixing the walls her mother had built, even if she wasn't her mother's match when it came to construction. Miara knew how Kaeden felt and for the first time was absolutely merciless in leveraging it against her. By the time she'd given up and gone to bed, Kaeden had almost been the one to change her mind. Then she'd dreamed of Tibbola getting shot; only it was Vartan getting shot in his place, and then Miara, and then Ashla, all while Kaeden had to watch.

In the morning, she'd been shaken and conflicted, and mostly useless. She didn't tell Ashla what the others were up to, and she didn't help Miara much, either, despite her sister's glaring. Instead she mostly stared at the map and hoped that no one asked her any questions she didn't want to give the answers to.

It had worked pretty well, for the first few hours. She and Ashla couldn't make any marks on the map, in case it fell into the wrong hands, Ashla said, but they did discuss where the caves Ashla had found were and where they might set up an encampment big enough for all the people Vartan was recruiting under the guise of field meetings. Then all Kaeden had to do was commit it to memory, which was what she was ostensibly doing while Ashla was out on her mysterious errand.

"Where do you think she went?" Miara asked. Kaeden hoped her sister was trying to change the subject and was more than happy to help with that.

"I have no idea," Kaeden said. She pointed at the map. "This is the main cave system. There are tunnels to others, but most of them are too small to drag gear through. They're only big enough for a person with a small pack. She might have gone to bring something around from one of those caves to this one. We talked about a door, or more likely a cover for the entryway to conceal it a bit."

"A door would be a good idea," Miara said. "I can secure it, if we can get it installed."

"There's also her stores," Kaeden said. "I know she has private ones, because her ship's still out there somewhere, but she has one for us, too, the one she set up with Selda."

"I wish she'd tell us where her ship is," Miara said.

"I wish you'd tell her about the bombs," Kaeden fired back. "But you won't, so stop complaining."

"I just don't know why she's so eager to help," Miara said, echoing Neera from the evening before. "She could leave whenever she wants."

"Do you want her to go?" Kaeden asked, all but daring her sister to voice the taunt about Kaeden's feelings for Ashla that had so far been left unspoken. Miara didn't take the bait.

"Of course not," Miara said. "She knows more about this sort of thing than anyone else on Raada does. I just want her to tell us how she learned it."

"Well," Kaeden said. "Maybe give her some more time. I think whatever happened to her was very bad and she doesn't want to talk about it yet."

Miara made a noncommittal sound and went back to the intricacies of her engineering work. Kaeden ran a finger along a line on the map, one that delineated a steep-sloped gully. That was where she'd hide a ship, if she had a ship to hide. She wasn't about to share that information with Miara, though.

Ashla appeared in the entrance of the cave, startling both girls. She was carrying a pack so massive that Kaeden wasn't sure how she'd been able to carry it at all. Ashla wasn't broad-shouldered like Neera or tall like Vartan, and she didn't have years of experience working in the fields to bolster her strength, but somehow she was clearly very strong though she looked delicate. Maybe it was a Togruta thing. Kaeden didn't know much about their physiology, but she liked it.

"Here's all the supplies I had stashed away in the first cave

I found." The pack made a loud clunk when she set it down. "I started to set it up before I knew I was going to be sharing. But it's probably better to have everything in one place."

Miara was about to make a biting remark about the ship, but Kaeden cut her off before she could.

"Why did you set up a stash as soon as you got here?" she asked. "There weren't any Imperials yet."

"Old habits," Ashla said. She tried to make it sound like a joke, but there was something deadly serious in her eyes. "I wasn't sure how safe the house was, but now I know better."

Kaeden got up to help her unload, and they spent the next couple of hours organizing where the medical supplies should go and trying to activate a power converter that looked like it was older than all three of them combined.

"What's that?" Miara asked as they settled in with a ration pack each and one canteen of water to pass among them.

Ashla was holding a small cloth bag. Kaeden had seen her pick it out of the larger bundle earlier in the afternoon but hadn't said anything.

"Oh, just some odds and ends I've collected," Ashla said. She opened the bag so Miara could look inside.

"There's a lot of junk in here," Miara said dismissively. "I mean, I can't use any of it. They don't even match."

"It's just something I do," Ashla said. There was an odd note in her voice, a mix of defensiveness and longing that Kaeden thought she recognized.

"Our mum was like that," Kaeden said. "Always had pockets full of scraps she'd found. It drove our father crazy, the things he'd find when he did the washing."

"They used to fight about it," Miara said. "But in the good way, you know?"

Kaeden realized it was quite likely that Ashla didn't know, but it was a question she couldn't resist asking.

"Did your parents bicker?" she asked. "The adoptive ones, I mean."

A slow smile broke across Ashla's face, curling first one side of her mouth and then the other. Whatever she was remembering, Kaeden could tell it was good.

"All the time," Ashla said, almost as if she were talking to herself.

Miara launched into a story about their parents, a small power coupling, and the horn that sounded to mark shift change. It was a story Kaeden remembered well, so she only half listened as her sister talked. The rest of her attention was concentrated on what she was going to do next: if she would listen to Ashla's advice or stick with her sister and her crew.

She knew she couldn't abandon Miara, but a lot of what Ashla suggested seemed like a good idea. In the end, she reached a compromise that suited both sides of her warring conscience. She would stay with Miara and listen very carefully to what Hoban planned. If Vartan thought it was a good idea, she'd go along with it, but the second things got out of hand, she'd find Ashla and tell her everything. The solution wasn't perfect, but she could work with it, and Kaeden was good at working.

"What are you looking so serious about?" Miara asked when Kaeden didn't laugh at the funny part of the story. Ashla did, which at least made Kaeden smile.

"I'm sorry," she said. "I'm tired, and a little worried about all of this."

She waved her hand at the cave in general but knew her sister would interpret the gesture differently than Ashla would.

"We should get some rest," Ashla said. "We've got a few more days out here, and all the jobs require attention to detail."

The cave floor was hard, but they were able to set up a place to sleep on a flat part of it, where no rocks protruded from the floor.

"Medical cots," Ashla mused as she unfolded a blanket. "I have no idea how we'd carry them out here, though."

"Selda will have an idea," Kaeden said, and they bedded down for the night.

◆ ◆ ◆

For the next two days, Miara built explosives to Ahsoka's specifications. It took more parts than Ahsoka was expecting, but weapons manufacture had never been her strongest suit. While Miara worked, Ahsoka and Kaeden installed the door, using an old metal hatch Selda had somehow procured and a spot welder that short-circuited at the most inopportune moments. Then they carefully collapsed most of the other cave entrances. They left a few intact, the ones that were most hidden from view and the one that had a straight line of sight to the settlement. It was risky, but Ahsoka decided that entrance was strategically necessary. There was no good in setting up a camp if they couldn't keep watch from it.

On the fourth day, they slipped back to town just as the sun was setting. Kaeden and Miara went straight home, since they would have to report to the fields the next day, but Ahsoka went to Selda's to meet up with Vartan. Over a crokin game, which Ahsoka lost with astounding incompetence to Vartan's superior play, the crew lead outlined how his work had gone.

"I picked the other crew leads carefully," he said. "Not just the ones who have been on Raada the longest but the ones who have worked with the same teams for the longest time."

Ahsoka took a shot and missed. It was a difficult game when she couldn't use all her abilities to the fullest.

"I watched the stormtroopers, and they have units and patrol groups. I thought it would make sense to keep ourselves organized, too, and we already have teams we're used to working with, so that's how I recruited people," Vartan continued. "It worked out well."

"How many people?" Ahsoka asked. Vartan landed another disc in the center of the board, and his points showed up in flashing lights on the scoreboard.

"Eight crews, including ours," Vartan said. "So that's about forty, once we account for additions like you and subtractions like Malat and her husband."

There was no bitterness when he spoke of Malat, even though she had been on his crew for longer than any of the others. Ahsoka knew that Malat had tried to arrange for Kaeden and Miara to go with her family, but she didn't think anyone had told the girls. It had come to nothing in the end, but Ahsoka knew Vartan appreciated the effort.

"I have to get home," Ahsoka said. "It's later than I thought, and I've been gone from town for long enough that someone might have noticed. We'll do a full briefing tomorrow."

"Stay safe," Vartan said.

She replied in kind and headed out, with a brief pause to say good-bye to Selda as she passed the bar.

She didn't notice Hoban, who sat in the opposite corner. He watched her go and then leaned forward to catch Vartan's eye. The older man nodded, and Hoban got up to go set his own plans in motion.

12

AHSOKA SWUNG UP OVER the back wall of the ship-yard and adjusted her hood so she could pull it down over her face. Selda had given her a new cowl, and it fit her better. It was also a darker color, which helped her blend in with the night. With her were Miara, Neera, and a young Rodian male named Kolvin, from another crew. Ahsoka was ostensibly in command, Miara was needed to put the final touches on the charges, Neera had been selected because she was a quick thinker, and Kolvin was included because he was an agile climber. Each of them wore hoods like Ahsoka's to obscure them from any surveillance and walked with light steps, staying as quiet as they could.

That part of the shipyard had been commandeered by the Imperials as a place to stage their walkers. Ahsoka had seen them being offloaded when the occupation began, but it had taken a couple of days for Vartan to figure out their exact models and where the Imperials had decided to keep them. After that, it was relatively easy for Ahsoka to plan her first strike.

They waited in the shadow of the wall until the Imperial patrol came into view. They knew that the whole yard was covered by only a handful of stormtroopers and that the rear wall they'd climbed over was thought by the occupiers to be unassailable.

"No imagination at all," Vartan had muttered under his breath when Ahsoka told him the intel. Then they had set about altering the repulsors on the bottoms of the threshing machines to help Miara and Neera make the climb.

Miara shifted her pack very carefully. Not only did she need to keep the parts from making any noise, she also had to ensure that none of the circuits activated prematurely. It was finicky work, but Miara was endlessly patient with it, even though she was restless about other things.

"Are we ready?" she asked Ahsoka, making sure to lean close so her voice wouldn't carry.

"I want to see the patrol a couple of times," Ahsoka said. "This might be our only chance to break in here this easily, and we should take advantage of it."

"She's right," Neera said. "Get comfortable, kids."

Miara grumbled but did as she was told. Kolvin, whom Ahsoka still didn't know very well, settled in without protest, apparently used to both waiting and following orders.

It was ten minutes until the patrol came back, the same two stormtroopers. They didn't even step into the yard. They just shone their lights around for a few moments and moved on. Behind the crates, Ahsoka and the others were never in danger of being discovered. It was almost too easy, which made Ahsoka nervous. She pushed the feeling away. She needed to focus on what was in front of her, and nothing else.

They waited another ten minutes, and the patrol came again. After they moved on, Neera leaned close to Ahsoka.

"We should go now. The others will get antsy waiting for us to come back if we don't."

Ahsoka nodded. These were farmers, she had to remind herself constantly. She had helped train farmers to fight before, back on Felucia, against pirates. They were smart and they learned quickly, but they still weren't soldiers. They didn't have the adaptability or patience of the clones, and she'd had to remember to treat them differently because of that. She had learned a lot on that mission that she could use on Raada now.

"Okay," she said. "Miara, give me your bag and follow me. Neera, you and Kolvin give us a few moments and then follow to install your part of the charge."

Their goals were simple, as befitted their first real mission. Miara had built several devices that she would activate at the last minute, and then Ahsoka would install each of them in the knee joints of the walkers. Then Kolvin, who had steadier hands than Ahsoka—since she couldn't overtly use the Force—would climb up with the second piece. Once the liquid in Kolvin's half started mixing with the liquid in Ahsoka's, it would become corrosive enough to melt not only the charge but also the knee joint itself.

"If we're really lucky," Ahsoka had told Vartan and Selda while the others listened, "the devices will be corroded entirely, and the Imperials will think something about Raada's weather is responsible for the damage."

"You really think so?" Kaeden had asked.

"No," said Ahsoka. "No one's that lucky. But we can hope for the best."

The only problem with the plan was that the liquid in Ahsoka's half of the device was quite corrosive all on its own. She'd have to let Miara open the seal on the device at the base of every walker and then climb with it very carefully. It was not a good place to make mistakes.

Ahsoka waved at Miara to get her attention and then pointed to their first target. The two of them slipped off into the dark, leaving Neera and Kolvin behind to wait until they were done. The chances of getting caught were slim, but splitting into pairs meant that if two of them did get nabbed, the other two might escape.

At the base of the first walker, Miara placed the device carefully in Ahsoka's hand. It limited her ability to climb, which slowed her down, but the knees on the walker weren't very high anyway. She remembered training the Onderon rebels to take out Separatist weapons by exploiting their weaknesses, and tried not to think too hard about the fact that she was exploiting the weaknesses in the equipment she'd once served in.

She placed the first four charges without incident. If she listened very hard, she could hear Neera and Kolvin working behind them, but they were doing well at keeping quiet. The patrol was due back any moment, so Ahsoka and Miara hunkered down behind the feet of one of the walkers, which would conceal them from the searchlight the troopers lackadaisically employed. Ahsoka was already holding the next charge, ready to climb as soon as it was clear, but she noticed something different about it, even in the dark. It wasn't a corrosive charge at all. It was an actual bomb.

"Miara, what is this?" she whispered, after checking to be sure the Imperials weren't back yet.

"Oh, sorry," the girl replied. "I passed you the wrong charge. I must have packed that by accident."

Miara spoke like it was no big deal, but Ahsoka couldn't let the subject drop so easily. She didn't remember Miara's making that kind of charge, and it certainly wasn't included in any of the plans Ahsoka had gone over with Vartan.

"Are you planning your own operations without me?" she hissed in Miara's ear, but before she got an answer, the searchlight turned on.

Both of them froze, and Ahsoka hoped that Neera and Kolvin were similarly concealed. This time the troopers stepped into the yard—only two or three steps, but far enough that Ahsoka prepared for the worst. Tucked in beside Ahsoka, Miara wasn't breathing at all, but Ahsoka could feel her trembling. For the first time, Miara was really scared. After a few more nervous moments, the searchlight went off and the troopers moved on. Ahsoka put the more dangerous charge in her pocket and held out her hands for a proper one. Miara handed it to her without asking for the other one back.

They didn't speak for the rest of the mission, not until all the charges were placed and Neera and Kolvin had caught up with them at the other end of the yard. Ahsoka could already hear the sound of failing metal struts, straining to stay upright, and knew they had done their job well.

"Back to Selda's," she commanded.

Neera shot her a surprised look. That hadn't been the plan. Ahsoka didn't give them any time to protest. She led the way back over the wall and then down the unlit streets to the cantina.

There were more people inside than there should be, Ahsoka could see, but they were staying away from the windows at least. She barged right through the front door.

"Hey, now!" Vartan had jumped to his feet, a blaster in his hand. There was the sound of several chairs scraping back as others leapt up. "Wait, wait," he said. "They're friends of ours. Put your weapons down."

Something was very wrong. Kaeden wasn't there. Ahsoka couldn't imagine she was at home if Vartan was in the cantina. And yet if she were present, she would have run toward Miara immediately. Worse, Kaeden wasn't the only person who was missing.

"Where's Hoban?" Ahsoka demanded.

There was no immediate answer. Neera slumped into a chair and gestured to Vartan as if to say, *It's your problem now, boss*, so Ahsoka turned her attention back to him. She took a tally of who wasn't there. It was fully half of Vartan's recruits. He'd mixed up the crews. The older ones, the *slower* ones, were all there. The ones who could run were gone.

Wearing her most fearsome expression, Ahsoka pulled out the chair opposite to where Vartan was standing and they both took a seat. He leaned as far back as he could, scared of her even though he held a blaster and she was, to all appearances, unarmed. When she reached into her pocket for Miara's charge and set it on the table, he flinched as if she had struck him. Ahsoka didn't care. Kaeden was out there, doing something stupid, and Ahsoka didn't know if she'd be able to set things right.

"Let me see if I have this figured out," she said. "You

thought I would be distracted by the walker operation and it would be a good time to run your own mission."

Nobody said anything. She wasn't even sure they were still breathing.

"You picked a target. The admin building, maybe? I hope it's not the barracks." Vartan flinched again, and she knew her guess was right. "You sent them out, your own crews, to lay explosives."

"We had to do something." That was Kolvin's crew lead. Ahsoka didn't know the woman's name. "We can't just sit here."

"Any moment now, a pair of stormtroopers are going to find out that their walkers are damaged," Ahsoka said. "All of their walkers. And they're going to raise an alarm, and that will wake up all the other troopers. And where do you think those troopers are going to go to receive their orders?"

Miara gasped and made a break for the door. Selda caught her and held her until she stopped struggling against him.

"We didn't know," Vartan said.

"You didn't even try," Ahsoka said. "What were you thinking?"

"We can go help them," Kolvin's crew lead said.

"No," Ahsoka said. "Now you are going to listen to me.

Those of you who are here have to go home. Right now. If anyone asks, you disavow any knowledge of what went on tonight. You lie."

"We can't leave them," Vartan protested.

"You have to," Ahsoka said. "Or every member of our group is going to end up arrested, dead, or on the run tonight. We need operatives in town."

"She's right," Selda said. His tone brooked no argument, and he received none. He pointed to the door. "And I think the bar is closed."

"I'm not going home," Miara said, pushing through the crowd to stand next to Ahsoka. "I'm sorry, Ashla, I'm so sorry. She's everything I have."

Ahsoka looked at Vartan, who was directing people through the door with Selda's help, and then locked eyes with Neera. Ahsoka could see that she was just as determined as Miara was.

"Fine," Ahsoka said. "But you do everything I tell you to."

They both nodded.

"And bring the charges."

13

STEALTH WAS IMPOSSIBLE, so they just had to run for it. The streets were mostly deserted, thanks to the curfew. Ahsoka and the others were almost halfway to the Imperial compound when the alarms sounded. The damage to the walkers had taken a while for the troopers to detect. That was good news, as far as Ahsoka was concerned. Anything that bought them more time was good news.

As she ran, Ahsoka put aside her anger. It would do her no good in the coming confrontation. She also put aside her desperation to make sure Kaeden was all right and every thought about her failures over the past year. She focused on her strengths: her speed, adaptability, and familiarity with military procedure. That was going to get them through this.

They were a block from the compound when the first explosion rocked them back on their heels. Ahsoka looked at Miara with some surprise. She'd had no idea the girl was capable of building anything that big.

"That wasn't one of mine!" Miara said. "They must have found something else. That or . . ."

She trailed off, unwilling to voice the other option.

Ahsoka waved them both close. They were behind the cover of the last non-Imperial building before they'd be exposed to the artillery. She needed to know more before she stepped out into the fray. Once they went around the corner, they'd be in full view and wouldn't have time to confer.

"Tell me everything about the plan," she said. "Numbers, objectives, all the details. Quickly."

"Hoban split the group into three, one for each door," Neera said. "They all have explosives, and most of them have blasters, too."

"Where did you get blasters?" Ahsoka asked.

"Here and there," Neera said. "Vartan said most of them are in pretty bad shape, but they'll get the job done for a little while at least."

"I hope it's long enough," Ahsoka said.

They walked the last block cautiously, even though they met with no resistance. The Imperials must have been busy with the others. It wasn't exactly a cheery thought.

"Miara, can you find the caves again in the dark?" Ahsoka asked when they stopped again. She took a look around the corner, to see how the fight was unfolding, and then came back to finalize the plan.

"Yes," Miara said. She sounded sure.

"Then you wait here," Ahsoka said. Miara started to protest, but Ahsoka held up her hand. "This is one of those things I said you were going to listen to me about, got it? You wait here, and Neera will start to channel our people toward you. Tell them where to meet up on the edge of town. Not Selda's. Pick someplace random. Then lead everyone out to the caves as quickly and quietly as you can.

"Neera, you come with me. There's a line of Imperial tanks pointed away from the compound. They must have set them up for defense, and they haven't had time to get them turned around yet. I'm going to disable as many as I can. You go to the doors on the left side of the compound and get those people out. They aren't being pressed as hard, so they should be able to get free." Neera nodded. "If you can get to the right-side doors, try for that, too, but if you can't, leave them, do you understand?"

"Where's Hoban?" Neera asked, shrewdly seeing the information Ahsoka had omitted.

"I didn't see him," Ahsoka said. "I'm sorry, but you need to focus, too."

"I understand," Neera said.

"What are you going to do, Ashla?" Miara asked. For the first time, she sounded very small.

"I'm going to the front," Ahsoka said. "The fighting is the thickest there, but I might be able to help out long enough for our people to retreat."

"Where did you come from?" Neera asked. She didn't sound like she was expecting an answer, but Ahsoka decided to give it to her. In all likelihood, they'd find out soon enough anyway.

"The Clone Wars," she said. "I fought in the Clone Wars."

She didn't give them any more specifics. Let them think

she was part of a planetary militia. She was pretty sure that's what Selda and Vartan thought already. They weren't even wrong. She *had* been part of a planetary militia. But she'd also been a part of something else.

There was another explosion. They couldn't afford to wait anymore.

"Are you ready?" she asked Neera.

Neera held the blaster she'd gotten from Vartan in one hand and a couple of explosives in the other. Ahsoka carried most of the explosives, because she had no blaster of her own. She was sure she'd be able to pick one up after a few minutes of fighting.

"Good luck," she said to Miara. The younger girl swallowed hard and crouched to wait.

Neera and Ahsoka turned and ran into the yard.

Ahsoka's initial tactical assessment had been immediate, instinctive, and not at all promising. Now that she could see the whole compound at once, she was no more optimistic. She had warned them that this kind of strike was a terrible idea, for exactly this reason: the farmers were outmatched, and she still wasn't entirely sure what they were up against. They hadn't listened. Now she had to either leave them to their fate or go to their rescue. No choice, really. Her only advantage was that they were up against the Empire's new stormtroopers, not the formidable clones. She couldn't use the Force for anything as showy as deflecting blaster bolts, but she could jump and she could run, and that would have to be enough.

Most of her friends had already retreated, and Neera was rounding them up. The left side was clearing, and even the fighters on the right side were starting to retreat now that they knew their options. It was the disastrous attempt to take the front gate of the Imperial compound that was causing the biggest problem. It had ended almost before it began. As Ahsoka had suspected, the heavy artillery was too much for the ill-equipped farmers to deal with, even with the element of surprise and Miara's explosives to back them up. The five who remained alive were pinned down, with the Imperial ground reinforcements closing in. Through the smoke, Ahsoka could see both Hoban and Kaeden crouched among the survivors. They didn't have a lot of time, and Ahsoka was their only hope.

She moved forward cautiously, staying as low to the ground as possible to present a minimal target for the guns that lined the compound walls. She was far enough away that the troopers couldn't target her more easily than they could her friends, and she didn't want to draw attention until she had to. She listened for incoming fighters but couldn't hear anything over the noise of battle and the hammering of her own heart.

"I am really out of practice," she said, talking to companions who were no longer with her. She spoke out of habit, falling into the banter as easily as she took stock of her surroundings, even though there was no one left for her to banter with. She shook her head and refocused: it was not the time to get lost in the past. There were plenty of people, living people, who needed her at that moment.

Staying behind the line of Imperial tanks, Ahsoka attached charges to every one of them she could reach. Apparently, a backwater like Raada didn't merit entirely new weaponry, and Ahsoka knew these Clone Wars—era vehicles like the back of her hand. The charges wouldn't destroy the tanks completely, but they should render them immobile, and Ahsoka needed all the help she could get. The explosions started just as she jumped clear of the last tank, earning her friends a momentary reprieve from bombardment.

"This way!" she shouted, waving them toward her so that she could guide them to the questionable safety of the hills. At least it would be harder for any fighters to maneuver in there.

The five survivors moved, but three of them were wounded, and that slowed them down. They didn't get very far before stormtroopers from the compound caught up with them. Ahsoka engaged a trooper in hand-to-hand combat, taking him down with a vicious kick to the midsection and keeping him down with a blow to the head. Kaeden gaped at her, but Ahsoka didn't have time for that. She picked up the fallen stormtrooper's blaster and did her best to cover their retreat with her newly acquired weapon. Despite her best efforts, the distance between the Imperials and her friends kept shrinking.

"Leave us!" Kaeden shouted. She was half carrying Hoban even though he was twice her size, and she was bleeding from a cut on her forehead. "You told us not to get in this mess. You shouldn't pay for it."

"Not an option!" Ahsoka shouted back.

Anything else Kaeden might have said was drowned out by an enormous explosion in front of them. A crater opened, blasted by one of the tanks that still had a working gun. It would take too long to go around the smoking hole in the ground, and if they went into it, they were as good as dead.

"Freeze," said the closest stormtrooper.

"It's our lucky day," said Hoban sarcastically as Ahsoka lowered her gun. "They want prisoners."

Ahsoka didn't have the heart to tell him it was more likely the stormtroopers just wanted clean shots. Sure enough, when she turned around she found a line of blasters and no signs of mercy.

Obi-Wan would have had a clever remark in this situation, something that belied the danger of the moment and confused his adversaries into doubting themselves. Anakin wouldn't have surrendered in the first place. Ahsoka usually fell somewhere between the two, but right now she didn't have the luxury of deliberation.

Hoban threw himself toward the line of stormtroopers. It was pointless, but Ahsoka couldn't stop him. She heard Neera screaming behind her, but then the sound was drowned out by the whine of Imperial blasters as they ripped Hoban apart at close range. When he was dead, there was a horrible moment of silence. Someone must have shut Neera up, or dragged her far enough away that Ahsoka couldn't hear her anymore.

Then the Imperial lieutenant raised her hand, giving the order to fire, and Ahsoka raised hers at the same time. Since she'd started helping the Raadians organize themselves, she'd used the Force only to sense her friends and avoid her enemies. She'd been careful, contained, making sure she would not be detected. That caution was gone now. For the first time in too long, she felt the full power of the Force flow through her, and she welcomed it.

Blasters flew backward through the air, some even dragging the stormtroopers who held them. Metal screamed as it was bent away from her and her friends, and even the ground seemed to shift as Ahsoka pushed the Imperial firing line back. The lieutenant gaped at her, staggering as if someone had struck her across the face.

"Ashla!" Kaeden was staring at her, too, which was when Ahsoka realized exactly what she'd done.

"Run now," she said. "Talk later."

The Raadians did as they were told, making for the hills. Ahsoka lagged behind. With her cover well and truly blown, she had no qualms about continuing to deflect the heavy artillery aimed at them. It took longer than she would have liked and she could only imagine what a spectacle she made, but eventually she and the farmers reached the temporary security of the hills and the cave where they could hide until they came up with a better plan.

As soon as Ahsoka walked into the cave, all eyes turned to her. Kaeden, who was sitting next to her sister on a medical cot, turned and bore down on her.

"So," she said, her eyes blazing with anger, "was there something you wanted to tell us?"

14

THIS COULD STILL BE MANAGED. Fixed. Jenneth could rework his calculations, accounting for the new variables, and come up with a workable solution. He just had to know what resources were currently available. He called up the incident reports that the Imperial officers had already entered into the system and read them quickly so he could begin his extrapolations.

The loss of the walkers was rough. They were newer than the tanks, built since the rise of the Empire, and much better suited to patrolling, because they were operated by smaller crews and covered more ground. Without them, the storm-troopers would have to search on foot while the tanks were being repaired. At least the gun turrets were still operational. The Imperial compound was not defenseless.

What he really needed were more stormtrooper units. Although they weren't suited to doing any of the actual farm-ing, they'd be more than capable of supervising the local labor. The initial plan had been implemented well, but it was time for harsher measures. Curfew, which had been laxly enforced, would be strictly monitored, and those who disobeyed would be punished. In broad daylight. Preferably in the center of town. He would also have to make sure the ringleaders were rounded up. They wouldn't be executed—that would just make the farmers angrier—but publicized torture and visible suffer-ing did wonders to break morale.

He could work with that.

What he could not work with was also his biggest prob-lem. He hadn't seen the raid, had in fact slept through it, but there were simply too many corroborating reports for him to discount. There had been a Force user in the uprising. She had come out of nowhere, and by all accounts she was very good. She was old enough that she must have had Jedi train-ing. Jenneth wanted to scoff, to dismiss the notion. All the Jedi were dead. And even if some had escaped, why in the galaxy would one show up on a backwater like Raada?

He turned the calculation in his head and found the answer. The Jedi was here *because* it was a backwater. She thought the Empire wouldn't come to Raada, and he, Jenneth Pilar, had surprised her. That made him feel much better about the whole thing.

He had no idea how to report a suspected Jedi. He would let the Imperial commander take care of that. He just had to submit his new report and analysis, and make his suggestions as soon as possible to maintain his good reputation.

Jenneth thumbed to a blank screen on his datapad and began entering his new tabulations.

In the end, they'd had to sedate Neera to keep her from harming herself. Ahsoka covered her with a blanket, tucked Neera's hands underneath, and checked her breathing. Neera inhaled and exhaled quietly, at the proper rate. It wouldn't be a solution for the long term, but for now, they needed quiet and time to think. And Ahsoka had some explaining to do.

She sat down at the table where Kaeden and Miara were building more explosives. Neither sister looked at her, even to glare. Ahsoka sighed. This wasn't going to be easy.

"My real name is Ahsoka Tano," she said. "I'm sorry I couldn't tell you."

Ahsoka always found it best to start with the apology and then work backward to the explanation. It was something Anakin had never mastered.

"It's not very safe to be like me," she continued. "The Empire pays handsomely for Jedi, and it doesn't show mercy."

"We noticed," Miara said curtly. She still wouldn't look up, but her hands were shaking with anger, and probably fear.

"I never meant to put any of you in danger," Ahsoka continued. "I didn't think anyone would find out, and I hoped that would keep you safe."

"Safe?" Kaeden said. She gave up all pretense of working and looked Ahsoka right in the eye. "We're not angry because your existence put us in danger, Ash—Ahsoka. We're angry because you didn't do everything you could to help us sooner."

It felt like Kaeden had struck her across the face. Ahsoka had done everything she could possibly think of. She'd set up a place to hide. She'd stockpiled food and water and medical supplies. She'd helped them get organized.

But she hadn't used the Force to save Hoban.

"Kaeden," she said as gently as she could manage, "even a

Jedi can only do so much. And I promise I did my best to help your friends and your family."

"What do you even know about family?" Kaeden said. "You never had one. And you probably never had friends, either. Just clones who had to do everything you said, because you were their superior officer."

She stalked off before Ahsoka could think of a reply. Miara pointedly gathered up all the pieces she was working on and moved them to another table, leaving Ahsoka alone. No one would look at her or talk to her, though aside from the girls, the farmers looked more exhausted and scared than angry. Ahsoka got up and walked out of the main cave. She crawled through the tunnel that led to one of the other chambers, the one with the entryway that looked toward town, and then sat there alone, staring at the lights.

"We take a piece, you take a piece," she said quietly. She wasn't sure why it helped to think of a crokin board. She'd always been able to visualize tactics in plain terms before. She decided that the difference was her comrades. The clones knew battle. It was in their blood. The farmers knew crokin. It was the easiest way she could think of to explain it to them, and now it was a habit.

She was going to have to leave soon and confirm all Kaeden's worst suspicions about her. If the Empire was interested in the moon before, knowing there was a Jedi on it would increase the Imperial presence tenfold. They'd be slow without their walkers, but they'd be out looking. And even the people who had stayed in town wouldn't be safe, especially once the officers realized that the farmers had used their field crews to organize the uprising.

Ahsoka closed her eyes and took a deep breath. She meant to meditate, but instead of the serenity she usually found, the first thing she saw was the solemn face of four-year-old Hedala Fardi. That was almost worse than the blank space where Anakin used to be. At least her former master could take care of himself. The little Fardi girl deserved much better than being forgotten.

Blinking to regain her focus, Ahsoka made a decision. She couldn't go back for Hedala, not now, but she could stay for Kaeden and Miara and the others for as long as possible. Her ship was still safely hidden, and now that her secret was blown anyway, she didn't have to be subtle in any sudden escape attempts. She would stay on Raada and continue to help the farmers resist, assuming they'd let her, of course. After that night, there was a fairly decent chance they'd run her out of town themselves. She would at least stay long enough to apologize and to see if there was anything she could do for Neera.

"Ahsoka!" The cry came from behind her. It was Miara, her voice thin with worry and tears and no small amount of resentment for having to talk to Ahsoka in the first place.

"What is it?" she asked.

"It's Kaeden," Miara gasped, winded from crawling through the tunnel. She must have done it in a hurry. "She stalked off after yelling at you, and I thought she'd gone back to the medical area to sit with Neera, but she didn't. The door guard said he let her out, and she hasn't come back."

Ahsoka whipped around, staring out at the grassy hills between the caves and town. It was too dark to see anything, and there were too many people concentrated close together for Ahsoka to get an accurate read through the Force.

"If she goes to town, will they catch her?" Miara asked.

"She wasn't wearing a mask, and you can see her injury as soon as you look at her face," Ahsoka said. "They know what she looks like. They'll catch her for sure."

She didn't add that the Imperials would torture Kaeden, too. They would assume she knew where the rest of the insurgents were hiding; they would assume she knew where Ahsoka was, and they would really, really want to catch Ahsoka.

"What are we going to do?" Miara asked.

"You are going to stay here with Neera," Ahsoka said. "She is going to need a friend very badly when she wakes up, and you're the only one she's got right now."

Miara swallowed hard, but nodded.

"You're going to go?" she asked. "Even though Kaeden was so angry at you?"

"Yeah," Ahsoka said. "I'm going to go."

She didn't look but assumed that Miara followed her through the tunnel to the main cave. She stopped only long enough to pick up the cache of tech pieces from where they were hidden, in case she wasn't able to return for them, and to reclaim the Imperial blaster she'd stolen during the battle. No one tried to stop her, and she disappeared into the dark.

Kaeden realized her mistake almost as soon as she stepped back into town. Of course there would be more patrols, given that night's two-pronged attack. Of course they would be actually searching now, not just showing off their presence and letting fear do the rest. Of course they would know what she looked like. At least she had stolen Miara's hood to cover the wound on her forehead. It throbbed, but the bleeding had stopped, and the medic-trained insurgent who'd sewn her up said she probably didn't have a concussion. Anyway, it was too late to turn back now.

She didn't go home. She went to Vartan's, but he wasn't there. He must have stayed with Selda, waiting for news. She didn't want to try to make it to them until it was daylight. At least once curfew was over it would be easier to move around. She had just finished disarming the lock on Vartan's door when eight stormtroopers rounded the corner at a trot. They were clearly on their way to Vartan's house, and they were just as clearly surprised to find her instead of him, but they were not about to let the opportunity pass them by.

"Take her," said the one with the pauldron.

Kaeden thought about fighting, but eight to one was not good odds. She put up a bit of resistance, but not enough that they did more than knock the wind out of her.

"Careful with this one," said the troop leader. "They'll have a few questions for her back at base."

The way he said it made Kaeden's blood run cold. *Ahsoka,* she thought, wondering if Jedi really could read minds, *Ahsoka, I'm sorry.* Then the commander hit her again and everything went black.

15

AHSOKA WATCHED. Ahsoka waited. Ahsoka was not afraid.

◆◆◆

Kaeden had heard stories all her life of the cruel things men did for power. Orphaned on a remote world, and with next to nothing to her name, she'd seen more than a few of those stories play out in real life. She knew of spouses who hit. She'd seen bruises on her playmates' eyes. One time, one of the overseers had tried to set up a food-rationing sideline, controlling everything his laborers had access to. It had fallen apart quickly—Vartan had been the one to break the overseer's fingers—but Kaeden remembered those few days of watching her every move, and Miara's, too, to keep out of the line of fire.

After she was captured and thrown in a cell, they left her alone for what felt like hours. She knew it couldn't have been more than four, because there was a window in her cell and it was still dark outside. But it was more than long enough for her to relive every terrible story she'd ever heard and for her imagination to work her mind into a frenzy. She didn't bother hiding her tears. She knew the Imperials would see them— and more—eventually.

The first interrogator didn't ask her any questions. She pressed a machine to Kaeden's chest, and when it was activated, all Kaeden could do was scream from the pain. She would have said anything, given up anyone, to make the pain stop, but the woman didn't ask, and she never let up long enough for Kaeden to talk. When she finally removed the apparatus, Kaeden fell sideways onto the floor, her throat too raw from screaming to say anything at all.

The second set of interrogators asked, of all things, about her health. They wanted to know if she had heart problems and if she was fully human, or if she had some genetic quirk. Kaeden's voice was slow to return, so she mostly nodded or shook her head in reply, and when they were satisfied with her answers, they strapped her to the chair, palms up. Kaeden realized that this exposed all the veins in her arms. One of the interrogators went into the corridor for the medical tray and wasted no opportunity for drama in showing Kaeden the needles and vials they were about to use on her. After all the injections, Kaeden felt too cold and too hot at the same time, and she had trouble holding her head upright.

"Give her a few minutes," she heard one of them say to someone who stood in the hallway. "We might have under-guessed her weight. They're all a bit scrawny in the Outer Rim. It makes them hard to medicate."

Kaeden blinked stupidly and wished very hard for a glass of water. Then she laughed out loud. Water! Why not wish for free arms and a clear head and a ship that would carry her to safety. What she really wished for, more than anything, was that the first interrogator and her terrible machine would never come back into her cell.

The door opened again. Kaeden tried to look up, but her head was still too heavy for her neck. A very bright light came on, and something hummed loudly, uncomfortably close to her ear. She turned slightly and saw the round black interrogator droid hovering there, bright needles protruding from it. The threat was clear: talk or pain. Kaeden honestly wasn't sure yet which one she was going to choose.

Another chair scraped against the floor, and a figure sat down across from her. He was dressed in Imperial gray, and his hat was pulled down over his eyes. Kaeden couldn't decipher his rank, but he carried himself like someone who was used to being obeyed.

"Kaeden Larte," he said. She was a little surprised he knew her name but tried not to show it. She failed. "Human female, legal adult, caretaker of Miara Larte, a sister. You were not born here, but you were orphaned here, you have never been indentured, and your work record is spotless. Your crew lead thought you might actually replace him, when he got around to retiring."

That was a surprise. Vartan had never mentioned it, and Kaeden had never considered it. It was somehow reassuring to know he thought well of her, even though it did her no good whatsoever at the moment.

"More recently, however, your prospects have dimmed somewhat," the man continued. "Larceny, vandalism, conspiracy, murder, and treason. That will probably put a stop to your upward career mobility."

She wished she had something clever to say, like a character in a holonovel, but her tongue was too heavy and her brain too slow. Also, she was too scared.

"The only decision you have remaining is how you wish your sentence to be carried out." He pulled his hat up, and Kaeden was struck by the pitiless look in his eyes. "You'll die for your crimes, of course, but if you were to cooperate with us, we would make sure you left this mortal coil with, shall we say, no worries on your chest."

Kaeden flinched so severely that she wrenched her arms sideways in their straps. Her shoulder joints scraped agonizingly, but before she could fully register the pain, the chair toppled over. Her arm had moved just enough that it was crushed under the metal chair, and it was that pain, real and concrete, that finally broke through the fog in her brain. Two stormtroopers rushed into the cell to pick her up and set her right.

"I see we understand each other," he said, as though nothing had happened. "I need you to tell me two things, Kaeden, two little things, and you'll die with a single blaster bolt to the heart. Where are your friends hiding? We know they ran off and left you to get captured, but you must know where they went. Tell me."

She tried to answer him but only croaked.

"And what is the Jedi's name?" This time, the look in his eyes was demonic. He didn't want to capture or torture Ahsoka. He wanted to kill her—for a promotion or for power or for the opportunity to say that he, personally, had killed a Jedi. He wanted Ahsoka dead.

Kaeden croaked louder this time. If he thought she legitimately couldn't talk, it might buy her a little time.

"Your lack of cooperation is unfortunate." He clicked his tongue at her. "But not altogether surprising. Consider carefully, Kaeden Larte, and I will be back when the sun comes up. Or perhaps one of my colleagues will come instead."

Kaeden managed to control the flinch a bit better this time. The ache in her arm helped, giving her something else to focus on. It was definitely broken.

They left her strapped to the chair.

◆ ◆ ◆

Ahsoka perched on the roof of the Imperial admin building. Climbing up had been easy. Now that she was no longer being careful to hide her true self, she had managed it in two jumps.

The hardest part was waiting for a break in the patrols and finding the best spot to make her ascent. The rear of the compound was still underprotected.

Her examination of the prefab building yielded some interesting results. Ahsoka had seen the tanks, of course, but the building itself was of the style used during the Clone Wars, which meant she could guess the layout of the inside without actually seeing it. She allowed herself a small smile at the idea that Imperial monotony was working to her advantage.

She crossed the roof to the left side, her right since she was approaching from the back, because it had suffered the most damage during the day's attack. She ruled it out as soon as she saw it, though, because the guard had been quadrupled to compensate for the damage. There would be no easy entry that way. Ahsoka slid down the wall to the lower roofline, still at the rear of the building. If the design was consistent, the holding cells would be there anyway.

She looked over the side, down the steeply slanted walls, and saw narrow windows that she remembered being at the tops of the cells. They were included in the design for air circulation and deemed an acceptable security risk because they were thought to be too small for escape. They were, Ahsoka noted, also designed with full-grown adult humanoids in mind. That would be her way in.

One of the windows was emitting a very bright light, the sort that an interrogator might use to keep a prisoner as uncomfortable as possible. The light went out suddenly, and Ahsoka made herself count to one hundred before she lowered herself headfirst, with her toes clinging to the ledge, to check the room. There was no point getting caught because of impatience.

She peered through the dimness and felt something in her stomach uncoil. There was Kaeden, and she was alive enough to be sitting upright in a chair. Ahsoka reached into her pocket and drew out the last of Miara's corrosive charges. She couldn't risk the noise of blasting the window, even though this way would take longer. Upside down, the charges were difficult to install, and Ahsoka nearly burned her thumbs off, but she managed it in the end and moved to the side to wait.

Her head was pounding by the time the glass was brittle enough for her to push it into the cell. It made more noise than she might have liked, but the thick walls muffled it somewhat. She crawled through, biting her tongue as she brushed against the leftover chemicals, and then dropped to the floor.

"Kaeden," she whispered. "Kaeden, wake up."

Kaeden stirred and looked at her, and her head lolled to the side. Drugs, then, in addition to whatever else they'd done to her. Her arm was broken, and the wound on her head had reopened, trickling blood into her eye. Ahsoka went to work on the restraints. She didn't bother with breaking the locks; she just cracked the straps using the Force.

"Kaeden, I need you to wake up," Ahsoka said. "I need your help for the next part of this."

"Ashla—Ahsoka, you shouldn't have come," Kaeden said. It sounded as if she were talking to a dream, but at least her voice was low. "They want you so bad, Ahsoka. They want you dead."

"Shhh, I know," Ahsoka said. "It's okay. I can take care of myself. But first I need to take care of you. Can you help me?"

Kaeden tried to answer, but her eyes rolled back, and Ahsoka wasted precious seconds trying to decide if it was safe to shake her. She pulled Kaeden to her feet and took measure of the girl's wobbly stance and broken limb. This was going to be difficult but not impossible. She put her hands on Kaeden's shoulders, gently, mindful of the injured arm, and breathed a sigh of relief when the girl's eyes refocused.

"Okay," Ahsoka said. "I am going to climb out the window and then pull you out behind me. It's going to hurt, but I need you to be as quiet as you possibly can."

Kaeden managed a nod, but nothing else. They were going to have to do this one step at a time, because every step forward was an improvement over their current situation.

Ahsoka hoisted herself out the window and then leaned back in for Kaeden. It was an awkward position. Her head was too big, and her shoulders were at a wrenching angle. She used the Force to pull Kaeden up and maneuver her through the narrow opening, and then lowered her to the ground before jumping down after her.

"Can you run?" she asked.

Kaeden cradled her arm against her chest, her head clearer now that she was in the open air. Ahsoka couldn't carry her all the way back to safety, but something—either panic or determination—had reinvigorated Kaeden. She was solid on her feet, and her eyes had lost a bit of their drug-induced glassy sheen. They had about three minutes before a patrol came around the corner, and quite a bit of ground to cover.

"I don't really have a choice," Kaeden said, and they took off, moving as quickly as they could.

Ahsoka led the way. There was no time for diversion, and no real need of it, so she just went straight to her tiny house on the edge of town. It was unguarded, and the lock was still intact. She and Kaeden went inside just as the sun was coming up. It was all Kaeden could manage for now.

"We'll wait until dark," Ahsoka said, "and then head back to the caves."

"No, Ahsoka," Kaeden said. She lay down on the bed, completely spent. "You have to go now."

"I'm not leaving you," Ahsoka said. She filled a canteen with water and helped Kaeden as she struggled to sit up and drink.

"Yes, you are," Kaeden told her as Ahsoka eased her back down. "I saw his face when he talked about you, the Imperial commander. Ahsoka, he wants you dead just to see you die, and he's not going to be nice about it. You have to take your ship and leave. Now."

The worst part was that Kaeden was right, and Ahsoka had known it since before she'd pulled her out of that cell. Staying wouldn't just endanger Ahsoka, but everyone else, as well.

"I'll come back for you. I promise," Ahsoka told her, her voice as steady as she could manage.

It wasn't just that she was leaving her friends; she was leaving her friends *again*. This time, at least, she'd been able to commit one act of heroism before being forced away. Kaeden was safe.

"You've done more than enough for us already," Kaeden said. "We were just too stupid to see it."

"I'm coming back," Ahsoka repeated. Then she paused. "Thank you. For taking me in when I got here. Even though I kept things from you."

"The galaxy's a lot bigger than Raada," Kaeden said. "It took me a while to understand that."

Ahsoka reached into her pocket, where the pieces of discarded tech were still tightly wrapped in their packaging. She was close to something, but she wasn't close enough.

Ahsoka didn't need darkness for cover the way Kaeden would. She was faster and she could deal with any pursuit. She could get to her ship and make her escape. She had to let go of her feelings. She looked over at Kaeden one last time, and then she left.

THE MIDDLE OF *a battlefield was a less-than-ideal place for in-depth self-reflection, but Anakin Skywalker was a well-trained Jedi and more than up to the challenge. In the time since he had ceased to be Obi-Wan's Padawan learner, he'd come to appreciate the independence of being his own master. Of course, he still had to follow the Temple rules and go where the Jedi Council sent him, but he was a general now. And the clones were his to command.*

It was all very different than he'd imagined, when he was still that little boy back on Tatooine who had looked up at the stars and known that there was something better for him. The galaxy was much more complicated than Master Qui-Gon had let on, and while he was grateful for Obi-Wan's teaching, sometimes Anakin couldn't help but wonder how things would be different if Qui-Gon had lived. For all the Jedi disapproved of attachments, there was nothing in the galaxy that was ever truly untethered. Anakin's own unofficial return to his birth planet had proved that well enough.

And now Anakin was attached: by his oaths to the Temple and to Padmé, his unspoken but no less sincere promises to Obi-Wan, his responsibilities as a commander of troops in the Republic army. The clones had been intended as a faceless mass, but already they were exhibiting undeniable signs of individuality, and Anakin didn't doubt they would continue to do so.

Perhaps this new Padawan that Obi-Wan had requested would help give him perspective. Anakin was reluctant to bring someone with no practical combat training this far out into the war. Christophsis was a dangerous place, even for two Jedi of Anakin and Obi-Wan's skills, and they'd already proven that they could take the planet only to be at risk of losing control immediately afterward. At the same time, Anakin knew that there was no guarantee of safety for a Padawan anywhere anymore, and he knew from personal experience that Obi-Wan Kenobi was the best of teachers. Plus, this time around, he'd have Anakin to help him.

Or at least, he would if Obi-Wan wanted.

Anakin wasn't entirely sure what his place next to Obi-Wan would look like once his friend had a new student. Jedi weren't as married to the concept of two as the Sith were, but most of them acted singly or in pairs. It was one of the reasons Anakin had never put in for a Padawan of his own. He didn't want it to look like he was pushing Obi-Wan aside. Now, Obi-Wan had gone and done it first, and Anakin still wasn't sure how he felt about it.

He surveyed the battlefield below him for the hundredth time since the shooting had stopped. It would only be a matter of time before the Separatists tried to take another crack at the Republic heavy weaponry, and Anakin wanted to be sure he was ready for anything when that happened, even if it involved incorporating Obi-Wan's Padawan into his strategy.

Maybe it would be for the best. The addition of a younger Jedi would constantly remind Obi-Wan that Anakin was old enough for more responsibilities, that he was that much closer to being a master in his own right. And getting different assignments than Obi-Wan wouldn't be so bad, either. It might even give him the opportunity to spend more time with Padmé. On strictly official business, of course.

Anakin looked upward as a new sound split the air above where he was perched. A Republic messenger ship had broken through the Separatist blockade. He hoped it would carry the beginnings of their reinforcements, enough to start turning the tide of the battle on the planet's surface. Anakin told his clone commandos to hold their positions and then went off to meet Obi-Wan. He couldn't quite shake the feeling that his life was about to change.

CHAPTER

16

BAIL ORGANA felt like he was being buried in bureaucracy. His office in the royal palace on Alderaan was roomy, and he'd never felt overwhelmed in it before. There was more than enough space for chairs, a desk, and the aquarium full of brightly colored sea creatures he'd had installed to keep his daughter from getting under his feet, but he felt like all the room in the galaxy wouldn't accommodate the double weight of responsibility he now carried. He did what he could to represent the people of the Alderaan sector in the Imperial

Senate, and he did what he could to help the people of the galaxy when he was sure no one was watching.

He was almost positive no one was watching him now.

He risked a glance sideways to be sure his daughter was distracted by the fish and then opened the latest of his secret files. It was encrypted, of course, but he had it decoded soon enough. He looked sideways again. The trouble with adopting the child of two prodigies was that there was a decent chance she would turn out to be unusually intelligent, as well. He was reasonably certain that Leia hadn't learned to read while he was on Coruscant for the last senatorial session, but with her, he could never be sure. He wouldn't be able to keep her out of the mess forever, but he and Breha had agreed they should keep her clear of it at least until she could reliably speak in coherent sentences.

He started reading and almost forgot that Leia was in the room at all.

The moon was called Raada, a small satellite of an uninhabitable planet that he had to look up on a star chart. He had no idea why the Empire had gone there, but they had, and the local population—mostly farmers, according to the report—had not reacted well to occupation. During their resistance, several of them had died or been captured. All this informa-tion pulled at Bail's heartstrings, but it was the note at the end that made his heart nearly stop: *Jedi activity confirmed.*

He still dreamed of that last night, when the Temple had burned. Sometimes he was able to get the Padawan into his speeder in time. Sometimes the clones shot him, too, when they shot the boy. Every once in a while, he failed to rescue Yoda and woke in a cold sweat, with the sound of blasters and lightsabers echoing in his ears and visions of a tiny, bro-ken green body haunting him. When he had the dream on Coruscant, there was nothing he could do about it but accept his defeat and yet another night of lost sleep. When he had the dream on Alderaan, he would get Leia out of her bed, hold her close to his chest, and hope against hope that she exhibited only her mother's gifts, not her father's. He would stand there, cradling her, until Breha found them and guided them both back to bed.

The idea that there was a survivor out there filled his chest with equal parts anticipation and dread. Dread because the Empire would never stop hunting the Jedi and anticipation because a Jedi was a natural ally to his cause. There was no description of the Jedi in question, so he didn't know who he was looking for. He knew it couldn't be Obi-Wan, at least. There had been thousands of Jedi before the purge. It was likely that this one would be a stranger to him and would have no reason to trust him if he made an overture of friendship. That said, it would have to be someone relatively powerful to have survived for so long, making it worth the effort to find them.

He debated sending a message to Obi-Wan but almost immediately dismissed the idea. They had agreed to no contact, except in the direst of emergencies, and as much as a Jedi survivor might make his old friend feel better, Bail knew it wasn't worth the risk. Someday, if he had a reason to reach out, he would. But the toddler in his office was all the reason he needed to keep silent, and there was another child, one he'd met only for a few moments, who needed his discretion just as badly.

Bail deleted the report and scrubbed the drive clean. At some point, it would be useful to have a way to store these files, but right now he simply had no way of securing them once they were decrypted. He currently relied on verbal transmission and living memory, which was inconvenient but generally safer for everyone involved. He looked out the window, the green-and-blue mountains of his home world a comfort to him, as they always were.

He would get the R2 unit back from Captain Antilles. The droid was trustworthy and capable of defending himself. Bail would just have to make sure not to leave the droid alone with his daughter, in case either of them got any ideas.

Thinking about her made Bail look at the aquarium again. Leia had pulled herself up, her hands and her nose pressed against the glass, as she watched an orange-and-purple tentacled creature move through the water like a dancer. She laughed every time it changed direction, which it did by emitting a stream of bubbles. He couldn't imagine his life without his daughter. He couldn't imagine not working for a better galaxy for her to grow up in. He still wasn't entirely sure how he was going to do all that *and* manage to keep her safe.

He closed all the files on his desk once the message to Captain Antilles was sent. He'd get a reply soon, and until then he would need to think about the next step and discuss the options with his wife. Bail crossed the room quietly, counting on the tentacles to keep his daughter from seeing his reflection in the glass, and then swung her up into his arms. Her surprised giggles echoed through the office, the perfect counterpoint to his deeper laugh.

"Outside," she said, not willing to relinquish his attention, even if they left the aquarium behind.

E. K. JOHNSTON

"Outside," he agreed, and carried her onto the balcony, where he'd first introduced her to her mother and the planet she would grow up calling home.

◆ ◆ ◆

The main problem was that after a certain point, despite his training as an Inquisitor and skills of observation, all children looked the same to the Sixth Brother. That point came fairly early in his inquisition this time, because of the sheer number of children this family seemed to have produced. He was able to rule out the older ones; who would have come to the attention of the Jedi Temple before it fell, but there were at least a dozen younger ones, and they seemed to travel everywhere in a pack.

The report hadn't been entirely reliable to start with, either. Static-laden surveillance holos of a shipyard weren't all that useful, and he hadn't even seen the replay himself before some inept underling managed to ruin it. All he had were the statements of four stormtroopers and a lieutenant who had seen the recording before it was destroyed, and none of them had been able to say for sure if it had been a child in the recording. No one else had actually seen a child do anything, or at least he hadn't found such a person to question yet. The family didn't seem to be aware that they might be concealing a traitor in their midst.

So he was reduced to this: sitting on a backwater planet, watching an unruly mob of children until one of them exhibited Force sensitivity that she may or may not actually possess. More than once, he wished he could just arrange an accident for all of them and solve the problem that way. The Fardi family was important on Thabeska but virtually unknown everywhere else in the galaxy. There would be no complaints if an entire generation of them met with an untimely end. Sadly, that was against his current directive. He didn't kill children. He only acquired them for his masters.

The console he was seated at signaled an incoming message. It was a holorecording from a moon even more backward than the planet he was already on, so he very nearly ignored it altogether. Then he noticed the message's code. It was a new one, created especially for him and his brothers and sisters. It might be another wild mynock chase, but it might also be something he very much wanted to see.

"Attention, Imperials," the recording began. It was a low-level district commander, though his rank was unusually high to be stationed on a moon that far out. There must be something on the moon that the Emperor really wanted. "We have detected the presence of a Force-sensitive being. Identity cannot be determined, but ability to use the Force has been confirmed by several parties. Age indicates a certain level of Jedi training. Suspected Padawan, no higher. Report made according to standard procedure while we await further instructions. Please advise."

This was much better than looking for a child. A child was to be captured and taken for experimentation and corruption. A Jedi, even a lowly Padawan, he could kill. Moreover, he was granted unlimited Imperial backing when it came to tracking down a Jedi, and he'd been meaning to brush up on his interrogation tactics. Now all he had to do was make sure he got there first.

He recorded a quick reply, using the same code, so the district commander would not find his arrival unexpected. From what hadn't been said in the message, he guessed that the Jedi had already managed to escape and the commander needed all the help he could get before the full measure of his incompetence was brought to light. The Inquisitor sent a longer, though still quite terse, message to his own headquarters, detailing where he was headed and why. None of the others had replied yet, which meant his claim was solid. He was not above poaching, though, so he couldn't really expect the others to be. He had to get to the useless little moon as soon as he could.

With no hesitation, he closed the file he'd been monitoring and marked it as noncritical. If one of the children had any power, it wasn't enough for him to find or track and was therefore nothing to be concerned about. The Empire could always send another Inquisitor if it was deemed necessary in the future, but he was done with this dusty world. And an adult was better prey. He stood up, pulled his helmet down over the gray skin of his face, and strode across the shipyard to where his sleek vicious little ship was docked. He had no belongings, save the weapon he carried on his back, and he was in orbit and calculating the jump to hyperspace before much time had passed.

In the dust on the planet's surface, Hedala Fardi played with her cousins in the empty yard where her family's ships docked. The ugly feeling that had been bothering her for the past few days, like a toothache or a dark spot in the corner of her eye that she could never quite bring into focus, suddenly lifted, like the sun coming out from behind a cloud. She took her turn at the toss-and-catch game and was perfect as usual, making her shot with no real effort. Her older sibling and cousins didn't question her skill at the game. It had long since ceased to be a wonder to them.

17

IT WAS MUCH WORSE than Ahsoka had expected. Every system she passed through had an Imperial presence, and they weren't just discreet bases set up to monitor local governments. They were oppressive, controlling resources and populations alike, with no regard for personal rights and needs. Any overt resistance was crushed. Ahsoka had nearly wept when she read the updated bulletins of what continued to happen on Kashyyyk while she'd been out of contact on Raada. She wondered what had become of Chewbacca, the Wookiee with whom she had escaped from captivity on the hunter moon. She hoped he had survived and that he hadn't regained his freedom only to lose it again, but she was starting to lose that hope.

The planets that weren't under the control of the Empire had all been overrun by crime lords, none of whom were friendly. Ahsoka didn't think Jabba the Hutt would feel obliged to pay her any kindness, let alone keep her presence a secret. She briefly considered Takodana, a green world covered with water and more plants than she felt comfortable around, but decided against it without even making landfall. There were just too many unknowns.

After the seventh Outer Rim system that she deemed too Imperial to approach, Ahsoka made a decision. She couldn't go back to Raada yet. It was safer for everyone, safer for Kaeden, if she stayed away until she came up with a way to rescue everyone at the same time. The Imperials would still be looking for her, and it would be better for her friends if they didn't know where she was.

She also couldn't go anywhere in the Core. Even the Inner Rim would be too exposed. As much as she would like to find a hidden valley on a mountainside on some planet like Alderaan or Chandrila, she couldn't risk it. Her life as a Jedi meant that she knew too many people there.

What she could do was go back to the Fardis. The Empire was already installed there, so things were stable, but the world wasn't terribly important to galactic politics. She wasn't even sure who the senator was, despite having lived on the planet for almost a year. The guilds and federations that had held so much power under the Separatists had mostly been obliterated at the same time as the Jedi. That was what had allowed the Fardis to step into power in the first place, without allying with a larger family like the Hutts. She could dodge patrols, and she knew she could get by without raising suspicions as long as she kept a low profile and made absolutely sure not to use the Force for anything. Ever.

In her heart, she was willing to admit a secondary motivation. She needed to check on Hedala Fardi. She'd failed the child before, and since she couldn't help Kaeden, she could at least try to help someone else who needed her. If she had another rescue to organize, she needed to know about it as soon as possible. She owed the family that much.

She was close enough that the jump through hyperspace was short—an easy calculation, and then she was in orbit. She looked down at the familiar dusty landscape she'd briefly considered home and sighed. She was going to have to do some fast talking to convince the Fardis to take her back, even though they had all but given her clearance to leave in the first place.

She could just hide. Bury her head in the dust, eat only what she could hunt, and disappear from civilized life entirely. It wouldn't be easy, but she'd be safe. She'd also be completely cut off. Hiding wouldn't protect anyone except herself, and it wasn't like she had anything to wait for. She'd just atrophy, alone. It would be better to try lying low again, until she figured out her next move. She squeezed the package of metal pieces, but it didn't make her feel better. Not having a mission was hard.

The last time she'd landed in the Fardi shipyard, the girls had met her. This time, it was the chief Fardi, the man who'd bought her Republic vessel, and he didn't look particularly happy to see her.

"Back, I see," he called out as she disembarked. "Are you returning my property?"

"I think I'll keep it for a little longer, if that's all right," Ahsoka said. "If you have anything that needs fixing, though, I'd be happy to help out again."

He looked at her in a measuring way. She knew he didn't know the truth about who she was, but he did know that she'd taken the opportunity to leave when it was presented to her, rather than stay and face Imperial scrutiny. Maybe he would decide she wasn't worth the risk.

"There's always room for a good mechanic," he said after a long moment. "Or even a competent one, like you."

Ahsoka smiled. Competency was tolerable.

"Even less luggage this time," Fardi commented.

"I travel light," Ahsoka said.

"Well, you might as well come back to the house with me," he said. "We'll attract attention if we stand around for too long. Usually, we're ignored, because the Imperials can't tell us apart, but you're definitely not related, so it's best to get out of the open. The girls have missed you, and there'll be food."

Ahsoka followed him down the dusty road. It was different than it had been when she left—quieter, an air of expectation hovering on every corner, but not the expectation of anything good. People kept their heads down, and Ahsoka would have to do the same, but keeping her head down wasn't the same as ignoring what was happening around her, and Ahsoka had no intention of doing that. She'd check on Hedala, mend relations with the Fardis, and then see what she could do for Kaeden back on Raada.

◆ ◆ ◆

Hedala Fardi knew Ahsoka was coming. That was the only explanation for the girl's appearing in the door of the family house by herself, away from the gaggle of children she usually ran around with. Even her uncle noticed the strangeness of it, though he let it pass without remark. Perhaps they'd grown accustomed to Hedala's being strange.

The little girl walked over to Ahsoka and hugged her around the waist. Ahsoka was pleased to see that she was alive and safe. She knelt down to give the girl a proper hug.

"I'm glad to see you," she whispered.

"Me too," Hedala said back. The girl was about a year past the age when the Temple might have found her, as far out from the Core as she was. Her baby lisp was gone, vanished in the weeks Ahsoka had been absent. "There was a shadow while you were away."

Ahsoka wanted to ask what she was talking about, but before she could, the Fardi cousins swarmed her. Already on the ground, Ahsoka had no choice but to submit to the hugs and remonstrations about her absence.

"We're happy you're safe, though, Ashla," said the oldest girl. Ahsoka still couldn't remember the girl's name. She'd have to do better this time.

"I'm happy you're all safe," Ahsoka said. "The galaxy's starting to be kind of an ugly place."

"Shhhh, don't let Mama hear you talk like that," one of the girls said. "She doesn't like politics, and she'll make us talk about something boring instead. We'll wait until we're alone."

Ahsoka nodded, happy to be involved in so innocent a conspiracy if it led her to good intelligence, and fought her way back to her feet through the hugs from the littler girls.

"I'm really sorry," Ahsoka said, "but I've forgotten which name goes with which of you."

Instantly, a babble of giggles and names assaulted her. Ahsoka held up her hands in protest.

"One at a time!" she said. "That's probably why I could never keep you straight in the first place."

"No one ever keeps us straight," said a girl who was older than Hedala, but not by much. "That's how we avoid the law."

"Too many secrets, lovelies," Fardi said. He'd come up behind them and was laughing. "But there's no problem telling Ashla your names. Just get out of my hair while you do it. You babble worse than my own sisters."

The girls reacted to the perceived insult to their mothers by attacking, and Fardi pressed a hasty retreat toward his office.

While they pursued him, Hedala stood quietly next to Ahsoka. She took the opportunity to warn the girl to be careful.

"I need you to tell me about the shadow," she said. "But you mustn't tell anyone else, do you understand?"

Hedala nodded, small and solemn.

"We'll talk later," Ahsoka said. She took the little girl's hand. "Come on, let's go save your uncle."

It took very little to divert the girls. They brought Ahsoka out into the courtyard, where they all sat on colorful pillows. The high walls made Ahsoka feel safe, even though she knew an Imperial walker could blast right through them. The oldest Fardi girl appeared with a tea tray that held an enormous pot and more than a dozen little cups.

"I'm Chenna," she said, pouring a cup and handing it to Ahsoka. Despite the heat of the day, the tea was very hot, and Ahsoka blew on it before taking a sip.

Chenna passed out all the cups, naming each girl as she received hers. It was really quite lazy to say they all looked the same. Similar, yes, but that was genetics. Ahsoka catalogued each name as she heard it, linking it with something unique to each girl. Finally, Chenna got to Hedala.

"And this is Hedala," she said. "But you already knew that, because everyone always remembers Hedala's name."

"She will have trouble with the law," said Makala in a sing-song voice.

"You'll have trouble with the law," said Chenna, "if you don't pay more attention to your pilot lessons."

Makala went off to sulk while the rest of the girls laughed. They started talking about learning to fly, a family requirement, and all the other things they'd done since Ahsoka had left. Eventually, as the sun lowered in the sky, they began to wander off in search of their dinners, and just Chenna, Ahsoka, and Hedala were left sitting in the courtyard. Hedala was seated on Chenna's lap, and the older girl was brushing her fingers through Hedala's straight black hair. By this time, Ahsoka had figured out that Chenna was Hedala's sister and took special care of her on that account.

"Did you see terrible things out there, Ashla?" Chenna asked. "You can tell me in front of Hedala. Nothing scares her."

"Yes," Ahsoka said. It was important that Hedala know, but Chenna needed to hear it, too, if she wanted to survive. "The people I met suffered, and there wasn't anything I could do about it."

"So you left them?" Chenna asked. She held Hedala tighter, and the little girl squirmed.

"It was more complicated than that," Ahsoka said. "They went into hiding, and I couldn't hide with them."

"Why not?" Chenna asked.

Ahsoka considered it for a moment and then selected a lie that held just enough truth to be reasonable.

"There aren't so many Togruta at large in the galaxy that I fit into a crowd," she said. "It would be different if I were Twi'lek, and it would be very different if I were human, but I'm neither. I'm not ashamed of who I am, but I have to be extra careful because of it."

"We all look like each other, everyone in my family," Hedala said. She had the manner of someone reciting a lesson, which Ahsoka reasoned was why she sounded suddenly mature. "Our long hair and our brown skin. People don't try to tell us apart, and we fool them. It helped us avoid the shadow, and it keeps us safe from the law. I wish you looked like us, too."

"My smart baby sister," Chenna said. Her tone was full of warmth, and it made something inside Ahsoka ache. Hedala was too young to be so wise, and she would never get to prove her cleverness to Master Yoda like she should. "It's probably all thanks to my influence."

Ahsoka laughed, and the Fardi girls laughed with her. She was safe enough for now.

CHAPTER

18

IT WAS FIVE DAYS before Ahsoka managed to get Hedala alone. She spent that time working on one of the bigger Fardi transports, tuning the engine and installing a new compressor. She didn't ask what the cargo would be. The Fardis were welcoming because she was useful, but they weren't about to tell her the secrets of their operation. Frankly, Ahsoka wasn't sure she wanted to know.

In the end, Hedala sought her out, padding into Ahsoka's tiny room in the family compound after she was supposed to be in bed. Ahsoka had wanted to turn down the offer to stay in the family house but couldn't think of a way to do it politely. Her old house had been taken over by someone else, and she couldn't sleep on the ship. It wasn't like she had a lot of options. The house was loud and noisy, but at least she could keep an eye on things.

"Sit, little one." She said it the way she might have spoken to a Jedi youngling.

Hedala sat down on Ahsoka's bed platform. She crossed her bare feet and put her hands on her knees. It was Ahsoka's favored position for meditation, and she mirrored the little girl without thinking about it.

"Hedala, I need you to tell me about the shadow," Ahsoka said. "Anything you can remember about it. Can you do that?"

"Yes," Hedala said. "I never saw it, but I knew that it was here, in the city."

"How did you know?" Ahsoka asked. "I mean, how did you know if you couldn't see it?"

"I could feel it," Hedala said. "Like I feel the sun when it's too hot, only dark, not light."

"And then one day it was just gone?" Ahsoka asked.

"Yes." The little girl tapped her fingers on her knees.

Ahsoka considered how best to proceed. She didn't want

to terrify the child completely, but she did want her to be cautious. She wished she'd spent more time with younglings. Master Yoda always seemed good at talking to them. She tried to imagine what he would say and then found herself fighting off unexpected giggles when she remembered Master Yoda's unique way of talking. Maybe that was why the younglings had liked him so much.

"You were very smart to stay out of the shadow's way," Ahsoka told her. "It's always wiser to wait and learn when something is unfamiliar and scary."

"I didn't tell anyone," Hedala said. "Do you think that was foolish? I didn't think they would believe me."

"But you knew I would?" Ahsoka asked.

"Chenna says that well-traveled people always believe more things," Hedala said matter-of-factly. "They have seen more, so they have bigger imaginations."

"Chenna might be right," Ahsoka said. "I think you were right to keep the shadow to yourself. It's easier to hide from something like that if no one else is looking for it."

"I'm very good at hiding," Hedala said.

"I'm glad to hear it," Ahsoka told her. "But I think you should get to bed before someone comes looking for you, just to save your reputation."

Hedala giggled and went on her way, leaving Ahsoka with her thoughts.

The shadow was almost certainly one of the dark side's creatures. Ahsoka had no idea what sort of thing it might be, but whatever it was couldn't be that powerful, because it hadn't been able to track down Hedala. That ruled out Palpatine himself, not that the Emperor could just show up on a planet without causing a great deal of alarm. It also ruled out whatever Palpatine was using to track down surviving Jedi. Ahsoka had heard rumors of a dark lord who served the Emperor, but nothing confirmable. As usual, she felt rather cut off without her former channels of intelligence. At least Hedala said the shadow was gone.

Ahsoka spared a momentary thought to wonder where it went. She tallied the days on her fingers, accounting for time spent in hyperspace, which always made things a bit fuzzy, and realized that Hedala's shadow had left shortly after Ahsoka had rescued Kaeden on Raada. It was probably a coincidence, but at the same time, Ahsoka had been around long enough to know that coincidences and the Force rarely went together. There was always some sort of link.

She drummed her fingers on her knees, the way Hedala

had earlier, and wondered what the shadow would do to Raada once it learned Ahsoka was gone. It hadn't done anything to the Fardis, but they weren't already the targets of an Imperial investigation. Perhaps she should try to draw the shadow back.

Except, of course, that would put Hedala in danger again and Ahsoka, as well. Ahsoka resisted the urge to smack her head against the wall. It was difficult to keep one's own counsel. She missed being able to ask for advice. Imagining what her masters would do was only so useful, and she always felt foolish when she talked to herself. When she meditated and thought about the quandary, the voice that came to her with a suggestion was, somewhat surprisingly, Padmé Amidala's. Ever the politician, the Naboo senator prized gathering information and playing to her strengths.

At this particular moment, Ahsoka's strengths were all inside the Fardi compound. She was as protected as she could be, she had access to the Holonet for news, and if she invested a little more time in making the older members of the family trust her, they would probably be able to give her a very good idea of what was going on, even if she had to construct it backward from shady trade deals. It wasn't the way Ahsoka was used to thinking about politics, but with any luck, it wasn't the way her unknown opponents were expecting her to act, either.

Ahsoka lay down, putting her head on the pillow and thinking, as she always did, how much softer it was than anything she'd slept on when she was a Padawan. If she was going to learn about intergalactic trade in the morning, she might as well be rested.

Fardi had been surprised when, only a week into her stay, Ahsoka had come to him with a request for a new job. He'd insisted on watching her piloting skills firsthand, which made sense given the stakes of the family business. Ahsoka knew she had impressed him, both in the atmosphere around Thabeska and on a circuit of the system at large.

"It's not as if you can't do both jobs," Fardi said as Ahsoka landed the freighter, their last test run completed. "We'll let you know when we have need of a pilot. Nothing else will change."

That suited Ahsoka just fine.

They started her off with small jobs. She flew to other cities on Thabeska, controlled by other branches of the family, and made deliveries. Sometimes she flew her own ship, and sometimes she was assigned a larger one. She never asked what was in the crates, so if her cargo didn't match the manifest, she didn't know about it. After her tenth trip, she was starting to think that the Fardis smuggled just to stay in practice, except that every time she dropped something off, in some dark alley or behind an isolated warehouse, the people receiving it were emaciated, desperate, and *grateful*. It was oddly fulfilling work.

She learned that the main weapon of the Empire, after fear, was hunger. She had seen this strategy at work on Raada and also during the Clone Wars, but to see it applied on such a large scale made her very uncomfortable. The Empire was still new, still establishing itself in the outer reaches of the galaxy, and yet it was already incredibly powerful. And she realized that she had helped build it. The mechanisms put in place during the Clone Wars had been twisted for the Empire's use, and every day the Emperor's hold grew tighter. She almost admired Palpatine for his ability to pull off a long-term plan—except for his being evil and all.

By the time the Fardis trusted her with off-world transport missions, Ahsoka was more convinced than ever that the Empire must be resisted. Unfortunately, she still had no idea how. She understood, finally, how the farmers on Raada had felt as they were forced to poison their own fields. She felt their frustration and their anger and saw how it had pushed them to recklessness. She was going to owe Neera an apology when she returned, assuming Neera would even listen to her.

In the meantime, her only option was this passive resistance, and Ahsoka was grateful for it while she sought out other options, even though it wasn't much of a distraction.

All that changed very quickly when Ahsoka picked up a distress call in the middle of one of her routine off-planet runs. It was coming from an escape pod, and Ahsoka hesitated only briefly to consider her options. The transport she was flying had a big enough cargo bay for a pod, and the pod wasn't very far away. Quickly, she set course, and before long she had three shocked, though relieved, humans standing in front of her. From their expressions and general alarm, she didn't think it had been a mechanical error that lost them their ship.

"It was pirates," said the woman. She was the first to calm down enough to talk. "They attacked the shuttle we were on and took several prisoners. We barely made it into the pod."

"Why would they attack you?" Ahsoka asked her, speaking as gently as she could.

"Ransom, I suspect," the woman said. She shifted uncomfortably. Ransom was something that the Black Sun crime syndicate peddled in this sector, and they were not known for being courteous to their hostages.

"You don't have to tell me your business," Ahsoka told her. "Just tell me why you were targeted."

"We were underbid by a well-known firm for a large project," the taller of the two men said, after considering his words for a moment. The only large projects were Imperial ones. "We were reworking the numbers to see if we could match the lower bid when we were attacked."

"You think your competitors would like to bankrupt you enough that you can't afford a lower bid?" Ahsoka asked.

The woman nodded.

"If I help you and you save the credits, are you still going to get involved?" she demanded. She was willing to help people who needed it, but she was far less comfortable making it easier for them to serve the Empire. The fact that she was forced to make that sort of distinction made her feel ill.

"No," the woman said emphatically. "No credits are worth this kind of trouble. We just want our people back and we're out."

The way she said *people* made Ahsoka think she wasn't just talking about employees.

"All right," said Ahsoka. "Give me the coordinates."

After that, it seemed like she kept running into people who

needed help. The missions—if she could call them that—were random and unorganized, and sometimes they ended badly. More than once, she was betrayed and escaped only because she'd been trained to fly by the best pilot in the galaxy. But little by little, she carved out a reputation. Or Ashla did. After the first time, she did what she could to prevent those she was helping from seeing her face. They usually understood. Anonymity was the best defense she could muster.

If the Fardis knew what she was up to when she took their ships and cargo off-planet, they didn't complain. She made sure the ships she flew were hard to track, and she scrubbed off all evidence of carbon scoring every time she was back on the ground. Soon, she thought, she would be ready to go back to Raada. Soon she'd find a ship big enough for her friends. And the rest of the farmers, too. It wasn't a big town. She would think of something.

If she was being honest, being a hero again felt *good*. She had been trained for this, for justice, and the fact that she was working against those who had hurt her so badly only made it better. She was careful and did her best to resist her reckless nature. And she made life a little easier for the people of the Outer Rim.

Her good work did not go unnoticed.

19

THE SIXTH BROTHER did not hold the district commander's failure to apprehend the Jedi Padawan against him. After all, if just anyone could catch Jedi, there would be no need for Inquisitors. He did make sure to file a report detailing where the commander had fallen short and outlining his suggestions for reprisals, but he did not hold a grudge. He was too much of a professional for that sort of pettiness.

He was significantly less impressed by the nonmilitary lackey who called himself Jenneth Pilar.

"You weren't exactly what I had in mind," Pilar said,

winding down a long series of complaints about how he felt the Imperial base was understaffed and why his suggestions should be followed to fix it. "I am sure you are good at whatever your job is, but I need men to patrol, to enforce order, and to make sure the fieldwork gets done on schedule."

"Then you will have to do it yourself," the Inquisitor said. He enjoyed the way Pilar recoiled from the harshness of his tone. "The Empire has other priorities on Raada now."

Pilar huffed for a while longer but finally fled as the Inquisitor's expression got blacker and more threatening. That was the easiest way to deal with weak-minded bureaucrats. They didn't listen anyway, so it was best to intimidate them until they gave up.

The Inquisitor called up the interrogation report on the girl called Kaeden Larte. She'd given no indication that she knew anything about a Jedi, but of course her interrogation had been mostly botched. They'd pushed her too hard, trying to scare her, and then she hadn't been physically capable of speech before her rescue. The rescue itself was almost certainly carried out by the Jedi. No one had seen anything, and the window was far too high for a girl who had a broken arm to climb through on her own.

A map of the surrounding area replaced the report on the Inquisitor's screen. There was nowhere to hide in the agricultural region of the planet. It was too well patrolled, there was no cover, and it would take too long to cross. The insurgents couldn't be hiding in the town itself. They would have been uncovered by now, by even the most inept stormtrooper patrol. That left the hills. Without use of the walkers, the commander had been slow to search the area, because it would require too much manpower. Maybe that wretch Pilar had a point about being understaffed.

It didn't matter. The Jedi Padawan was long gone. Her ship had been seen leaving the planet after the successful rescue mission. What the Sixth Brother needed to decide was the order in which to take his next steps. He was going to find the insurgents and torture them, but he thought it might be wiser to track down the Jedi first, so she would be sure to hear about the suffering of the people she'd left behind. Then she'd come back to save them, and he'd have her. He knew, or at least suspected, the general direction she had gone. He'd received reports of a series of seemingly random heroic actions that, when considered together, he felt a Jedi could be responsible for. He simply required confirmation. He'd hate to go to all the effort of setting the trap without making sure his prey would be able to find it.

Decision made, he prepared to go back to his ship. Let the Empire drain Raada of its resources for a while longer. It wasn't as if the people had anywhere else to go. He'd get the Jedi's attention and then crush all of them at the same time. He deleted the report on the district commander before he left. He hated having to reestablish his authority, and if the incompetent man were replaced before the Inquisitor returned, he'd have to do just that. It was much easier to leave Raada as it was for now, ripe and ready for his return.

◆ ◆ ◆

The casual observer might have thought it a regular meeting between a senator and his staff. Bail Organa sat behind his desk and discussed logistics while his underlings took notes, and everything looked absolutely aboveboard. Outside the window behind him, Coruscant traffic moved endlessly in ordered lines.

What Bail was really doing was making a list. There had been several lucky coincidences in the Outer Rim of late that had come to his attention. An Imperial contract had fallen through. A planet in desperate need of food aid had received it.

A pirate ship known to run operations for Black Sun that had been preying on passenger shuttles had been thwarted. There was no pattern in terms of time or location, but for reasons he couldn't explain, Bail was certain it was the Jedi he sought.

So far, none of his tracking methods had paid off. He wasn't entirely surprised. The Jedi would be hiding from Imperial watchers, and the Empire was far more likely to employ unsavory types to do its dirty work than Bail was. He'd gotten R2-D2 back from Captain Antilles but had left the droid with Breha on Alderaan when it was time to return to the Senate. Although the droid was eager to help, Bail didn't have a mission for him yet. He'd left the little astromech happily working through the Alderaanian historical database and hoped to have a more practical job for him soon.

"It's tricky, Senator, but I think if we actually went out there and started tracing these supply lines, we might succeed in finding the source." Chardri Tage was a pilot Bail had known since before the Clone Wars. He trusted the man, both to keep secrets and to plan strategy. The fact that Chardri could keep up with a spoken code only reaffirmed Bail's instinct to ask the pilot to do the job, and the fact that he'd maneuvered the pilot into thinking it was his own idea helped with Bail's cover.

"I agree." Chardri's partner and long-time copilot, Tamsin, was a small woman who was not at all reluctant to use her pretty face to lull enemies into underestimating her and then use her pretty blaster to shoot them.

"Will you need a ship, or can you use your own?" Bail asked. He didn't have a lot of resources to work with when he was acting as a rebel instead of a senator, but there were some benefits to being married to a ruling planetary queen.

"We can use ours," Chardri said. "I get the feeling we might have to do some tight flying, and it's always best to do that in something familiar."

Bail hadn't told them they were looking for a Jedi. He trusted them, but he wasn't stupid. Also, to be completely honest, he was a little wary to say the words out loud. He knew his offices on Coruscant couldn't be completely secured. But even if they could, Bail didn't think he would have said anything to them about the Jedi. There was just too much at risk. As far as Chardri and Tamsin knew, they were looking for some sort of ringleader, a person like Bail himself but on a much smaller scale—and presumably someone who wasn't currently late for a vote in the Senate.

"Where do you want us to meet next?" Tamsin asked delicately as she rose to her feet.

Bail considered it. Alderaan was out, as was Coruscant. In fact, any planet at all was too risky. He'd be calling in another favor from Captain Antilles, it seemed.

"We'll meet your ship," Bail said. "Contact me when you've secured the objective, and I'll give you the coordinates."

Chardri and Tamsin exchanged a look but didn't protest.

"If you'll excuse me, I'm late for a vote," Bail said. Both pilots took that for the dismissal it was. "Good hunting," he told them as they preceded him out of his office. *And may the Force be with us,* he thought.

◆ ◆ ◆

Ahsoka landed her ship, took her hands off the controls, and cracked her neck. It had been a very long flight, and while nothing had gone wrong, her nerves were on edge. She couldn't shake the feeling that something was coming, something that would change everything she was working to build. She did her postflight inspection as quickly as she could, eager to eat real food, take a decent shower, and then sleep in her own bed.

None of the Fardis came out to meet her, which was unusual enough to upset her nerves even further. She made her way toward the big house, looking carefully for any disturbance and even going so far as to reach out with the Force. When she got to the door, it was open, so she went inside.

All the family members currently in residence were gathered in the living room, and there were four stormtroopers with blasters standing in the doorway. They spotted Ahsoka instantly, so there was no point in running. She might get away, but the Fardis wouldn't. She held their lives in her hands, and she could see that the older ones knew it. She thought fast.

"Your ship's repaired," she said. She had no idea what, if anything, the Fardis had told the Imperials about her. It was best to start with an easy lie and hope they followed her lead. "I took it for a spin around the system, and all the kinks seem to have been worked out."

"Excellent," said Fardi. There was sweat on his brow, but the room was hot with so many people in it. "This is the mechanic I was telling you about," he told the stormtroopers. "When you keep as many ships as my family does, it makes sense to employ one full-time. She lives here, as a matter of fact, so that she's always ready to work."

"We don't care about your mechanic," said one of the troopers. "We're just conducting a routine search of the house."

Ahsoka made sure to keep her face neutral, but the trooper's words surprised her. There was no such thing as a routine search of private property. They were looking for something, or they wouldn't be there.

"Of course, of course," Fardi said. "Anything we can do to help."

Ahsoka went to sit beside Hedala, who was sitting in Chenna's lap. Ahsoka leaned forward carefully and whispered in the girl's ear.

"Any shadows today?" she asked.

"No," Hedala replied, just as quietly. "Clear skies for good flying."

Ahsoka breathed a little easier. She hadn't felt anything, either, but the girl knew exactly what she was looking for, so it made sense to ask for surety.

Two more troopers and an officer came into the room. The stormtroopers who were already present straightened to attention.

"We were in a small room in the back of the house," the officer said. "Whose room is that?"

"Mine," Ahsoka said, standing up again. She tried not to measure how far it was to the door or to calculate how she might jump out the window.

"Please explain this," the officer said, holding up the package of metal pieces that Ahsoka kept under her pillow. Her skin crawled to think of their searching her room to that degree.

"Oh, those are just bits of junk I've picked up doing various jobs," Ahsoka said, deliberately underplaying the value of the tech she'd collected. "I can show you if you want."

"Open it," the officer said.

Ahsoka pulled on the ties. The Imperials must have thought it was rigged to explode or something. The package was only sealed with knots. The wrapping fell away to reveal the bits and bobs Ahsoka had collected on Raada. She still couldn't have said why any of them were important to her, but she knew she didn't want to hand them over to any Imperials.

"Nothing here, sir," said one of the stormtroopers. "Just scrap metal."

The officer drew himself up in front of Fardi.

"It might be wise to limit your exposure to those people who are outside your family," he sneered. His eyes trailed to Ahsoka and then back to Fardi. "We've noticed a certain criminal element in this city, and we would hate to trace it to your home."

"I'll take it under consideration," said Fardi.

"Good," the officer replied. He signaled to the stormtroopers, and they all marched out of the house.

Fardi deflated as soon as they were gone.

"Everyone out," he said, sounding defeated. "Except Ashla. We need to talk."

CHAPTER

20

"I'LL GO," AHSOKA SAID, getting to her feet once the room was clear. "It won't take me long to gather my things."

"Ashla," Fardi said. "I'm sorry we've put you in the cross fire here. We didn't mean for the Empire to pin our activities on you."

That brought her up short.

"Your activities?" she said. "But I've been—"

She and Fardi looked at each other in stunned silence for a moment, and then, of all things, Fardi began to laugh.

"You used our ships to run mercy missions of your own,"

he said, and Ahsoka realized he hadn't known for sure until just then. "You thought the Imperials were here for you."

"Um, yes," Ahsoka said. "They weren't?"

"Well, they might have been here for all of us, as it turns out," Fardi said. "I don't know what you've been up to, but we have taken contracts and moved merchandise counter to Imperial regulations. You did some of the runs for us. My wife was furious that I was putting you in danger, but apparently you could handle it."

"I thought it was ordinary smuggling," Ahsoka admitted. "And it bothered me a bit at first, but then I saw how needed your supplies were throughout the sector. Every time I dropped something off, it felt like I was making a difference—but it wasn't enough. The first time I heard a distress call, I knew that I could do more."

"I did wonder why you were deviating from your schedule so randomly," Fardi said. "Perhaps if we had talked about this, organized it for real, we could have had a longer run at it. As it is, I think you'll have to leave, and we'll have to go straight for a while to get our reputation back."

"I'm in your debt again," Ahsoka said. "This is the second time you've taken me in when I had nowhere else to go and the second time you've turned me loose instead of turning me in."

"You're a good mechanic," Fardi said with a grin. "There aren't so many of those that I am willing to throw one away just because of a few Imperial entanglements."

"Thanks," Ahsoka said. She started to move toward the door and then stopped. It was a risk to say the words out loud, but she had to do all she could before she left. "Fardi, you need to be careful with Hedala."

The change in the older man was instant. His brow furrowed, and there was a determined gleam in his eyes.

"What about her?" he asked.

"She's . . ." Ahsoka trailed off. She wasn't sure how to say it without giving too much away. "She's special. It's important that no one realizes how special she is."

Fardi blinked, putting the pieces together. Ahsoka wondered what he'd seen the little girl do, if he'd ever found her behavior odd and then dismissed it because he was busy. If he had, he was remembering it now.

"Do you think she'll grow up to be a mechanic?" he said, and Ahsoka knew he'd understood everything she hadn't said.

"There isn't anyone to teach her," Ahsoka said, choosing

her words carefully. It was more than she wanted to reveal about herself, but so far the Fardis had given her every reason to trust them. "She won't exactly grow out of it, but eventually she'll grow into other things."

"I'll keep an eye on her," Fardi said. "I promise."

"Thank you," said Ahsoka. "I'm sorry I can't do more."

"I am very much aware of what you have done, Ashla," Fardi said. "And now that I know why you came back, I think we are even."

Fardi held out his hand, and Ahsoka shook it. Then she picked up the package of tech pieces and went back to her room. She stood in the center of it, looking at her bed and the little shelf where she kept her few belongings. Then she knelt and spilled the contents of the bag onto the mattress to examine them again.

The bag was starting to fray, which wasn't really a surprise considering all the oddly shaped pieces it contained. She spread them out, finding the pairs and the few pieces that had no match. She liked the colors of the metal and the weight of the pieces in her hands.

What she really wanted to do was close her eyes, reach out with the Force, and see if all the pieces somehow fit together.

The door was open behind her, though, and she could hear the noises of the house. She trusted Fardi and his family, but there was a difference between suspecting something and knowing it, and that difference was dangerous. There was no reason for Ahsoka to put any member of the family at more risk than she already had. She'd be alone again soon enough. She'd be able to test her theory then.

Carefully, she slid the pieces back into the bag and retied the fraying ends. Then she put it into the carrying pack Neera had given her on Raada and added the other knickknacks she'd picked up, mostly from the children, who apparently thought she needed more shiny things to look at.

Ahsoka hoisted the bag onto her back, adjusted it around her lekku, and turned around. Hedala was standing in the doorway, looking at her with a serious expression.

"I don't want you to go," the little girl said.

"I have to, little one," Ahsoka said. "It's dangerous for everyone if I stay."

"The shadow isn't back," Hedala said. "But I guess there are other shadows."

Ahsoka wasn't too surprised that Hedala could sense something she could not. It happened frequently with younglings.

They'd be good at one aspect of the Force and not at others until they were trained. Obi-Wan told her that Anakin had been found by Obi-Wan's master, Qui-Gon, because of his quick reflexes. It was her ability to sense people's feelings and intentions that had marked her. Hedala was apparently good at sensing danger from a distance. Not a bad skill to have, untrained, at a time when having any skill at all was enough to make her an automatic target.

"I can handle it, thanks to your warning," Ahsoka said. She was almost positive that she was telling the truth. "Your job is to avoid the shadows altogether, do you understand?"

Hedala nodded and then threw her arms around Ahsoka's waist, as high as she could reach. Surprised, Ahsoka rested her arms on the little girl's shoulders for a moment, and then Hedala drew away.

"Good-bye, Ashla," Hedala said. "I'll miss you."

"I'll miss you, too," Ahsoka replied.

Hedala held her hand until they reached the front door and then waved until Ahsoka disappeared around the corner. Ahsoka didn't like that she was leaving the little girl behind again, but there wasn't anything she could do about it. Her position was too tenuous to include child minding. It was better for Hedala to stay with her family. At least Fardi knew to keep an eye out now, and he would tell the family what they needed to know.

What gnawed at her even more was that she knew Hedala couldn't be the only Force-sensitive child in the galaxy. There had been thousands of Jedi because there had been thousands of kids like Hedala, and there still were, even though they had nowhere to go for training. And the Empire was hunting them down. It was another entry on the list of things Ahsoka could do nothing about. She was starting to really dislike that list. It was heavy, and she had no choice but to carry it.

She walked up the ramp onto her ship, both the hull and the navicomputer scrubbed clean since her last mission, and stowed her bag. When she sat in the pilot's seat, her view was clearer. This, at least, was something she could do. She ran the preflight checks quickly, even though she wasn't in any particular hurry, and took off when she had clearance. With no real destination in mind, she set a course at sublight speed and headed for one of the neighboring planets in the system. It was sparsely populated and covered with mountains. She couldn't stay in isolation for very long, but taking a couple of days to clear her head and formulate a new plan was probably a good idea. There was no need to rush off half-cocked.

While the ship cruised along, she ran a scan of the hull and computer system, searching for any kind of tracking device. The sudden appearance of Imperials at the Fardi house was too alarming to overlook entirely. She hadn't been away from her ship for very long, but it was more than enough time for someone to install a device. She found nothing, but she couldn't shake the feeling of unease that Hedala's warning about the new shadows had stirred in her. At least her stolen Imperial blaster was on board, so she'd have something to fight back with, if it came to that. She got it out of its hiding place so she would have it handy.

Her ship slid into the planetary atmosphere with only a small tremor, and she began scanning for a good place to set down and stay for a few days. Eventually, she found a spot with a wide enough platform to hold the ship. It was quite high up, so the air was crisp. The planet was smaller than the one where the Fardis lived but larger than Raada, so she was accustomed to the gravity. All told, it was not a bad spot to set up shop for a while and check the ship. It seemed to be running just fine, but since she had some time, she could give it a thorough onceover.

She was fine-tuning the plasma manifold when she heard it: the unmistakable hum of approaching engines. The blaster was still next to the pilot's chair, so she had to run up the ramp and back into the ship to fetch it. She clipped the blaster to her side and cautiously walked back down the ramp.

Ahsoka could see the approaching ship now. It was flying low, skimming the tops of the mountains and weaving to avoid the highest peaks. It was definitely following her. If it were randomly scanning, it would have been higher up. She wondered how it had found her, and then she realized that since she hadn't gone into hyperspace, whoever was flying that thing could have just tracked her visually.

The ship was not new, but it was well maintained. Even from a distance, Ahsoka could tell that much. It didn't have space for cargo. Single pilot, she suspected. Maybe one or two crew. It began to descend toward her, which was interesting. At least whoever was flying in wasn't going to blast first and ask questions later.

Ahsoka waited, calm and collected, until the ship landed. The other vessel's ramp descended, and then a single figure emerged. Ahsoka couldn't begin to guess if the being was male, female, or otherwise. Their armor was dark, and covered them from head to toe. They carried at least two blasters that Ahsoka could see immediately.

"Pilot Ashla." The voice was heavily modulated. "Congratulations. You have come to the attention of Black Sun."

OBI-WAN REACHED *and found nothing.*

It took him a while to get to this level of deep trance, and now that he was here, he was reluctant to pull up, even though he had failed once again. There must be other things he could see, other Jedi he could find and possibly aid.

Images flickered across his eyes. Padmé, dying, with the babies beside her. Yoda, exacting a promise and giving him a new goal. Anakin, burning on the volcanic slopes of Mustafar, blaming him for everything that had gone wrong.

And it had all gone so wrong.

Now he was back in the place where his carefully

ordered life had begun to unspool. Not the exact location, of course. The Lars family lived in the middle of nowhere, and it was a part of Tatooine where Obi-Wan had never gone until he had brought Luke to them. But it was the planet where his whole existence had been forever altered.

He'd gone to Shmi Skywalker's grave to apologize for losing her son. He had never met her, knew her only from Anakin's stories, but Qui-Gon had made her a promise and Obi-Wan hadn't been able to keep it. As he stood there, looking at the stone, he felt an even deeper shame. Qui-Gon had left her there a slave, and Obi-Wan had done everything in his power to prevent Anakin's return. It was only the love of a good man, here on Tatooine, that had saved her—the kind of love the Jedi were supposed to eschew. Yet it had done something the Jedi could not.

But that was the past. What he did now, he did for an uncertain future and for hope. He had trusted in the light side of the Force for his entire life. There was no call for him to stop now. He found the center of his meditation, the quiet place where there was no emotion, no resistance, no worldly bonds. He rooted his feet in that place and reached again.

Still nothing.

Obi-Wan shook himself out of the trance, more annoyed with his failure than disappointed, and found he was still sitting on the floor of Ben Kenobi's house. It was sparsely appointed, only the basic necessities. He hadn't been there long, but he got the feeling that even if he stayed until Luke Skywalker had a long gray beard, he still wouldn't accumulate many possessions. Tatooine wasn't that sort of place.

He stood up, his knees creaking in a rather alarming fashion. Surely he wasn't that old yet. It must be the desert climate that affected him strangely. He got a small cup, filled it with water, and then returned to his seat on the floor. Something caught his attention, one of the few pieces of his old life that he'd taken with him to his desert solitude.

Anakin Skywalker's lightsaber.

It was all that was left of the man who had been, often simultaneously, Obi-Wan's greatest annoyance, his brother, and his closest friend. If any other part of Anakin had survived, it was lost to evil and darkness. Obi-Wan couldn't save him any more than he could save any Jedi who was still at large in the galaxy, trying to find footing in the new order. All Obi-Wan could do was make sure the child Luke survived to adulthood, and train him if he exhibited his father's talents.

He wondered briefly how the daughter was faring under Bail Organa's tutelage.

Then he closed his eyes and took a deep breath.

Down he plunged, through memory and dream. There was Commander Cody, handing him back his lightsaber only to blast him off the cavern wall moments later. There was Anakin, laughing as he made some improbably difficult landing, saving all their lives again. There was Ahsoka, her hands on her hips, her endless questions challenging him at every turn. There was Palpatine, as Chancellor, his disguise so complete that Obi-Wan couldn't detect his villainy even when he knew where to look.

He made himself pass them all by. It was easier this time. It grew easier every time. That made his heart hurt, to think he was so fickle that he could turn his back on them to achieve his own ends. When he thought it, he heard Yoda, reminding him that his work was important, that he must focus on the future alone, obscuring the past and even ignoring the present if he must. He had to break through.

He reached the bottom again, the quiet place where his doubts, loves, and fears were gone. Then he realized it wasn't the bottom, not quite. There was another level below.

Obi-Wan let go of Ben Kenobi's house, the last place in the galaxy where a piece of Anakin Skywalker rested, and broke through the wall between life and death.

It was dark there if he wanted to take anything with him or leave anything behind, but he wished for neither of those things, so he stood in the light. His senses were sharp. He could hear every sound at once, and also none of them. It took him a moment to focus on the voice he wanted most to hear.

Alone and connected. Aloof and hopelessly entwined. Obi-Wan had only a moment before he was wrenched back into the physical world, but it was long enough to renew his hope.

"Obi-Wan," said Qui-Gon Jinn. He was sure the voice was stronger this time. "Let go."

21

THE SIXTH BROTHER'S return to Raada had not been as triumphant as he had hoped. He had not been able to make a positive identification of the Jedi, but he was fairly certain that any news of his forthcoming actions on the farming moon would reach the Padawan's attention. He'd tracked a series of happy accidents—happy, that is, for the people who had been saved from run-ins with the Empire. The events had Jedi do-gooding written all over them: low death count, grateful civilians, and a lack of official records. All he had to do was make sure that someone on Raada was left to send a distress call in the right direction and the Jedi would come to him.

His first order of business, after he landed and squared away his ship, was to read the situation updates on the insurgents. As he'd suspected, the local troops had made no inroads in capturing them, which suited him just fine. The district commander seemed to be avoiding him, which also suited his purposes, so he called in the chief interrogator instead.

"I require information on the girl who escaped your custody," he said, cutting straight to the chase. Interrogators usually appreciated the direct approach, which was something he admired about them. "Her appearance, preferably. Not her character."

"She had dark skin," the interrogator said. "And her hair was in braids when I saw her, but unless she's found someone to redo them, I imagine she'll be wearing a scarf or something now."

"Why couldn't she fix them herself?" the Inquisitor asked.

"Her arm is broken," was the reply. "The right. I think there may also be damage to her shoulder, but I couldn't be sure."

"Are your methods so callous?" It was always nice to trade professional information.

"No, the arm was an accident," the interrogator said. "Our

initial torture scared her so badly that when I mentioned the possibility of revisiting it, she knocked herself over and pinned the arm under her chair."

"You have been most helpful," the Inquisitor said. "You're dismissed."

The interrogator was smart enough not to take umbrage at someone with no discernible rank issuing orders. That sort of person was likely to do well in the Imperial hierarchy, which required a certain amount of flexibility. The Sixth Brother made a note to write a commendation. His job, and the jobs of his brothers and sisters, would be easier if the upper ranks were populated by people who listened to them.

Alone, the Inquisitor called up the map of the moon's surface, to refresh his memory of the geography. It took him only a few moments to identify the best places to hide a large group of people, and then he closed the terminal and headed for the door. It was time to stop asking questions and go hunting.

◆ ◆ ◆

Kaeden had played, in her estimation, approximately ten billion games of crokin since Ahsoka had rescued her and left Raada. It had been Miara's suggestion. With a broken arm and limited medical options, Kaeden needed to learn to use her other hand, and crokin was the easiest way to do that. She played with her sister frequently, but her most common opponent was Neera. Once the sedatives had worn off, Neera had shambled around the cave like part of her was missing, and Kaeden thought that wasn't far from the truth. The only time Neera showed any spark was when they played. Neera always trounced her, but if it made her feel better, then Kaeden was happy to lose.

Aside from the board game and the ability to take herself to the bathroom, living in hiding from the Empire was not all that different from being imprisoned by it. The food was terrible. The lighting was bad. She was nervous and jumpy, startling at every sound. But there were no torture machines, so at least she had that going for her. And her sister was with her and safe, mostly, so she had that, too.

Reaching up with her good hand, Kaeden readjusted the scarf she was using to contain her hair. Her usual braids had fared about as well under torture as she had, and she hadn't been able to fix them one-handed. Miara had given it her best shot, but despite her ability to make tiny circuits that could explode when properly triggered, Miara had no gift for braiding. Kaeden ended up taking them out entirely and then had to do her best to deal with the bushy volume hanging loose.

She should probably have cut it, but she knew her arm would get better eventually, and she liked the long braids. She could be patient.

Or she could be patient with her hair, at least. Being patient while they hid out from the Empire was an entirely different matter. No one talked about it, because it felt too much like speaking ill of the dead, but Kaeden could tell that even the most hotheaded of them was wishing they'd never listened to Hoban. As their supplies ran low, there was talk of who should go into town for more and arguments about whether or not they should just try to leave the planet altogether.

"Do you think it's strange that the Imperials haven't found us yet?" Miara said. She sat down beside Kaeden, who was flicking crokin pieces at the center of the board. Her aim was getting better, but not by much.

"We did take out the walkers before things went sideways," Kaeden said. "But you're right. They have to know there are only so many places we could hide. Even the densest stormtroopers should have checked here by now."

"What do you think they're waiting for?" Miara asked.

"I think they're busy looking for something else," Kaeden said. "It's not like we're a threat to them."

"But Ahsoka's gone," Miara said.

"She said she'd come back," Kaeden reminded her. She'd said it a hundred times if she'd said it once, and every time, a little more of her surety died.

Miara looked at her witheringly. It was an old look for a young face, and Kaeden didn't like it.

"Why would she come back?" Miara asked. "There's nothing here."

"There's us," Kaeden said, ignoring Miara's implication that Kaeden believed Ahsoka would return solely on her account. "She might come back for us."

"Her and what army?" Miara asked. "Or would you leave everyone else behind to save yourself?"

Kaeden couldn't say it, couldn't see the look of disgust she knew her sister would give her if she did, but the truth was that she would leave Raada in a heartbeat if she could. If it would save her, or Miara, from ever feeling that machine on her chest again, she would do it. Guilt was a long pain, but it was survivable. She wasn't sure how long she'd hold up if she was tortured again.

"Stop that," Miara said, and Kaeden realized she was rubbing her chest. The machine hadn't even left a mark. All Miara could see was that Kaeden was twitchy and constantly scared. At least no one accused her of being lovesick, even when they might have needed a laugh.

Neera sat down opposite Kaeden, across the crokin board, and began dividing the discs by color. She never asked if Kaeden wanted to play; she didn't do much talking at all anymore, so this was how their games usually began. Kaeden was preparing to lose spectacularly again when Kolvin, who was on sentry duty, crawled out of the connecting tunnel, an alarmed expression on his face.

"There's something coming," he said.

"Stormtroopers?" Kaeden asked. "In the tanks?"

With the walkers out of commission, the tanks were the only ground transport option the Imperials had. They were slow and lumbering and didn't do well in hills, but storm-troopers didn't seem overly fond of walking.

"No," Kolvin said. "Just one person. But moving really fast. They'll be here soon."

The main entrance was always locked. They'd spent time increasing the camouflage around the hidden entrances. It was one of the few activities they could manage safely with-out attracting attention. The weak point in their defense was the sentry door. They had to decide if they wanted to collapse it and lose their vantage point permanently or risk leaving it open. For Kaeden, it wasn't a hard choice at all, but she wasn't the one issuing orders.

Everyone looked at Miara. She wasn't in command, either. No one really was, but the charges were her design. If they were going to be set off, she was the one to do it.

"It'll take me a few moments to get everything ready," Miara said. "Kolvin, do we have that kind of time?"

"We do if we go now," he said. His wide black eyes gleamed, even in the dim of the cave.

"I'm coming with you," Kaeden said.

Miara paused. "You can't crawl yet," she said. "And you can't help with the charges."

"I don't want us to be separated," Kaeden insisted.

"Then let me go so I can come back in a hurry," Miara said.

"Your sister's right," Neera said. "They can kill one of you together as easily as they can apart. You might as well stay here and play crokin with me. It's your turn anyway."

Kaeden gaped at her, shocked that even in grief Neera could say something so awful. Miara took advantage of her sister's distraction and dove into the tunnel with Kolvin on her heels. Time seemed to stretch out forever, but then the ground shook slightly, and Kaeden knew that the sentry point had been taken care of. She wished she'd gotten a look at the approaching figure. She didn't like not knowing what was coming for them.

Neera tapped her on her injured shoulder, and she winced. The older girl gestured to the board.

"It's your turn, Kaeden," she said, as though they were sitting at Selda's at the end of their shift.

Kaeden picked up a disc and debated her next shot.

◆ ◆ ◆

Jenneth Pilar was packing. There was no rhyme or reason to the Empire once Force wielders got involved. Every one of his painstaking calculations was ignored and all his formulae were unbalanced by the very presence of such mythology, and he had no more patience for it. The one who called himself the Sixth Brother was back, and that meant that all Jenneth's well-planned methodologies were about to be jettisoned in favor of some scheme involving a so-called Jedi.

Everyone knew the Jedi were dead. So far from the Core, there were few people who had any faith in the Jedi Order at all. Jenneth didn't admire much about the Outer Rim, but he could respect that. The Force had no place in an ordered galaxy. It simply couldn't be accounted for in the math.

He paused, looking around his quarters for anything he might have forgotten. His eyes fell on the datapad he'd used to calculate exactly how much of what the Empire needed could be extracted from the moon's surface before destroying it for future generations. All that fuss for a plant. Just a simple plant that could be processed into a nutritional supplement that allowed people working in low gravity to process oxygen more efficiently. He couldn't imagine it was worth the trouble the Empire had gone to in order to procure it.

He threw the datapad into his case and shut the latches. It was hardly his problem. He'd been paid, and he'd seen the job along as far as he could before it got out of his control. There was no reason for the Imperials to think he'd slighted them, and there was no reason for him to stay on the benighted moon a moment longer. He was going back to a planet with real trees, real food, a real bed, and no lingering smell of fertilizer.

In the fields, the farmers labored under duress and the little plants grew taller. A few more days and the harvest could begin.

22

IN HER FAVOR, the armored figure hadn't yet drawn a weapon. They really did want to talk. Ahsoka's own blaster still hung at her side, but she could get to it if she needed to. It didn't matter how quickly the figure could draw and fire, Ahsoka would be faster. Her Jedi-trained reflexes were more than sufficient for that. At the same time, she knew that there was no point in a firefight unless she was provoked. The Black Sun agent had come looking for Ashla, so Ashla could deal with them.

"I'm surprised Black Sun has heard of me," Ahsoka said. She relaxed her shoulders but stayed alert, her eyes scanning the visitor's armor for weaknesses and her feelings seeking out the surge of aggression that would precipitate a fight.

"My organization keeps watch on this whole sector," the agent said. The voice modulator made the words difficult to understand. It must be an old machine. Either this agent was new and couldn't afford good tech yet, or they were seasoned and had had their gear for a while. "We tend to notice when our business ventures go awry."

Business ventures was not the term Ahsoka would have used. She considered all forms of sentient-being trafficking abhorrent. She absently calculated how long it would take to get her ship in the air from her starting position at the bottom of the ramp. The freighter wasn't designed for quick takeoffs, but you could generally push a ship to do anything once, and this might be her one time.

"Well," she said. "I don't know much about that sort of thing. I'm just a hired pilot."

"My organization is aware of that, too," the agent said. "You're much better than those petty Fardi scum. Whatever they're paying you, we'll double it."

"You're offering me a job." Ahsoka's voice was flat.

"We are," the agent said. "Lucrative contracts, and all the benefits that come with working for such a high-level organization."

Ahsoka almost wished the agent had come in firing.

"I had a certain amount of freedom with the Fardis," she said. "I doubt your employers would continue to let me be so independent."

"There are some limitations they would expect you to accept," the agent conceded. They shifted, and Ahsoka saw that the knee plating on their armor was cracked. That would be her first target, if it came to that. "And there's also the matter of the credits you owe them."

"I don't owe anyone anything," Ahsoka said.

"Oh, but you do," the agent said. "You've cost Black Sun thousands of credits, and you'll pay them back one way or another."

"This is sounding less and less like a job," Ahsoka said.

"Your corpse is also acceptable," the agent said.

"Do I get some time to think about it?" Ahsoka asked.

"Not long," the agent said. "There will be others searching for you. I'm lucky I found you first."

If Black Sun wanted a smuggler they felt had snubbed them badly enough to send out bounty hunters, then a suspected Jedi would be an even better target. She couldn't reveal herself to this agent any more than she could have to the Imperials back on Thabeska. It would mean more people chasing her, and while she knew that she could handle them, she had others to consider. Wherever she set down next would become a target, just by virtue of her presence. She had to be careful.

"I'm very flattered," she said. "But I don't think I'm interested."

To their credit, the Black Sun agent didn't hesitate, but they were still too slow. Ahsoka was halfway up the ramp of her ship before the first salvo of blaster shots sounded and closing the door before the second round. The agent could have charged the ramp but chose instead to retreat back to their own ship. It seemed they now had fewer qualms about shooting her and were going to try to take her in the air.

There was good reason for this. The freighter was bulky and hadn't been designed for speed. The agent's vessel was sleek and vicious, a predator in ship's clothing. Ahsoka was going to have her work cut out for her. She started the takeoff sequence before she even had the hatch shut. As soon as she was airborne, she turned around. Looking down, she saw the agent running up the ramp of their own vessel. The ship's guns were powerful but would fire slowly. All she had to do was avoid a direct hit.

"Easy as anything," she said.

She fired the engines, putting as much distance between her and the Black Sun agent as she could while they were still ascending. Maybe they would be a terrible pilot and this would be easy.

"Or maybe not," she said, as the agent's ship closed the gap on hers.

She gave the engines more fuel and took the ship down toward the mountain peaks. She'd have to lose her pursuer that way. A flurry of stone erupted on her port side as the agent's artillery laid waste to a mountainside. She dodged the rubble and flew lower, trying to force them to fly down after her.

"Cloud cover would be very handy," she said to no one in particular. Even R2-D2 couldn't control the weather.

She spotted a peak and swung around it, banking so hard that the metal around her screamed with exertion. It was worth it, however, because for a few precious seconds, the Black Sun vessel crossed into her line of fire. She didn't waste the opportunity. Her guns fired much more rapidly than theirs did, shorter bursts and less concentrated power but still effective. One of their cannons was disabled by the time she finished her pass, and they had to turn around to follow her.

She used the time, brief though it was, to start her computer's hyperspace calculation. There was no point in sticking around any longer. So much for a few days to clear her head!

As she continued to evade the agent, though, she realized that her head did feel clearer. For better or worse, she had made a choice: she'd chosen to protect the friends she had and the friends she might yet make by concealing her identity once again, even though it made her escape more complicated. Choosing, even under pressure, had made her see that she was capable of deciding on the fly. She'd been right to reveal herself on Raada, even though it had led to problems, and she'd been right to conceal herself on Thabeska. There was no one way forward for her anymore. She would have to make decisions like that over and over again, but it was always going to be *her*. Ahsoka Tano. She was ready to put Ashla away for good, even though she didn't know exactly who the new Ahsoka was going to be just yet. She'd have to write Black Sun a thank-you note.

"Or maybe not," she said, as the agent successfully targeted her starboard engine. She was going to be much slower now, if that smoke was any indication. At least her hyperdrive was still online.

She pulled her ship around. It was time for drastic measures. The other ship was careening toward her. The agent either hadn't noticed her direction change or didn't care that they were about to ram her. Ahsoka fired everything she had, landing almost all her shots, but they didn't deviate from their course.

She screamed, wrenching the helm sideways so her ship went spinning out of the path of the other vessel. It took her a few moments to regain equilibrium—both the ship's and her stomach's—and by then the agent was coming about for another pass at the same speed.

Both of the agent's engine manifolds were smoking, greasy black stuff that looked as terrible as Ahsoka knew it would smell. Her starboard engine was almost stalled. It would be only a matter of time until it gave out completely, and she'd be unable to run.

"Come on, come on," she said to the navicomputer.

In that moment, several things happened. The first was

that her starboard engine failed and she began to spin out of control. The second was that the Black Sun agent pulled up, as though they wanted to watch her crash from a distance. The third was that there was another ship in the sky with them, and it was much bigger than hers.

Ahsoka saw it only in flashes as she spun. It was a new ship, shiny hull fitted with state-of-the-art cannons. There were markings on it, but she couldn't make them out. What she could make out was that the ship wasn't targeting her. It was targeting the Black Sun vessel.

Under onslaught from a ship that size, the sleek little craft didn't stand a chance. The agent must have known it, because they turned tail and fled after the first salvo. Ahsoka used the reprieve to stop her ship from spinning out. She leveled off just above the treetops and began the climb back up, trying to break orbit and get away so that she could make the jump to lightspeed. It was slow going with only one engine, and she had to use her full strength to hold the ship on course.

Between that and her fading adrenaline, she couldn't locate the bigger ship. She tried to see it on her scanners, but steering required too much of her concentration.

"Just a little more," she said. "Just a little more."

She broke into space and killed the port engine before it could burn out, too. Out of the planet's gravity and atmosphere, she was able to relax a little bit and use the thrusters to maintain stability while her inertia carried her toward a location where she'd be able to make the jump.

"About that hyperdrive," she said, turning to the navicomputer and preparing the manual parts of the calculation.

Her proximity alarms went berserk. The bigger ship was right on top of her. It must have waited for her to break orbit and then pounced when she paused to catch her breath.

"Come on, come on!" she said to the computer, but she had a sinking feeling that it was too late.

Sure enough, a few seconds later, when the computer beeped and she tried to make the jump to lightspeed, nothing happened. She was caught in a tractor beam.

23

MIARA WENT OVER the circuitry as carefully as their current predicament allowed. Generally speaking, it was not a good idea to rush explosives. Plus, she needed these ones to blow discreetly. It wouldn't do them any good to blast the hillside, only to have whatever was out there follow the explosion back to its source. She kept her head clear and calm and worked with steady hands. Beside her, Kolvin was not so patient.

"Will you stop that," she said, when his fidgeting got to be too much for her slowly fraying nerves.

"It's getting closer, Miara," Kolvin said.

"I know that, you idiot," she said. "But if I rush now, I might blow you up instead."

"Right," said Kolvin. "Sorry."

"Just go stand somewhere else, would you?" she requested. "You're blocking my light."

He gave her some space, and she went back to work. Just another couple of switches and she'd be ready to go. Fortunately, when she'd first rigged this, she had anticipated a stealth blast would be necessary. Everything was already in place. She just needed to lay the final ignition sequence.

"Okay, Kolvin, back into the tunnel," she said, closing up the final circuit board.

"You're really going to blow me up?" he asked, but he was already moving.

"No," she said. "Though it's tempting. It's going to get dusty in here, that's all. Most of this blast is directed downward."

Kolvin crawled into the tunnel and she followed him. When they were both entirely covered by the lower ceiling, she hit the detonator. There was a quiet rumble beneath them and a louder clamor behind them as the rocks fell inward. They both started coughing.

"Go," she said, sputtering. It was going to take her weeks to get the taste of the smoky crap out of her mouth.

Kolvin went, and she followed. A few seconds later, they emerged into the main cavern. Kaeden was still playing crokin with poor Neera, but she got up and walked over as soon as she saw Miara, and started dusting off her sister's back and shoulders as well as she could with one arm.

"Hey, hey, cut it out," Miara said, though to be honest, it felt nice to know that Kaeden was watching out for her.

"I'm sorry," Kaeden said. "I just really hate all this waiting, even when we're not split up."

"I know," Miara said.

They had never spoken about it, but the night and day Miara had spent waiting for Kaeden to come back after the raid was the worst time of Miara's life. Even though she'd known, logically, that Kaeden wouldn't be able to return until it got dark, every minute of daylight seemed to taunt her. When she'd heard Ahsoka's ship take off, she'd almost given up and run out onto the hillside, screaming like Neera. Kolvin had practically sat on her chest until she'd calmed down. When Kaeden had finally arrived, her hair a mess and her poor arm trailing uselessly at her side, it was hours before Miara was willing to leave her.

"I hope Ahsoka does come back," Miara said. "I mean, obviously I'd like her to rescue us again, but more important, I want to tell her that I'm sorry."

"You have strange priorities, little sister," Kaeden said. "But I guess I already got to apologize."

"Yeah," Miara said. "I don't really blame her for anything that happened. I know she helped us as much as she could."

They didn't talk about the others, about Vartan and Selda, or any of the rest of the farmers who hadn't been part of the raid. Not knowing was bad, but speculating would only make it worse.

They waited.

Neera lost interest in the crokin board and started pacing in a corner, muttering under her breath. Kolvin went off to check on the vaporator, which had been making strange noises for a few days. The rest of the insurgents checked their weapons, even though nothing had changed since the last time they used them. Anything to keep distracted while they waited to see if the mysterious creature would find them.

Then, from outside the cave, there came a very loud voice.

"Kaeden Larte! I know you are in there."

Kaeden started, jerking her arm painfully. Miara's eyes widened, and everyone in the cave, even Neera, froze.

"Come out, Kaeden Larte," the shouting continued. "Surrender or I will collapse your little hiding spot, and your sister and your friends will die gasping for air."

Kaeden was on her feet before Miara could stop her.

"What are you doing?" Miara said. "You can't just go out there."

"I can't stay here, either!" Kaeden said. "We knew they'd get us somehow, and we knew they wouldn't fight fair when they did. I'm just the name they know, that's all."

"He might blow us all up anyway." Neera materialized next to them, her face completely still and her blue eyes focused in a way they hadn't been since her brother died.

"Ahsoka picked the escape doors because they have lines of sight with each other," Kaeden reminded her sister. "I'll go out the smallest one, and you can keep watch from the others. Maybe you'll get a clean shot."

"If he didn't bring any friends," Kolvin said.

"Kaeden Larte," came the voice again. "I grow tired of waiting."

"Look, just get in position," Kaeden said. "I'm going."

"I'm coming, too," Miara said. "You said it yourself. We shouldn't be separated."

Kaeden locked eyes with Neera, hoping the older girl would

understand. Kaeden couldn't watch her sister tortured the way she had been. Then she would definitely tell the interrogator everything he wanted to know. Neera nodded and raised her blaster. It was a newer model, stolen from a stormtrooper during the raid, and it had a stun setting. Miara never knew what hit her.

"Tell her I'm sorry," Kaeden said, and then she was gone.

It was difficult to crawl through the connecting tunnel, even though she picked the shortest one. She couldn't put any weight on her right arm, so it was more like dragging herself through the dust. *Fantastic,* she thought. *Not only am I about to be captured by Imperials again, but I'm going to be absolutely filthy when they catch me. If they grant me a last request, I'm going to have to ask for a bath.* At least her slowness gave the others time to get into position.

She studied the creature before she walked out to meet him. He was tall with broad shoulders, and of a species she had never seen before. His face was gray, and it didn't look like the color was natural. There were other markings, too uniform to be scars, on his cheeks, nose, and chin. They gave his face an evil look, though Kaeden imagined that without them, and without those piercing ice-blue eyes, he wouldn't be so intimidating. As it was, he was intimidating enough. He wore a gray uniform, too, but not a typical officer's. There was no rank insignia. It was like he had been designed to be as unremarkable as possible, except for one thing: he held a massive double-bladed red lightsaber.

Somehow, Kaeden found the courage to keep walking.

She stumbled out of the cave, squinting against the brighter light, and stood before him, waiting for him to tell her what to do next.

"I'm Kaeden," she said. "Now leave my friends alone."

The gray figure laughed. It was not a pleasant sound.

"But they've all come out to see us off," he said, and reached out a hand.

Kaeden had seen Ahsoka use the Force twice. The first time when she'd turned the Imperial blasters away and the second when she'd rescued Kaeden by lifting her through the window of the prison cell. This was nothing like that. Kaeden could almost sense the unnaturalness, the wrongness of it, and then Kolvin was dragged out of the cave to her left, clutching at his throat while his knees scraped along the ground.

"Stop!" Kaeden said. "I surrender, I surrender, just *stop!*"

But the gray creature didn't listen. Kolvin's struggles grew weaker and weaker as the life was choked out of him, and then everything got even worse. The hillside around Kaeden erupted in blaster fire as her remaining friends tried to shoot the creature down.

They did their best, and they were decent shots, but they didn't come close. The gray creature was more than a match for them, and he was without pity. His lightsaber spun so fast that it looked like a ring of red light instead of a blade, deflecting all the shots back at whoever had fired them. Kaeden heard the screams as her friends were wounded, and then she heard the silence as they died. When it was quiet again, she realized she was still standing and Kolvin was still fixed in place beside her. He'd stopped struggling, nearly all the light gone out of his massive eyes. She couldn't stop looking at him. Ahsoka had made her look away from death before, but now there was no escape from it.

"This is what happens to those who would resist the Empire," the gray creature said.

He threw his still-spinning lightsaber at Kolvin and sliced him in half. Kaeden screamed, expecting fountains of blood, but both halves of the body thudded cleanly to the ground and did not so much as twitch. The coldness of Kolvin's death was almost worse. The lightsaber flew back into the gray creature's hand. He turned it off and stowed it somewhere behind him. Kaeden didn't even think of trying to steal it. She wouldn't make it three steps.

"What are you?" Kaeden asked, surprised she had any voice at all.

"I am the future," the gray creature said. "And the only reason you are alive is because I need you to make my future come to pass."

He grabbed her good arm and forced her to walk in front of him. She thought about resisting, forcing him to kill her there and then, with the others, so she couldn't be used to further his ends. He had to be after Ahsoka. It was the only reason she could think of that anyone would target her specifically. Ahsoka had already rescued her once. They must want her to try it again. If she died now, then Ahsoka wouldn't have any reason to come back, and Kaeden would get to lie in the dust with the rest of her—

Miara. Who hadn't wanted to leave her. Who was lying unconscious back in the cave, thanks to Neera's quick thinking. Neera who was dead but who had saved Miara without even knowing it. Kaeden had to live for a little bit longer so she could get this terrible creature away from her sister.

"All right, all right," she said, shaking her arm free. It

hurt—her whole body hurt—but she could do this. "I can walk on my own."

"Excellent," the gray creature said. "We want you to be in your best shape for when your little Jedi friend gets here to save you."

He laughed again, cruelly, and pushed Kaeden between her shoulder blades. She stumbled but managed not to fall. She walked back toward the town as quickly as she could, not knowing how long an Imperial stunner would keep Miara out. She was sorry that Miara would wake up to discover the bodies of her friends, particularly Neera's, but at least she'd wake up. She was smart, too, Kaeden knew. She'd go to Vartan or Selda or somewhere else before she tried anything stupid like staging a rescue.

As for Ahsoka, she was a Jedi. She'd fought in the Clone Wars, and somehow she'd managed to survive the Jedi purge when the Empire began. That meant she was resourceful and quick thinking. She'd know it was a trap. She'd leave Kaeden to die, or she'd come prepared to fight.

Kaeden clung to that hope as though she had two good arms, grit her teeth against the pain, and kept walking.

24

THE TRACTOR BEAM seemed to take its time reeling her into the hold. It was almost like whoever had captured Ahsoka wanted her to have time to arm herself and get ready to fight back. Which was exactly what she did. She left the blaster where it was but rummaged through the weapon box that all Fardi ships carried. She'd never gone through hers before now, because she'd never needed to, but there was a first time for everything. She discarded several smaller blasters, a stun rifle, and three explosives whose yields were not clearly marked. At the bottom of the box was a pair of bastons. Not perfect, but they were as close to her former lightsabers as she was going to get. Then she went down to the main hatch and waited.

After what felt like forever, the hatch opened. Standing there were two humans, both with helmets covering their faces and with their weapons up. She didn't know if they were the only two people on board, and she didn't wait to find out. She jumped, flipping down the ramp to kick the taller human at the base of his helmet while striking the shorter one with the baston in her right hand. They were unprepared for the swiftness of her attack. The man dropped immediately, but the shorter one, a woman, managed to dodge the full brunt of the first blow.

"Wait!" she said. "We're here on behalf of—"

That was as far as Ahsoka let her get before she dropped the woman with another blow to the helmet. Both of them would wake up, but by then Ahsoka would be gone. First, though, she had to deactivate the tractor beam, and the easiest place to do that was on the bridge.

Bastons at the ready, she prowled through the ship. It was a fairly straight line from the hold to the bridge, but she wanted to be sure no one surprised her, so she took a quick detour to the engine room and the berths on the way. There was no one else on board, which was strange, because the ship could have accommodated many more crew members with no stress on the oxygen recyclers. Maybe her would-be captors just liked their privacy.

Ahsoka shrugged and opened the door that led to the bridge. The first thing she noticed was that there were no people here, either. The second thing she noticed was the beeping of an astromech droid, one that sounded exactly like—

"Artoo!" She didn't mean to shout at the little droid, but she was so startled and surprised that she couldn't help it. She'd had a very stressful day.

The little blue-and-silver droid disconnected from the console he was working on and rolled across the floor to her so quickly that she thought for a second he might have flown. He was beeping so fast she could barely understand him, but she could tell by his tone that R2-D2 was as happy to see her as she was to see him.

"I'm so glad you're okay," she said, dropping to her knees to give the droid a hug. She didn't care if it was a silly thing to do, and R2-D2 seemed to appreciate the gesture. "They didn't even memory wipe you?"

The droid beeped happily at her.

"You work for a senator? But you're not supposed to tell me who?" she said. The droid had always been good at keeping secrets. "What about your friends in the hold? Can you tell me about them?"

R2-D2 rolled back across the floor and called up two holos. They were labeled, and she read the names of the pilot and copilot, both of whom she'd left unconscious in the hold of their own ship.

"I hope they don't hold a grudge," she said. "Though really, what do they expect? Capturing people in tractor beams."

The astromech chirruped soothingly and went back to stand beside her. She was going to have to leave soon, but she really didn't want to part with the little droid again.

"What was their mission, anyway?" Ahsoka asked.

R2-D2 told her what he was permitted to, specifically that the pilot, Chardri Tage, and his partner, Tamsin, had been tasked with taking her to meet someone.

"The same senator you're not supposed to tell me the identity of?" Ahsoka asked. "Artoo, I need to know."

The droid seemed to consider it for a moment, rolling back and forth on his three legs. Then he said a name.

"Bail Organa?" Ahsoka said. "I can't believe they let him live. He's a known Jedi sympathizer. He must be in so much danger."

R2-D2 beeped that she didn't know the half of it.

"And you won't tell me," Ahsoka said. "I get it."

The droid reminded her that Padmé Amidala, too, had trusted Bail, not just the Jedi. Ahsoka sighed.

"Look, can you release the tractor beam on my ship?" she asked him. "And then I'll escape, and you can tell everyone you never saw me, okay? Just make sure I can track this ship. If I like what I see, then I'll come in. I promise."

R2-D2 rolled back and forth for a few moments. The little droid was used to espionage and high stakes. He would understand why Ahsoka wanted to do this under her own power, as much as she could. After a moment, he beeped his agreement and told her the code she could use to track the ship.

"Thanks, Artoo," she said. She turned to go, but he rolled over to her again. He made a series of sad sounds.

"I know, little guy." Her heart clenched around the empty spot where Anakin Skywalker used to be. "I miss him, too."

R2-D2 rolled back to the controls, and Ahsoka saw he was wiping all surveillance of their conversation. Then he beeped farewell to her and activated an electrical circuit that would make it look like she'd shorted him out. It wouldn't fool Bail, so he'd know to expect her if he was paying attention, but it would probably do the trick with the two pilots.

Ahsoka didn't waste any more time. She went back to the hold, dragged the pilots to the pressurized area, and then boarded her ship and fired up the engines, as much as they would allow in their damaged condition. She slipped out of the cargo bay and scanned around for a good place to hide and make repairs while she waited for the pilots to wake up.

In the end, she had to settle for one of the small moons that orbited the planet where she'd fought the Black Sun agent. She hoped they weren't hiding there to mend their ship, too, but honestly, she didn't think even *her* luck today would be that bad. She was nearly done with her repairs by the time the signal from Artoo started beeping at her, indicating which way he and the pilots had gone. She watched as it stuttered, meaning they had entered hyperspace, and then settled back for a nap. She wanted them to have a head start, and she'd need to be rested when she talked to Bail anyway.

Floating above some nameless moon, Ahsoka closed her eyes and fell asleep.

◆◆◆

Bail did his level best not to laugh through the report that Chardri Tage delivered to him. They hadn't even seen the Jedi long enough to give a description of her. She'd taken them out immediately, shorted out the R2 unit, and disabled the tractor beam with no real effort at all. Bail actually felt a little guilty. He hadn't told Tage what he was setting him and Tamsin up against, and apparently the Jedi was as well trained in combat as any Clone Wars veteran. She'd even scrubbed most of the security footage, but there was one clip she'd overlooked.

It was a shot of the engine room. Everything looked in order at first glance, but if he paused at the exact right moment, a pair of montrals was clearly visible above one of the coils as the Jedi checked to make sure the room was empty. Bail swallowed a shout of pure triumph. He knew those markings. This wasn't just any Jedi; it was Ahsoka Tano, and he had to find her immediately.

He paused. Ahsoka would have recognized R2-D2. More important, the astromech would have recognized *her*.

"Why, you little metal devil," Bail said, cursing the absent unit.

He couldn't really blame Ahsoka for her caution. He hadn't associated with her as closely as with Skywalker and Kenobi, and she hadn't parted well with anyone when she left

Coruscant. Also, he'd sent two people to kidnap her, essentially. She must have a plan, though, and the R2 unit undoubtedly knew what it was: the droid had all but told him to expect her, if not any of the specifics.

He recorded a new message to send Tage, giving coordinates to meet, even though they hadn't successfully apprehended the Jedi they were after. Tage didn't reply with a holo, merely sent a confirmation code, but Bail knew his orders would be followed to the letter.

Ahsoka Tano would find him, and he'd be ready for her. He didn't know what he would say to her, how much she knew already, and how much she should know. Perhaps it would be for the best if he didn't tell her anything at all. He thought of his daughter, safe on Alderaan, and the boy, safe in the desert. He owed them his silence, but he would do his best to sound out Ahsoka. If she already knew, she would be a valuable ally. He couldn't tell her that Obi-Wan lived, but he could gain her trust in other ways, and he would start by making his invitation in person.

He left his quarters on Captain Antilles's *Tantive IV* and made for the bridge. The captain was on duty, so it didn't take long to make his request. Antilles was loyal to a fault and knew better than to ask questions in front of the crew. They were working, slowly, to replace each crew member with a rebel or recruit the existing crew to the cause, but it was patient, cautious work. As it was, everyone was loyal enough to Alderaan, and to Breha specifically, to keep secrets. The rest would come in time. It was as safe a place as any to meet a Jedi.

The trip through hyperspace was short, and Tage's ship was waiting for them when they arrived. There was no sign of Ahsoka. The system they were in was mostly empty, but there were a few unpopulated planets nearby. Antilles liked to arrange meetings where there were hiding places available if he needed them. They waited for a few hours, with no sign of another ship. Eventually, Bail ordered Tage to return the R2 unit to the blockade runner and go. Perhaps he'd been wrong about Ahsoka's loyalties. Perhaps she was already settled into a new life and didn't want to be embroiled in another war. He couldn't say that he blamed her.

Bail saw the R2 unit returned to his flighty golden protocol droid companion, who immediately began to berate the little astromech, and then made his way back to his quarters. They were in the center of the ship, accessible by the main corridor. He'd never given much thought to the maintenance shaft that ran behind the row of guest quarters. It provided access to the panels that controlled the environmental systems in each suite and also connected the bridge to the engine room as an alternate route if something happened to compromise the main passageway. There were several escape pods located there and one airlock.

Bail walked into his temporary office, turned on the lights, and nearly had a heart attack. Sitting at his desk, wearing a pressure suit with the helmet off and resting on the table between them, was Ahsoka Tano.

"Hello, Senator," she said pleasantly. "I hear you wanted to talk."

25

"HOW DID YOU GET IN HERE?" Bail said the first thing that came into his head.

"Artoo opened the hatch for me as soon as he got on board," Ahsoka said.

"I should have him deactivated," Bail said with no real heat in his voice. "He is far too independent for a droid."

"He had a lot of bad role models," Ahsoka said dryly.

"That's true," Bail said. "Though Skywalker was your teacher, too."

"I was talking about Senator Amidala, actually," Ahsoka said. "Artoo belonged to her first."

"Where's your ship?" Bail asked, changing the subject to avoid the sudden tightness in his throat.

"Hidden on one of the lifeless rocks in this system. I knew that I'd be too small for the scanners to pick up, unless someone got very lucky looking out a window." Ahsoka glanced at the helmet. "I'm surprised I found one that fit."

"Why didn't you just come with Chardri Tage?" Bail said. "Save yourself the hassle?"

"In my position it's difficult to trust someone who employs a tractor beam before a hello," Ahsoka said. "I take it you didn't tell them who they were after?"

"No," said Bail. "I wanted to preserve your anonymity. I didn't know it was you until I saw the surveillance footage."

"Artoo was supposed to wipe all of that," Ahsoka grumbled. "I think you might be right about his independent streak."

"It's difficult to look for people without compromising their safety, I've found," Bail said. "The new order is harsh and unforgiving, so I thought if you didn't want to be found, I would give you the option."

"How did you even know where to look?" Ahsoka asked.

"I keep an eye out for acts of kindness in this new galaxy

of ours," Bail said. "When there's a concentration of them, I try to find out who is behind them, and then we have a talk."

"What do you talk about?" Ahsoka asked.

Bail gave her a measuring look and decided to go for it.

"The Rebellion, Padawan Tano," he said. "I look for people who will fight against the Emperor, the Empire, and everything it stands for."

"I don't deserve that title anymore, Senator," Ahsoka said quietly. "And I don't deserve your trust."

Bail let her sit on that statement for a few moments. Politics had made him good at getting people to talk.

"There was a planet," she said, finally. "A moon, actually. I tried to help them when the Empire came, but I couldn't. People died. I had to run and leave them behind."

"Raada," he said. "I heard about that, and what you did there."

"We tried to fight, and everything just got worse," Ahsoka said. "It's not like the Clone Wars. I was never alone then. I had an army, I had masters, I had—"

She'd had Anakin Skywalker.

"You can't fight the Empire alone, Ahsoka," Bail said gently. "But you don't have to, either. You can fight it with me."

"I can't command people anymore," she said with a shake

of her head. "I can't order them to their deaths. I've done that too many times."

"We'll find something else for you to do, then," he said. "I have a lot of job openings, as you can probably imagine."

He could see that she was very tempted. It would be safer than continuing to right wrongs on her own. Whatever was chasing her would have a harder time tracking her down.

"There are children," she said after a long moment. His blood ran cold. "All over the galaxy. I've met one, but I know there will be others. They would have been Jedi. Now they're just in danger. Something is hunting them down. I don't know what it is. I've never seen it. But if you will help find it, I will join your rebellion."

The casual way she had talked about Anakin and Padmé made him think that she might have known the true nature of their relationship but not the outcome. He was sure she didn't know about Leia, about the boy. She couldn't know his motivations, but he would overturn every stone in the galaxy to help her, if it was in his power to do so. Having someone else lead the search would work out well for him, too. Every layer of deception between him and anything connected to the Force was another layer in the safety net he was building for his daughter.

"That seems like a bargain to me," he said, when his voice came back. "And I have a mission for you, as it turns out. Are you up for it?"

◆◆◆

Ahsoka was exhausted, though she did her best to keep it from showing in her face. The fight with the Black Sun agent, her escape from Bail's hired hands, and then her trip through zero gravity had drained her. It was taking everything she had to stay upright behind the desk while she and the senator traded barbs, then words, and finally got down to negotiations. When he said he had a mission for her, she almost wilted, but she had been awake this long. She could manage a little longer.

"I might need a meal before I head back out," she said, "but I'd like to hear about anything you think I'd be interested in."

"It's on Raada," Bail said. Ahsoka felt immediately sharper. "My contacts in that sector have been getting spotty information for a long time—that's part of why it took me so long to find you—but then this, as clear as starshine."

Ahsoka held out her hands and Bail handed her a data-pad. She flipped through it as Bail continued to talk. It was mostly maps, and diagrams of the Imperial compound, things she already knew.

"It seems there's a new sort of Imperial agent there," Bail

continued. "Nonmilitary, but powerful. He has complete control over the garrison, if he wants it, and orders the officers around like they were stormtroopers. All of this is made more complicated by reports that he carries a double-bladed red lightsaber."

Ahsoka nearly dropped the datapad. It was getting too easy to surprise her. She needed to refocus, but she couldn't seem to find something to focus *on*.

"What does he look like?" she demanded.

"The overwhelmingly common descriptor is *gray*," Bail said. "Not terribly helpful, I think? Even the security footage doesn't reveal very much."

Ahsoka's mind turned it over quickly. *Gray* was not the sort of word anyone would use to describe any of the adversaries she was used to facing. This had to be someone else. Someone new. Someone like—

"A shadow?" she asked. "Gray like a shadow?"

"I suppose," Bail said. "He's rumored to be very fast, and he must be a Force wielder to carry a lightsaber, don't you think?"

"Not necessarily," Ahsoka said. "But it's probably true in this case. The Empire wouldn't send just anyone to hunt down Jedi."

"How do you know he's hunting Jedi?" Bail said.

"Don't you think it's a little strange that your intel was so spotty on Raada until now?" Ahsoka said. "Until I started drawing attention with my 'acts of kindness' as you call them? Until whatever this creature is was drawn away from the whispers he was hunting to follow bigger prey?"

"I didn't know about the last part," Bail said. "But yes, I did think it was strange. Also, there's something else you need to see. I thought it was just a trap set for anyone, but now that I've heard your side of the story, I think it might be a trap set specifically for you."

Bail picked up the datapad that Ahsoka had dropped and thumbed through to the final entry. It was a picture, taken by a security camera and beamed out across the stars, to be decrypted by Bail's agents. But it was astonishingly clear for an accidental transmission. Knowing that it was a trap made the clarity make much more sense.

Ahsoka took back the datapad and looked down at the picture. Her heartbeat sped up, and she felt like all the oxygen had been sucked out through the very airlock she'd used to get into Bail's office. There was the gray creature, his face obscured by a helmet but his lightsaber plainly visible. And there was Kaeden Larte, obviously his captive, with her broken arm bound tightly to her chest and her frizzy hair flying in all directions.

"Oh, no," Ahsoka breathed. "I have to—"

"Stop," Bail said sternly. She froze automatically and then glared at him. His expression softened and he came around the desk to stand close to her. "Ahsoka, you need to rest. You need to plan. They're not going to hurt her any more. They need you to show up first. The best thing you can do is make sure you're as prepared as possible when you do."

She slumped back in his chair, hands falling into her lap in defeat. He reached out to put his hand on her shoulder, and they both jumped when there was a clamor outside the main door of his suite. It hissed open and Captain Antilles burst into the room with several security officers.

"Senator!" Antilles said, and then stopped. He took in the room at a glance and dismissed the security force.

"Everything is under control, Captain," Bail said. "This is a friend of mine. She's going to be with us for a while. We'll need to pick up her ship before we leave, and she'll need quarters."

Antilles nodded sharply, and then left as quickly as he'd arrived.

"You didn't tell him who I was," Ahsoka said. "Are you really that vulnerable?"

"Yes," Bail said. "But we're getting more secure every day. Still, I don't like to give away other people's secrets. If you want to tell him who you are, that's up to you."

"Thank you," she said. Then: "You mentioned quarters?"

Bail showed her into the suite next to his and then went down to the cargo hold to make sure her ship was being secured. Ahsoka cleaned up, stripping off the pressure suit. She'd had to leave her bag in the ship, but the little package of tech parts fit next to her skin inside the suit. She opened it now and made sure everything was still intact.

"As if you could break any more than you already have," she said. Then she turned her attention back to getting dressed.

She debated for a moment between food and sleep, but the latter required less effort, so she lay down on the bed. She was asleep almost instantly.

◆ ◆ ◆

Ahsoka dreamed of ice, and an urgency she hadn't felt in years. She had to make it back to the mouth of the cave while the sun held the ice back or she'd be trapped on that frozen planet for much longer than she wanted to be stuck anywhere so cold.

But where was her crystal? Master Yoda had been no more helpful than he usually was, telling her only that she would know it when she saw it. But where was it? And how would she know?

She stopped running, closed her eyes, and thought about what she *did* know. Master Yoda was strange, and more often than not, she didn't understand him, but he was almost always right. She would just have to trust that he was right now, that she would find her crystal and she would know it when she did.

She opened her eyes. There, twinkling in the dark of the cave, was a light that hadn't been there before. It called to her, and she went to it. When she got close, she saw that it was a crystal, and just like Master Yoda had said, she knew it was hers. It fell into her hands, and she turned to run back to the mouth of the cave.

◆ ◆ ◆

It was warm in her quarters when she woke up, which is how Ahsoka knew the dream was over.

"Thank you, Master," she whispered, though she knew that Master Yoda couldn't possibly hear her, or help her even if he could.

Rising, she went to the low table that held her belongings and picked up the little pouch that usually rested in her pocket. She spilled out the collection of used parts and other derelict pieces she'd been carrying with her since her arrival on Raada. She could see now that several of them were useless, and she discarded them. The pieces that were left, however, might be worth something.

Lightsaber construction was a Jedi art of the highest order. Ahsoka had never done it unsupervised, as she knew she must do now. She also knew that she was missing important components, but since her vision was guiding her toward Ilum and the crystals that grew there, she would have to trust the path she was taking. The material she had would be sufficient to begin construction on the chambers. The hilts would be inelegant, but functional.

She finished after a few false starts and examined her work. She could almost hear Huyang fussing over her shoulder, but she still felt pleased with herself. She stood, stretched out her shoulders, and went in search of the senator. She found him in the mess hall, having a conversation with the captain.

"No, Captain, stay please," she said, when Antilles would have left them alone. "I think I'm going to need your help, too."

"What are you thinking, Ahsoka?" Bail asked.

And Ahsoka told him the plan.

THE CRYSTALS GREW.

Clear as ice and cold until they found the hands that waited for them, they added structure in an ordered way, one prism at a time. And while they grew, they waited.

From time to time, someone would arrive and call to them, like the harmony of a perfect song. Each crystal had a chosen bearer, and only that bearer would hear the music and see the glow. All others would pass by, seeing nothing but more ice.

There were larger crystals, visible to all but inert unless properly calibrated, and there were tiny ones, the size of a fingernail or smaller. Even the smallest could channel power and find a bearer. All they had to do was be patient and grow.

There was no particular pattern for where the crystals might be found. There were some planets that hosted them in countless numbers, and those places were often considered holy or special. Pilgrimages were made and lessons learned and lightsabers crafted. And thus the light crystals went about the galaxy to be put to use.

Dark crystals were made, too, but not in that holy place. They were plundered from their rightful bearers and corrupted by the hands that stole them. Even rock could be changed by the power of the Force, bleeding alterations until their color was the deepest red. The balance was finely staged between the two, light and dark, and it took very little to upset it.

When the first ships appeared in the sky over a planet where the crystals grew in number, nothing seemed amiss. Ships visited the planet all the time, and crystals were taken away, but this occasion was different. There were no young bearers to hear the songs, no attentive students to learn the lessons. There was only greed and a terrible, terrible want.

The planet was ravaged, its crystals broken by uncaring hands who thought to twist them to their own uses.

No more could the planet be considered a holy place, and no longer would pilgrimages be made. Instead, those who had once gone there would avoid it and despair for the loss of the crystals that once sang to them.

But in the wideness of the galaxy, there were many planets and many places where the crystals could appear. They would be harder to find, their concentration lower, but it would not be impossible for one who sought, for one who listened—for one who had learned the first lessons and had the patience to learn more.

The crystals grew, adding structure in an ordered way, one prism at a time.

And while they grew, they waited.

CHAPTER

26

BAIL OFFERED HER A SHIP, but Ahsoka turned him down. Everything in his manifest was new: sleek, fast, very obviously built on a Core world. Ahsoka elected to keep her own craft. She knew its foibles, for one thing, and she also knew it would stick out less on an Outer Rim world than any of the fancy ships in Bail's collection. She did let Antilles's crew fix the engine damage, though. Well, she let R2-D2 do it while she supervised.

While the droid worked, Ahsoka took the opportunity

to examine Bail's operation. He'd said that not everyone on board was fully aware of what he was attempting to organize, but it seemed like everyone at least knew that what they were doing wasn't entirely Empire business. She could tell from the conversations she overheard that the crew was loyal to Alderaan and to Breha and Bail themselves, which was a good start. Bail's work was slow, as he'd said, but his foundation was strong. Of course, it helped that he had more resources than she'd had on Raada and that the people he was working with were already trained to fight and follow orders.

Sitting in the hangar bay, with R2-D2 by her side, Ahsoka began to realize that what she had accomplished on Raada was more of an achievement than she'd thought. It wasn't like Onderon, where she'd had time and, most important, Rex to help her. She hadn't failed on Raada, even though her people had suffered casualties. She had learned a new way to fight, too, and she needed to have as much patience with herself as she did with the people she fought alongside.

R2-D2 beeped a question at her, and Ahsoka examined his work, even though she had a feeling they both knew he didn't require a second opinion.

"It looks great, Artoo," she said. "I've missed having you around for exactly this kind of thing."

The droid chirruped happily and made a few last adjustments to the engine. It hummed to life, and Ahsoka jumped to her feet.

"Thanks, little guy," she said. "I don't know if it's ever sounded so good."

R2-D2 made a smug sound, set the tools back in the crate, and rolled off without making any further comment. He passed Bail, who was walking in Ahsoka's direction. The senator was off that day, as well, on a mission no less dangerous than hers. He was headed back to Coruscant to play Imperial puppet in the Senate, and he was dressed for the part.

"Are you sure you don't want backup?" he said. "I'm sure Chardri and Tamsin don't hold a grudge, and they're good in tight spaces. Well, they are when they know what they're up against."

Ahsoka smiled as the test cycle of her engine spun down. She'd be able to leave soon.

"No, thank you," she said. "It'll be easier on my own."

"Is it some mysterious Jedi thing?" Bail asked. He hadn't pried the previous day when she had left out a few key details, but now that they were sure not to be overheard, she supposed he had a right to know the risk he was taking.

"No," she said. "It's just difficult to explain. I might not have a lot of time and might have to make decisions quickly that don't make sense to outsiders. It's nothing personal, I promise."

"That's all right," Bail said. "I've worked with enough Jedi over the years to know when to let them go their own way."

"I'm not really a Jedi, you know," she said. They hadn't talked about it before, but again, now that they were alone, it was only fair to let him know that his investment might not get the return he was counting on. "I left the Temple, turned away from the Jedi path."

"If you're not a Jedi, then what are you, Ahsoka Tano?" Bail asked. "Because to be honest, you still sound and act like a Jedi to me."

"I'll let you know when I figure it out," she said. She patted the engine pod. "Thanks for loaning me Artoo for the repair. The engine is perfect."

"Anytime," Bail said, and smiled. "I should get going. But we'll be there when you signal for us."

"I'll see you then," Ahsoka said, and watched him walk to his own shuttle.

Once the senator was gone, Ahsoka made a few last modifications to her ship and started her preflight checks. She'd had to make quick decisions the previous day, and she wanted to be sure that she hadn't put stress on anything besides the engines. She had time and security to do it now, and even though waiting galled her, she knew it would pay off.

She hadn't thought she'd be able to sleep at all the night before, the image of Kaeden with the lightsaber to her throat burned into her memory, but she'd been so exhausted that she'd dropped off almost as soon as she'd stopped moving. When she woke up several hours later, she'd felt much better and then instantly worse: Kaeden probably hadn't slept very well, whatever time it was on Raada.

She forced herself to clear her mind of worries. It wasn't easy, but she knew she would do her friends no good if she let emotion cloud her judgment. She might not be a Jedi, but she needed to act like one for a little bit longer. She knew how it worked, anyway: clear your mind and see the goal. She was determined to do that for the sake of her friends.

The preflight check ended, signaling that nothing new had been detected. She stowed her gear—the bastons, her carry bag, a few useful things that Bail had given her—but kept the pouch with the hilts on her. It was bulky now, but she was reluctant to store it anywhere else.

She asked for clearance to depart and received it, along with the deck officer's wish of good luck. She took the ship out of the hangar and then ran her calculations for the hyperdrive.

When that was ready, Ahsoka placed both hands on the controls, looked through the front viewport, and made the jump to lightspeed.

Ilum was a world of ice. Stark, cold, and beautiful as long as you didn't have to spend too much time outside. It had been a holy place for the Jedi. Ahsoka had been there three times, once for each of her own crystals and once with a group of younglings. The first two times had been unremarkable, except for her excitement over having the tools with which to build her lightsabers. The third time had been more of an adventure, complete with pirates. Ahsoka was very much hoping this visit would be a quiet one.

She'd calculated the jump to take her out of hyperspace some distance away from the planet itself. If she remembered what was buried in Ilum's crust, it was entirely possible that others did, too. She wasn't sure where those from the dark side got their crystals, but she knew they had to get them some- where, and she wasn't about to take any risks just to cut some time from her travel schedule. When she emerged back into normal space and saw what was waiting for her, she was very glad she'd been cautious.

There were at least two Star Destroyers and a massive mining ship in orbit around the planet. The Empire definitely knew there was something it wanted beneath the surface of the icy world.

The planet itself was much worse off than she'd feared. Before, it had looked like a giant white ball from orbit— uniform in color except the brighter spots where it reflected the light of its sun. It had been as striking from up high as it was on the ground, even though the great cliffs and deep crevasses that scored the planet's surface weren't visible from afar. Now it almost hurt her to look at it.

Great chunks of the planet had been carved away, exposing rock and lava that boiled up from the planet's core. With no real hope, Ahsoka scanned the usual landing site. Gone was the cliff-side entryway the Jedi had used for generations, the waterfall smashed to gain entrance to the cave beyond.

Ahsoka felt a swell of fury, which she had to work hard to pin down. They dared to invade Ilum, to spoil such a beautiful place, and for what? To carve out rock and dirt in the hopes of finding a few shards of crystal that none of them would be able to see? It was wasteful and terrible to behold, and also more than a little intimidating. Ruining the soil on a faraway moon was one thing. Destroying a planet, even piece by piece, was something else. The Empire had no sense of limitation and no respect for the order of life in the galaxy.

She was halfway through planning an attack run on the mining ship, analyzing it for weaknesses she could exploit if she was able to get past the Star Destroyers, when she remembered why she couldn't. Raada. She needed to go back to Raada. She couldn't die or get captured in some pointless skirmish. And it *would* be pointless, she reminded herself, even though it hurt to think of Ilum as expendable. No one lived there, and it wasn't like the Jedi needed the planet anymore. She wouldn't spend her life there, not when there were other places where it was worth more and when there were people who needed her.

She was still going to need crystals though. And she needed to get out of range of the Star Destroyers before one of them detected her. She flew to the outermost planet in the system, a nameless black rock with no air and little gravity, and set down on the surface. She powered down the engines so the ship would be more difficult to detect and then sat cross-legged on the floor of the cockpit, the pouch in her lap and her mind reaching for solutions.

It didn't bode well that her plan had unraveled at her very first stop, but she couldn't focus on that now. She had to focus on what came next and how she might achieve it without using Ilum as a resource.

Now that her mind was quieter, she could sense the icy planet, even though she was half a system away. The crystals there didn't sing to her as they had the first time she'd been there. Then, when she was younger, she'd felt them as soon as the ship dropped out of hyperspace, even though she hadn't known what she was feeling at the time. Now there was nothing—well, nothing that was intended for Ahsoka. She could still feel the crystals present beneath the planet's surface. She just knew that none of them was for her.

So where are mine? she thought. *Am I going to get another set? I could go back to Rex's fake grave and see if my lightsabers are still there, but I doubt it. They're worth too much, and I left them to be found.*

She called up a star chart, projecting it around herself and placing Ilum close to where she was seated. Then she closed her eyes and reached for the crystals on the planet below. She followed their structure, ordered and regular, searching for other sources in the galaxy. She knew there must be more crystals somewhere. Master Yoda had never said as much, but he had certainly hinted at it. It was, after all, a very big galaxy.

There, light-years away, she heard it: the familiar song that was hers alone. She slid her awareness of it through the star chart, hoping that when she opened her eyes, she would see a map with her crystals waiting for her at the end of it.

She opened her eyes and saw the planet that was her destination.

No, not a planet. A moon.

Raada.

27

AHSOKA SLIPPED INTO the atmosphere above Raada and landed as quickly as she could in the dark. By design, she was on the opposite side of the moon from the main town and fields. She'd have to leave the ship here. They were waiting for her, after all, and they'd probably be scanning, looking for her approach. She'd been in too much of a hurry when she left Raada to be stealthy, but now she needed to go undetected for long enough to complete the first part of her mission.

   She loaded everything she would need into the carry bag

and made sure her communication device was secured on her wrist. She hesitated when she got to the blaster. If all went according to plan, she wouldn't need it, and she wasn't sure what good it would do against the gray creature anyway. But someone else might be able to use it. She clipped it to her side. It wasn't that heavy, and it wouldn't be hard to carry it a little farther. Then she set out in the direction of the settlement.

She had been running for a little over two hours when she saw the first signs of life. A very small fire was burning. Whoever had set it had tried to conceal the light but clearly didn't know enough about stealth to be entirely successful. The pit wasn't deep enough. Ahsoka couldn't be sure, of course, but she thought that probably meant whoever had lit the fire was not an Imperial.

She crept closer. Soon she could make out a figure, small and hunched over the flames for warmth. The figure shifted, and Ahsoka saw a crop of dark bushy hair silhouetted by the fire. It was Miara.

Ahsoka got as close as she could before whispering the girl's name. She didn't want to scare her too badly, but in the dark she didn't have a lot of options.

"Miara," she said, as nonthreateningly as she could manage.

Miara still jumped, reaching for the old blaster she'd carried the night she and Ahsoka had taken out the walkers.

"It's okay, it's okay," Ahsoka said. "Miara, it's me, Ahsoka."

"Ahsoka?" Miara didn't look like she believed her own eyes.

Despite the dark color of her skin, there was a pallid, unhealthy sheen to it. She'd clearly been crying; muddy tear tracks lined each of her cheeks. Her hair was a mess, and there were bags under her eyes. She looked absolutely terrified.

"Ahsoka!" she said again, and threw herself into Ahsoka's arms, more tears spilling. "You came back! K-Kaeden said you would. She said you would."

"Shhhh, Miara," Ahsoka said soothingly. She helped the girl sit back down by the meager warmth of the fire. "Tell me what happened. What are you doing out here by yourself?"

Miara choked on her tears but managed to stop them. When she found her voice again, she started to talk.

"We were doing okay," she said. "I mean, it was awful, but we were hiding, like you said. Only then this terrible thing came, and he knew Kaeden's name. He said if she didn't come out, he'd blow the whole hillside up to kill us."

Ahsoka's heart sank.

"So she went," Miara said. "Her arm was still so bad she

had trouble walking, but she went. They were going to set up an ambush, see if they could catch him in the cross fire while she distracted him, but it didn't work."

"What happened, Miara?" Ahsoka asked again.

"I wanted to go, too," she said. "I know it was stupid, but I didn't want us to get split up again. Kaeden didn't want me to, and somehow she managed to tell Neera, and Neera shot me with a stunner. I was unconscious for whatever happened next, and when I woke up . . ."

She trailed off, horror in her eyes.

"They were all dead, Ahsoka," Miara said. "All of them. Neera, the others. Kolvin—Kolvin was cut in *half.* It was the worst thing I've ever seen, and there wasn't even a lot of blood."

Ahsoka put her arm around Miara's shoulder and held her close. It was exactly what she'd feared. The gray creature must have used her friends' blasters against them, redirecting their shots. She'd done it herself, though she preferred to deflect bolts rather than reuse them. And Kolvin must have died on the creature's lightsaber.

She gave herself a moment for grief. She might have prevented this, had she stayed, or her presence might have made everything even worse. There was no way to tell, so there was no reason to dwell on it. Ahsoka didn't like this cold, compassionless side of her training, but she needed it now if she was going to get the job done.

Beside her, Miara was rocking back and forth. The girl was so scared and so worried, Ahsoka didn't know if she could ask her for help. Maybe she ought to leave her and come back, if she could, once she was done. She dismissed the idea almost before she was finished thinking it. She couldn't leave Miara behind. She owed it to Kaeden to do what she could, and she owed it to Miara, as well. She would see if she could sneak Miara back to Selda's. The old Togruta would at least be able to feed her, and they could wait together.

"Miara," Ahsoka said. "I need your help to rescue your sister."

Miara looked up, shocked. "You're really going to?" she said.

"That's why I came back," Ahsoka said. "Do you think you can help me?"

"Yes," Miara said. "For Kaeden, I can help you."

"I need you to put out this fire and then stay awake while I meditate," Ahsoka said. "I'll be defenseless, so I'll need you to warn me if anything comes toward us. Can you do that?"

Miara nodded and started banking the fire. It would warm up as daylight approached, and the girl wouldn't be cold for too long. Ahsoka didn't have a cloak to loan her. She realized she had no idea where her cowl had ended up. Maybe she'd ask her new friend the senator for a nicer one.

"Focus, Ahsoka," she muttered.

"What?" said Miara.

"Never mind," Ahsoka said. "Just sit here. Are you ready?"

Miara nodded and sat up straight.

Ahsoka closed her eyes.

The first time, on Ilum, she hadn't been able to find her crystal until she'd made the decision to trust Master Yoda's instructions. After what had happened on her home planet when she was small, with the slaver posing as a Jedi, trust had not come easily to Ahsoka, even when her senses told her that she was in good company. The memory of the villagers' scorn when she'd refused to demonstrate her powers for the false Jedi, the burning shame at her inability to explain the danger to her elders, had lingered with her.

But she'd let it go in that cave. She had decided to trust Yoda, and that had led her to her crystal. From then on, trust had been easier for her, because she'd learned to trust her own

AHSOKA

instincts again. She had even returned to Ilum later for a second crystal.

Right now, her instincts were telling her that the new crystals were going to want something else before they let her find them. And she thought she might have some idea what that was.

The differences between Bail's organized rebellion and her operation on Raada had been stark. He wasn't more successful because he was better than she was but because he had more to work with. With his access, she would be a valuable ally based on her experience alone, not even taking her powers into account. She had to be willing to work in a system again, to accept the order of common purpose and the camaraderie that went with it.

Her heart clenched. She couldn't do it. She couldn't reforge connections with people who might betray her out of fear or because they had no choice. She couldn't face the deaths of her friends again.

But then, she already was. While on Raada, she'd learned that there was no escape from it. Even if she was no longer a Jedi, she had too much training to turn her back on people in need. She would help them fight, and she would watch them die, and every time her heart would harden a little bit more.

No. There must be another way. A middle road. Somehow, she wouldn't let the evil in the galaxy, the evil of the Empire, swallow her and change her nature. She thought of what had gone wrong on Raada and what had gone wrong with Bail, and in both cases, she thought she saw a similarity.

She moved without thinking about it, her hand shifting so it covered the communication device on her wrist. That was it. That was what she could do to help the galaxy and try to keep her friends safe.

Softly, but then louder as the sun began to creep up over the hills, Ahsoka heard the song. It didn't match the first one, though there were some similarities. She didn't doubt for a second, though. The song was hers, if she was willing to fight for it.

The sun broke over the horizon completely, and Ahsoka Tano was whole again.

"Come on, Miara," she said. "Let's go get your sister."

CHAPTER

28

THE FIELDS OF RAADA were ruined. Even Ahsoka's inexpert eye could see it. The soil that had once been a dark brown was now bleached to an unhealthy gray, and the life that she used to sense from it was almost entirely drained. The only things in the fields that looked healthy were the hectares of little green plants, the source of so much misery.

"If we get the chance," Ahsoka whispered to Miara, who crouched beside her, "remind me to come back here and burn this to ash."

"I'll help," Miara promised. "I've gotten pretty good at lighting fires."

"Come on," Ahsoka said. "We need to be through here before the first shift starts."

Miara had told her that the Imperials had extended the shift lengths again. Now the farmers worked for nearly the entire time there was daylight to work by, and there were rumors that once the harvest started, the Imperials were going to bring in floodlights so the farmers could work in the dark, as well. There wasn't a lot of time, and there wasn't much cover, so Miara led Ahsoka along the edge of the tilled ground, and as soon as they reached the outlying buildings of the town, they ducked down an alleyway.

"We're on the opposite side of town from the Imperial compound," Miara whispered. "We'll have to cross the entire settlement to get to Kaeden."

"Not we," Ahsoka said. "Just me. I need you to go to Selda and give him this."

She passed over the holo she'd recorded in hyperspace.

"If you can't find Selda, find Vartan or one of the other crew leads. But make sure it's someone you trust!"

"I want to come with you!" Miara said.

Ahsoka stopped and put a hand on each of the girl's shoulders.

"I know you do," she said. "I know you'd do anything for your sister right now, but I need you to listen. I can get your sister out, but my ship is too far away for us to escape Raada. And even if the three of us got away, what would happen to everyone else?"

Miara started to protest but then stopped. Ahsoka could tell she had seen reason.

"I need you to get to Selda," she said again. "Kaeden needs you to get to Selda. Okay?"

"Okay," Miara said. "I'll do it."

Ahsoka squeezed Miara's hand around the holo and then watched the girl make her way down the street. She'd learned to walk softly since Ahsoka had last seen her, and how to use even what little cover the street offered to her advantage. Ahsoka really hated war.

She let Miara get a good head start and then struck out in the direction of the Imperial compound. She did not use cover or make any pretense of attempting to conceal her approach. The gray creature knew she was coming and knew what her target was. Stealth was impossible, and she had one shot. Her only hope was that the Empire didn't have a secret piece hidden on the back of the board like she did.

She walked down the middle of the street, senses alert and ready for anything. Every part of her was like an energy coil, wound tight and ready for action.

She didn't have to wait very long.

"Jedi!" A harsh voice rang out. It seemed to come from every direction at once. Ahsoka cast out with her senses, searching for the source.

"You have something I want," she said. It would be easier if she could get the gray creature to keep talking.

"Poor little Kaeden Larte," said the creature. Ahsoka narrowed in on his location. "So hopeful that her Jedi friend would come for her. I had to tell her that Jedi don't have friends. Jedi don't have attachments of any kind. They're heartless and cold and don't even understand what love is."

"I don't know who taught you about the Jedi," Ahsoka said. "But they seem to have left out a few things. You should ask for better lessons."

"I told Kaeden that you weren't a real Jedi," the creature said. There! Ahsoka had him. Now she just had to wait for the right moment. "I told her that you were probably so scared of me that you were twelve systems away and never coming back. I'm actually happy to be wrong."

She felt him jump off the roof of the building behind her and turned. She could no more identify his species in person than she could from his picture. He was taller than she was, even with the height she'd added in the past few years, and very broadly built. He was clearly very strong, and with the body armor he wore, he was a formidable opponent. He was still wearing his helmet, and his face shield was up, as though he needed to see her clearly while they fought. That was another difference in their training, Ahsoka thought. She could fight completely blind if she had to, though blind *and* without her lightsabers might be pushing it.

She focused her attention on his chest, where movement began. She felt the Force flowing through her as his lightsaber flared to life. She could hear its hum, a dark counterpoint to the song of her own crystals, now quite nearby. Ahsoka cleared her mind of all distractions.

The creature struck, and Ahsoka deflected his blows before they fell. She read his feelings through the Force that connected them, and she tracked the movement of his shoulders, elbows, and wrists, pushing them away so that they always missed their targets. Furious, he doubled his efforts, striking for her head and chest.

What the gray creature lacked in finesse, he made up for in brute strength. He pushed Ahsoka back, toward the line of houses, and she let him, still taking his measure as a fighter. When she reached the front step of the house behind her, she jumped off of it, using the Force to propel herself in an elegant flip over his head. She easily avoided the frantic swing of his lightsaber as she flew over him, then landed in a crouch on the other side, ready to continue.

"Impressive," he said.

"You're easily impressed," she said. "I'm only just getting started."

She felt more people behind her and realized that someone in the Imperial compound had gotten wind of what was going on. The walls were lined with stormtroopers, all of them pointing blasters at her. At least it didn't look like they'd added any reinforcements since she left. She ducked down a side street, out of their line of fire, and the gray creature followed her.

He held his lightsaber aloft, and it began to spin. The effect was interesting—a deadly circle of light instead of a blade—but Ahsoka wasn't intimidated by it. The creature's entire strategy relied on overpowering his opponent. She had other options.

"What are you?" she asked. "Who made you like this?"

"I serve the Empire," the creature said.

"You certainly have a sense for drama," Ahsoka said.

She reached out for him again, this time for his hands and fingers, and for the balance of weight borne by his hips and knees. She felt something awaken in her, every combat lesson Anakin had ever taught. She remembered how to stand and how to hold the blades. She pushed her opponent's fingers too far apart and overturned his balance. She remembered, and she could make him forget. He staggered back, surprised at her power over him even at arm's length, but not yet overcome.

"I have a sense for power," he said. "And you do not have enough to resist me for much longer, weaponless as you are."

That was where he was wrong. She wasn't weaponless. No Jedi ever was.

The creature stepped toward her, close enough for her to touch. His spinning lightsaber held off attacks from the sides, but was vulnerable from the front. Just as she'd reached for her first crystal all those years ago, Ahsoka stretched out a hand.

Sensing her intent at the last moment, the Inquisitor tried to disconnect his weapon and fight her with two blades instead of one, but it was spinning too quickly for him to do it. Ahsoka's hand landed almost gently on the cylindrical metal, and the Force was with her. The hilt cracked at her touch.

A sharp whine reached Ahsoka's ears, the dark and light song of the crystals struggling for balance. She realized she needed to jump back even farther. She must have nicked the power connection that channeled the crystals inside his hilt, and now it was overloading. If he didn't deactivate it soon, it was going to explode.

Before she could even consider shouting a warning, the red lightsaber burst into a mess of noise and light. Bright spots pricked at her eyes, and then all was quiet. The creature wasn't going to bother her anymore.

He lay in the street, his face a burned mess, the shell of his lightsaber still clutched in his hands. If he'd been able to fight her with his face shield down, he might have survived the blast.

She wondered who had trained him and if there were others. Someone had twisted the potential for good in this creature and turned him to the dark side. Someone had made him like this. Someone, Ahsoka knew, who was still out there and who must be prevented from finding other children, if she could manage it. She reached down and closed his helmet, covering the ruin of his face. It was the only compassion she could show him. She had work to do.

Kneeling beside her fallen foe, Ahsoka sifted through the wreckage of his lightsaber hilt. The crystals that had powered his lightsaber were no longer contained by metal, but their song had not dimmed. She held them in one hand, almost shaking as the familiarity of them coursed through her, while the other hand retrieved the half-finished hilts she carried with her.

These lightsabers wouldn't have the decorative handles she preferred, and her grip would be affected until she had time to truly finish them. She was missing a few key components, parts that had to be specifically made, but the creature's ruined hilt was before her. Quickly, she picked through the wreckage again, this time paying closer attention to the inner workings of the weapon, and smiled when she found what she needed. They would do for now.

Ahsoka could hear the Imperials approaching. Her duel had made them hesitate, but now they were on high alert. She pushed aside her sense of urgency, even though she was in a hurry. Meditation came easily, as if she were sitting in safety in the Jedi Temple itself, instead of a dusty street with her enemies closing in. Her mind's eye sorted the preassembled components and those she had just retrieved into order, locking each into place with the others. When Ahsoka opened her hands, she was not surprised to find that two lightsabers, rough and unfinished, were waiting.

They would need more work, but they were *hers*.

When she turned them on, they shone the brightest white.

◆ ◆ ◆

Ahsoka found another side street that went in the direction she wanted and followed it back toward the compound. She was the Imperials' only target now. She was going to need all the cover she could get. In her hands, her lightsabers were a reassuring weight. Her fight had given her back the focus she had lost. She wasn't even breathing hard. This was something she could do.

She didn't bother with taunts or banter. She had nothing to say to these people. She took the wall with a single flying leap and landed in the middle of the compound, much to the surprise of the stormtroopers on duty there. They began to fire, and she began to work her way toward the front door, easily deflecting their blaster bolts.

It took her only a few seconds to get there, her approach heralded by explosions and blaster fire, and then a few seconds more to cut the door open. Once she was in the corridor, she pushed the Force behind her, knocking everyone who pursued her off their feet. Ahead, she saw uniformed officers readying themselves to defend the inside of the compound. Apparently, all the stormtroopers were outside. She hoped they were too busy to think of calling in a Star Destroyer.

Ahsoka fought her way through the corridors, using her lightsabers to deflect blaster bolts and the Force to push her attackers out of the way. The cells were in the back of the building, she knew, and she wanted to waste as little time as she could getting to them.

Finally, she reached the prison hallway. There was a master door switch, which she activated, and the cell doors all opened. She checked to make sure there weren't any ray shields and then went down the hall.

"Kaeden?" she called out. "Are you here?"

In her cell, Kaeden's head snapped up and she scrambled to her feet. It was still difficult to balance with her arm, but the sound of Ahsoka's voice encouraged her. She walked forward.

A few hapless prisoners had emerged from their cells, blocking Kaeden's view down the corridor. Kaeden heard Ahsoka shouting orders at them to get out, to get to Selda's cantina as soon as they could, and she followed the crowd toward her friend.

At last, Kaeden was face to face with Ahsoka. She knew her hair was a disaster, she was covered in dirt, her head wound looked terrible, and her arm was still bound uselessly to her chest—but she was on her feet. Ahsoka looked different: powerful, focused, completely beyond Kaeden's comprehension. Ahsoka wielded a pair of bright white lightsabers, and even though it was Kaeden's first time seeing them, she couldn't imagine Ahsoka without them in her hands. Despite the circumstances, she smiled.

"Kaeden!" Ahsoka shouted, and ran to help her move faster.

"Ahsoka!" Kaeden ran toward her, but stopped short of throwing her good arm around Ahsoka's shoulder. She knew that lightsabers were not to be trifled with. She could almost feel the power pouring out of Ahsoka anyway. It was amazing. "I could kiss you."

Ahsoka stopped in her tracks. The look she shot Kaeden was mildly confused.

"Not now, I mean," Kaeden said. She wanted to laugh for the first time in weeks but thought that might just be the hysteria setting in. "My timing is terrible and you have all those Jedi hang-ups. I just wanted you to know in case we die."

"Oh," said Ahsoka. "Well, thanks." She paused. "And we are not going to die."

"If you say so," Kaeden agreed.

Ahsoka deactivated the lightsaber in her left hand and attached it to her belt. She kept hold of the right one. With one arm free, she supported Kaeden, and together they walked away from the cells.

29

"NOW WHAT?" ASKED KAEDEN. They were free of the Imperial compound, but there were stormtroopers all over the place. "I hope you have a plan!"

"Of course I have a plan," Ahsoka replied. "Selda's. Now."

She activated the communication device on her belt and hoped that Bail wasn't doing anything he couldn't get out of immediately. She was going to need him right away.

By the time they reached Selda's, Kaeden was entirely winded but still pushing forward. They went through the door, and before Ahsoka's eyes had adjusted to the lower light, she saw Miara's small form leaping toward them.

"Kaeden!" she said. "You're safe. You're safe!"

"Yes, more or less," Kaeden said. She let go of Ahsoka so she could wrap her good arm around her sister. "Are you okay?"

"It was a bad time after you were taken," Miara said. "I couldn't stay in the caves. Not with . . ."

She trailed off, and Ahsoka knew she was thinking about Neera and Kolvin and the others. She held her sister as tight as she could and looked back at Ahsoka.

Ahsoka could hear the sound of Imperial tanks moving in the streets. It was only a matter of time before they were found, or the Imperials decided to just destroy them all from orbit.

"You said you have a plan, Ahsoka?" Kaeden said. "I hope it's already started."

"It is." Selda came up beside them. Gently, he picked Kaeden up and set her down on the bar. Then he began to examine her injuries. "Ahsoka sent us a message with your sister. Vartan is out right now, organizing people for the evacuation."

"Evacuation?" Kaeden said. "Where? And with whom?"

"Some old friends of mine," Ahsoka said. "I used to have a

lot of friends. Most of them are dead now, but there are some who survived. And I make new ones."

"I didn't believe what that . . . thing said about that, you know," Kaeden replied. "You lied to keep us safe. He lied because he enjoys the suffering. I may not be a Jedi who's seen the whole galaxy, but I can tell the difference."

"Thanks," Ahsoka said. "And I haven't seen the whole galaxy. Though I have seen a lot more of it than most people."

"You can tell her all about it later," Selda said. "Right now we have to make sure your friends find us before the Imperials do."

"I don't know if I'm going to be able to walk much farther," Kaeden said. "I'm already feeling pretty woozy."

"I was saving this for a rainy day," Selda said. He reached under the bar and came up with a syringe. Kaeden flinched but then mastered herself.

"It doesn't rain much on Raada," she pointed out.

"I realized that almost immediately," Selda said. "So I guess now's as good a time as any. Look away, Kaeden."

Kaeden did as she was told, and Selda injected her. The difference was immediate.

"Is this going to wear off, or am I actually better?" she asked as Miara helped her down from the bar.

"A bit of both," Selda said. "So try not to overextend too much."

"I'll keep that in mind as we run from Imperial storm-troopers," Kaeden said.

Ahsoka cocked her head, listening, and smiled.

"I don't think we'll have to run very far," she said. "Come on, let's go."

They went out into the street to find ordered groups of people making their way toward the edge of town. Well, mostly ordered. Every explosion made them jump, and there was no shortage of screaming. But the farmers managed to hold themselves together, following the directions of their crew leads, who in turn were being directed by Vartan. He waved when he saw them, stark relief clear on his face. Ahsoka was glad to see he was all right.

The Imperial compound was in flames. Looking to the sky, Ahsoka could see six or eight A-wings, the advance fighters Bail had sent, diving and firing on the Imperials. A few of the Imperial fighters had managed to get into the air, and as Ahsoka watched, four A-wings broke off to deal with them. The others turned toward the fields, where they laid down row after row of fire. The fields burst into flames.

"I want to learn to do that!" Miara said, her face alight.

"I'm sure one of them will be happy to teach you," Ahsoka told her, remembering her impressions about Bail's success getting recruits. Then she remembered that she was talking to a fourteen-year-old. "In a couple of years, maybe."

One A-wing took too much damage from the Imperial fighter it was chasing and spun out of the sky. Its engines were a mess of fire and smoke, but Ahsoka was sure she saw the bright orange of the pilot's uniform ejecting, and a few seconds later, she saw a chute confirming it. A second A-wing wasn't so lucky. It rammed into the Imperial compound before its pilot could eject, and the explosion rocked the ground as they ran.

Miara's fervor dimmed a little bit as she took in the danger, but she still looked determined. Ahsoka didn't imagine that Bail would have any trouble at all recruiting her, once she was old enough. Just because Ahsoka fought her first war at Miara's age didn't mean it was a good example.

More ships appeared in low orbit, and for a second Ahsoka's heart was in her throat. Then she saw that they couldn't be Imperial. It was Bail, or rebels he had sent, with enough transports and cargo ships to evacuate everyone on the moon. They set down in the grass between the edge of the settlement and the hills where Ahsoka's friends had spent their time in hiding.

"Keep them moving!" Ahsoka shouted to Vartan. He nodded and passed the orders along.

Ahsoka led Kaeden, Selda, and Miara to the blockade runner she recognized as Captain Antilles's *Tantive IV*. He was standing at the bottom of the ramp, waiting for her.

"We can't stay on the ground for very long," he said, shouting over the sound of so many engines. "We're going to have Imperials on our tails too soon."

"It's okay!" Ahsoka shouted back. "The evacuation is already begun, and your A-wings took care of the Imperial fighters."

That reminded her of something. She pointed in the direction she'd seen the chute.

"You had a pilot go down over there," she said. "I'm sure they ejected in time. Can you pick them up?"

Antilles nodded to spare himself from shouting again and typed a command into the small datapad on his wrist.

"Let's get your friends on board," he said.

"I'll wait until the end," Ahsoka told him. "If I'm the only ground cover we have, then they're going to need me."

Kaeden couldn't have heard the exchange, but she somehow realized what Ahsoka was going to do.

"No!" she said, grabbing Ahsoka's arm with her good hand. "Come with us!"

"I have to stay for a bit longer," Ahsoka said. "This is how it works sometimes, Kaeden. I'll be okay. Go with your sister."

She shook Kaeden off and went back down the ramp. She spared one look back to make sure that Selda had shepherded the girls on board and then turned her attention back to the evacuation.

All things considered, it was going pretty well. There was a lot of fire, and more than a few of the farmers were panicking, but Vartan had been able to make sure they weren't carrying too many belongings, and the other crew leads moved up and down the lines, keeping everyone as calm as they could. As Ahsoka watched the rear, ship after ship filled, took off, and disappeared into the upper atmosphere.

There were only three ships, and fewer than a hundred people waiting to board them, when the Imperials made their final rally. Three tanks, all in pretty good condition, considering, rounded the corner and opened fire, dispersing the orderly lines of refugees.

Ahsoka didn't have any charges, but she did have a pair of lightsabers, so she engaged the tanks without a second thought. She ran toward them, which always seemed to startle

Imperials. It was like they thought themselves invulnerable and when you charged them, they started to have doubts. She jumped, flying over the leading tank in a graceful arc that let her reach out with a lightsaber and cut the tank's gun clean off. This rendered the tank useless. She opened the hatch, hauled the driver out, and tossed him aside. Then she used her light-saber to cut through the control panels, careful to leave the trigger for the main cannon operational. She wanted the tank to be as unsalvageable as possible. When she was sure she'd destroyed as much of it as she could in a hurry, she pressed the trigger from the safety of the hatch. Unable to properly discharge, the cannon overloaded as Ahsoka leapt clear.

As she hoped, the explosion was enough to destabilize another nearby tank, as well, causing the hover mechanism to malfunction. It listed sideways, and Ahsoka leapt on top of it, slicing off its gun, too. It crashed into one of the houses on the edge of town and stopped moving.

That left her with only one target. Vartan had managed to get the farmers moving again, and one of the last remaining ships had taken off. Whoever was driving the third tank was smarter than the others had been and targeted Vartan directly.

"No!" Ahsoka shouted as the ground where Vartan was standing erupted in a shower of dirt.

She brought her hands together, and metal screamed as the last remaining turret deformed, destroying the gun and bringing the tank to a halt. She jumped clear and raced to the spot where Vartan had been.

"Keep going!" she shouted as she passed people. "Get on board!"

They made it through the dust and debris. Vartan was alive, but he was badly injured. Ahsoka put both her lightsabers back on her belt and hoisted him over her shoulder. She staggered for a moment under his weight, then used the Force to stabilize herself. She joined the last line of farmers as they made their way toward Captain Antilles's ship and then followed them up the ramp.

Antilles was waiting for her in the hangar. Kaeden and Miara both screamed when they saw Vartan, and Selda had to hold them back.

"Get a medical stretcher!" Antilles shouted. "And get us out of here."

The buzz of people around her was overwhelming as Ahsoka lowered Vartan onto the medical stretcher and watched him be carried away. She felt the ship take off, fighting even the low gravity of the moon, until the engines kicked in fully and the ship broke free. She saw the fire and ruin of Raada below her and felt the wash of emotions from the farmers, now refugees, who crowded around her.

And she felt Kaeden. Her gratitude and relief at being rescued. Her joy to see her sister and her sadness to lose her home. Ahsoka put her arm around Kaeden's shoulder, mindful of her injuries, and couldn't help the smile that broke across her face. She had done it. It hadn't been easy, and almost nothing had gone to plan, but they were free of the Empire, for a little while anyway, and they were safe.

"You know," said Kaeden after a moment, "when you first got to Raada, I thought you'd fit right in. I hoped that you would stay."

"I've never been able to stay anywhere for very long," Ahsoka said. "Even . . . before, I moved around a lot."

"It was a silly thing to hope for," Kaeden admitted. "I knew that almost right away, too. I just didn't listen to myself."

"You listened to your feelings," Ahsoka said. She smiled at a memory of a faraway place and a time that was lost forever. "That's something they teach Jedi, too, you know."

"Well, at least we have that in common," Kaeden said. She put her head on Ahsoka's shoulder for a heartbeat and then straightened, shrugging free of Ahsoka's arm. "And I don't mind finding out that the galaxy's a big place. I think I can handle it now."

"I know you can," Ahsoka said.

They were silent for a moment as the refugees and ship's crew milled around them.

"Will we ever see you again?" Kaeden asked.

"I think it will be a while." Ahsoka was already thinking about what came next, her mind moving quickly as the engine hum grew louder. "But as you said, the galaxy's a big place."

"Thank you," said Kaeden as they made the jump to lightspeed.

"Anytime," said Ahsoka—and meant it completely.

30

THIS TIME, Ahsoka didn't break into Bail's office until she knew he was already there. She tracked his consular ship from Coruscant. He stopped on a nearby moon and dropped off a few crates that were not at all suspicious. Everything looked entirely routine, but Ahsoka, who had landed some distance away and infiltrated the spaceport while the cargo was being offloaded, knew better. She took advantage of the *Tantive III* being grounded to stow away on board.

Coming this far into the Core was a big risk, but she wanted to show Bail that she was serious and also grateful for everything he'd done for Kaeden and the others. At last, she felt the ship take off and the little shift that meant they were in hyperspace, and she set off looking for him.

She cracked the security on his door pretty easily and slipped inside. As on Captain Antilles's vessel, Bail's quarters on the *Tantive III* comprised more than two rooms. She was in the antechamber, which was big enough for two seats and not much else. She could hear the senator's voice coming from the second room, which must be where he worked. She got closer to the door and overheard the end of the conversation, a series of repeated words in a child's prattle that she couldn't understand. He had no idea how Bail did it—maybe listening to all the shouting in the Imperial Senate was good for something after all—but he managed to answer.

"I know, love, but it's more secure if we just talk without any visuals to trace." There was a pause. Ahsoka couldn't hear the answer. Then Bail spoke again. "Tell your mother I'll see you both soon enough."

There was another pause as Bail disconnected the call. Then he coughed.

"Do I have another Jedi break-in to report?" he called out.

Ahsoka laughed. It was nice to know she couldn't fool him the same way twice. She got the feeling he knew exactly how much she'd overheard and that some of it had been for her benefit.

"Showing your vulnerabilities to put me at ease, Senator?" Ahsoka said, stepping into the main office. He waved her into a seat, and she took it.

"The whole galaxy knows I'm a family man, Ahsoka Tano," he said. "The Empire is counting on it. They think it means I'll be more amenable to certain suggestions."

"Don't you worry about her?" Ahsoka asked.

Bail shrugged, but there was some tightness around his eyes. Running a rebellion couldn't be easy.

"She's already a lot like her mother," he said.

Somehow that seemed like a test. Ahsoka didn't know the answer, so she let it pass. They were going to keep secrets, and they were going to trust each other anyway.

"I wanted to talk to you about what you're doing to fight the Empire," Ahsoka said.

"I thought you might," Bail said. "Captain Antilles sent a glowing report. Only fifteen casualties during the Raada evacuation—one of his A-wing pilots and fourteen evacuees."

It had almost been fifteen evacuees, but Antilles's medical staff had been able to save Vartan. He and Selda were a matched pair now, the Togruta had joked, with four limbs and four prosthetics between them, but at least they were both alive. She'd left them on Captain Antilles's ship with Kaeden and Miara. They were all impressed by the capabilities of real medical technology. Kaeden's arm was almost as good as new, which freed up Miara to prowl the ship, looking for A-wing pilots to pester. When they found out how good she was at explosives, they took quite an interest in her.

"I'm glad it wasn't worse," Ahsoka said. "I took out that gray creature before my backup arrived. I got the impression he wasn't the only one of his kind."

"Was he talented?" Bail asked. "Or does he just carry the lightsaber for show?"

"He's had some training," Ahsoka said. "He mostly relies on brute strength. If he was going to be facing Jedi, or someone with my level of training, I'd say he wouldn't be much of a threat. I defeated him without my lightsabers. But the others like him won't be facing Jedi."

Bail nodded. "We'll do what we can," he said. "What about Raada?"

"Well, the farmers can't go back," Ahsoka said. She slumped down a little bit in her chair. They'd won, but the cost had been high. "If they tried, the Empire would wipe them off the moon's surface without even landing first."

"I can resettle them on Alderaan, perhaps," Bail said. "There aren't that many of them, and there are enough refugees in the galaxy right now that Alderaan's taking in a few hundred won't raise any eyebrows."

"They don't want to be resettled," Ahsoka said. She straightened her shoulders. "They want to join up."

She could see Bail considering it. She knew he could use the extra people, but there were some obvious downsides. The Empire had no trouble using poorly trained people as cannon fodder, but Bail would refuse to do the same.

"They're farmers, Ahsoka," he pointed out. "They have only the training you gave them."

"They're resourceful," she said. "And anyway, your rebels have to eat, don't they?"

Bail laughed.

"I'll have someone talk to them, and we'll see what we can do," he said. "There are a few planets that would suit us for an agricultural base, and we can start training anyone who is interested in piloting or weapons use."

They sat quietly for a moment, and then Bail leaned forward.

"They told me your new lightsabers are white," he said, and she heard awe in his voice. "May I see them?"

It was safe enough in Bail's office, surrounded by the void

of space. Ahsoka stood up and unclipped her lightsabers from her side. She activated them, and Bail's office was filled with a soft white light, gleaming off the windows and reflecting the stars. The office was much smaller than a training room, being shipboard, but she did a few of the basic forms for him anyway. She would never get tired of the way they glowed. She hadn't thought she'd ever replace her original blue ones, and she still had to finish the handles, but these were all right.

"They're beautiful, Ahsoka," he said.

She turned them off, bowed slightly, and sat back down.

"I've never seen white ones before," Bail mused.

"They used to be red," Ahsoka said. "When the creature had them, they were red. But I heard them before I ever saw him on Raada, and knew that they were meant for me."

"You changed their nature?" he asked.

"I restored them," Ahsoka replied. "I freed them. The red crystals were corrupted by the dark side when those who wielded them bent them to their will. They call it making the crystal bleed. That's why the blade is red."

"I had wondered about that," Bail said. "I spent a lot of time with the Jedi, but I never asked questions about where their lightsabers came from. I don't suppose they would have told me anyway."

"These feel familiar," Ahsoka said. "If I had to guess, I would say they were looted from the Jedi Temple itself."

"That raises some very uncomfortable possibilities," Bail said. "Not to mention a host of potential dangers for a Jedi Padawan."

"I'm not a Padawan anymore, Senator, and it's not safe to be Ahsoka Tano," she said. "Barriss Offee was wrong about a lot of things. She let her anger cloud her judgment and she tried to justify her actions without considering their wider effects. She was afraid of the war and she didn't trust people she should have listened to. But she had a point about the Republic and the Jedi. There was something wrong with them, and we were too locked into our traditions to see what it was. Barriss should have done something else. She shouldn't have killed anyone, and she definitely shouldn't have framed me for it, but if we'd listened to her—really listened—we might have been able to stop Palpatine before he took power."

"The Chancellor played his hand very well," Bail said. He spoke the word *chancellor* with some venom, and Ahsoka knew it gave him great satisfaction not to say *emperor* when they were in private. "He kept us so busy jumping at shadows that we didn't notice which of the shadows was real."

"I thought I was done with the war, but maybe I don't

know how to do anything else," Ahsoka said. "I tried to cut myself off, but I kept getting drawn back in."

Bail thought of Obi-Wan, sitting by himself on some Outer Rim world. His sacrifice was to take himself out of the way, to focus only on the future and not give any thought to the present. It would be a lonely way to live, even if it was peaceful, and Bail did not envy him at all.

"I think," he said carefully, "that you and I are meant to focus on the present."

"What do you mean?" Ahsoka asked.

"In this fight, there will be people like Barriss who are focused on the past," he said. "And there will be other people who focus strongly on the future. Neither of them is wrong, exactly, but even if we don't always walk the same path as one another, ours must be the middle road."

Ahsoka smiled.

"That's what I thought when I was trying to find the crystals that power my lightsabers," she told him. "I didn't want to be alone, but I didn't want to be a general or even a Padawan anymore. I want something in the middle of that, still useful but different than before."

The ship dropped out of hyperspace. They were still some

distance from the planet, but Bail liked to look out at the system when he was returning home.

"I was thinking about what I did on Raada," Ahsoka said. "At first it was hard, because no one would listen to me. You told me later that you were aware that something was going on but you couldn't step in. And I couldn't figure out how to communicate with them. They had different priorities, and because I couldn't explain myself, a lot of people died."

"That's not your fault," Bail told her.

"I know," she said. "But it feels kind of like it is."

He nodded. She suspected he was also good at blaming himself for things.

"Then it happened again when you sent Chardri Tage and Tamsin after me," Ahsoka said. "They didn't have enough information, and I didn't know the priorities. All I saw was a tractor beam and two strangers with blasters."

"Chardri is never going to forgive me for that," Bail admitted. "I slipped up."

"My point is, both of those things could have been avoided if you had better channels of communication," she said.

Bail sighed.

"I know," he said. "Everything I'm trying to build is too

new and too fragile. We're not as secure as I'd like us to be, and things slip through the cracks as a result."

"I can help you with that, I think," Ahsoka said.

"How?" Bail asked.

"During the Clone Wars, I worked with a lot of people," Ahsoka said. "I fought alongside clones, who took orders from me even though I lacked their experience. I watched politics on a dozen different worlds. I helped train people who'd never held a blaster in their lives. When I did all that, I had the Jedi to back me up, but I think I could do almost as good a job with you."

"You want to recruit people?" Bail asked.

"Not exactly," she said. "Though if I found good people, I would certainly try to bring them in. I want to take your recruits and find missions for them. I want to be the one who listens to what people need, who finds out what people can do and then helps them do it."

"You want to take over running my intelligence networks," he said.

"Who runs them now?" she asked.

"No one, really," he told her. "That's most of the problem."

"Then that's where I'll start," she said. "Can you give me a ship? I've lost mine."

"We can modify something for you easily enough," he said, a smile on his face. "I know just the droid for the job."

"Thank you," she said. "It's good to have a mission again."

"I think I'm going to end up a lot further in your debt than you are in mine, but you're welcome," he said.

"Let's just call us even and stop keeping track," she said. "I'm going to be busy enough as it is."

"What am I going to call you, if I can't call you Ahsoka?" he asked. "You'll need a code name at the least, so you can deal with other operatives."

They looked out the viewport as Alderaan grew bigger and bigger. It really was a beautiful planet, though Ahsoka would always miss the whispering grass on Raada. Alderaan was blue and green, and a good staging point for a galactic uprising. The center, where the thread of all their hopes connected.

"Fulcrum," she said. "You can call me Fulcrum."

"Then welcome to the Rebellion."

THE GRAND INQUISITOR *stood in the smoking fields that had once been the pride of the farming moon of Raada and glared at the ground. Everything was gone, burnt from the surface as though it had never been built in the first place. By the time the Imperial Star Destroyers had arrived to provide backup, everything had already been in flames and the last of the traitors had fled.*

The Grand Inquisitor kicked at some loose soil. At least the scum could never come back. The Empire would show no mercy if they tried.

The traitors were gone, the buildings were gone, the resources were gone, and the idiot who'd sent the Empire so far out in the first place was also gone. The Grand

Inquisitor wished he had been assigned the task of tracking down the man to exact Imperial revenge, but his talents were needed elsewhere.

The Jedi had done more than anyone expected. Not only had she trained the traitors to fight and helped one of them escape from jail—twice—she'd had the ability to call in a large number of ships to help her. The Grand Inquisitor would have dearly liked to have been assigned the task of tracking her down, but that had also gone to someone else.

He hadn't come to Raada to follow someone's trail. He had come to see someone's work. To learn what she was capable of when pushed. To see how far she could go, would go, for her goals. In spite of himself, he was impressed. He had never razed a whole moon, even if it was a tiny and pointless one. There was something to be said for that level of destruction.

Moreover, one of his own kind had died there. He'd found the body, burned almost beyond recognition, but the Grand Inquisitor knew what to look for. The other one had been bold, too bold it seemed. He had gone fearlessly after a Jedi and paid the price. The Grand Inquisitor would not be so reckless. He would channel his hate more usefully, be more measured. He, too, longed to kill his enemies, but he was not stupid. He knew the value of a good plan.

He turned and strode back to his ship. No one else had disembarked, and as he stalked through the corridor, his agents scattered out of his way. They were all afraid of him, which he liked rather a lot. They didn't know exactly what he was, only that he was implacable and cruel. His kind was new to the galaxy, a fresh weapon for the dark side to wield. His agents must follow his every order as though the Emperor himself had given it. That sort of power made him feel very strong.

"Set a course back to base," he said. He took his lightsaber off its mounting on his back and held the rounded handle almost lovingly. It wasn't the first one he'd ever carried, but it was the first he'd borne in service of his new master, and he liked the viciousness of the design.

"And inform Lord Vader that we have found evidence of another survivor."

ACKNOWLEDGMENTS

I first told Josh Adams, agent extraordinaire, that I wanted to write a *Star Wars* book on December 3, 2014, at approximately 9:03 AM (which is when I e-mailed him a really vague proposal). He called not ten minutes later, very excited, and has remained my staunchest supporter throughout.

Emily Meehan and Michael Siglain matched that early enthusiasm and never left me hanging while we waited for updates (which goes a long way to maintaining an author's sanity, I have to say).

MaryAnn Zissimos sent me that GIF of Mark Hamill with a cat when I needed it the most.

Jennifer Heddle is an editor I'd hoped to work with, AND I GOT TO. She is amazing. (My *Star Wars* spelling is terrible, you guys. I had to double-check "Hamill" just now. But Jen got me through all of that and even more, because: see above re: amazing.)

I can't believe I get to thank Pablo Hidalgo, Dave Filoni, and the rest of the Lucasfilm Story Group, but here we all are. They know so much, and they take everything so seriously, and that is just so great. Also, I made them laugh! Twice! (Sorry about that thing with the [redacted for spoilers].)

Finally, I need to thank all the people I COULDN'T tell about this book: Emma, Colleen, Faith, and Laura, who usually read everything I write; Friend-Rachel and Cécile, who I flat out ignored for most of March because I couldn't take it anymore (we'll talk about *Rebels* when I've calmed down, I promise!); my whole family (though I think I could have told my dad everything and he STILL would have thought I was talking about *Star Trek*); but most important, my brother EJ, who got me into this mess in the first place.

Read on for a look at E. K. Johnston's second

Star Wars novel, the *New York Times* best-seller

QUEEN'S
SHADOW

CHAPTER 1

Padmé Amidala was completely still. The brown halo of her hair spread out around her, softened here and there by white blossoms that had blown through the air to find their rest amongst her curls. Her skin was pale and perfect. Her face was peaceful. Her eyes were closed and her hands were clasped across her stomach as she floated. Naboo carried on without her.

Even now, at the end, she was watched.

It was no more than was to be expected. Ever since she'd entered the arena of planetary politics, her audience had been unceasing. First they had commented on her interests and ideals, then later on her election to queen. Many had doubted her strength in the face of an invasion, when the lives and well-being of her people would be held ransom against her—hers to save if only she would give up her signature—and she had proven them all wrong. She had ruled well. She had grown in wisdom and experience, and had done both rapidly. She had faced the trials of her position unflinching and unafraid. And now, her time was ended.

A small disturbance, the barest movement through the

otherwise peaceful water, was Padmé's only warning before her attacker struck.

An arm wrapped around her waist, pulling her down into the clear shallows, holding her there just long enough to let her know that she had been bested.

The Queen of Naboo surfaced, sputtering water in the sunlight as her handmaidens—her friends—laughed around her. Yané and Saché, who had suffered for their planet during the Occupation. Eirtaé and Rabé, who had helped make sure their suffering meant something. Sabé, who took the most frequent risks and was the most beloved. Together—young and seemingly carefree—they were a force that was often underestimated. No matter how many times they were proven able, people who looked at them were blinded by their youth and by their clothing, and dismissed them yet again. That was exactly how they preferred it.

The lake country was renowned for its privacy. Here, even the queen could go unnoticed, or at least be easily overlooked. Naboo's natural heritage was to be protected and treasured, even before new treaties with the Gungans had been signed, and this had reinforced the isolation of the lakes in the region. The bustle of the capital was far away, and Padmé could have, for however small a moment, some time to herself. Well, to herself, her handmaidens, the guards Captain Panaka deemed appropriate, and all the household staff. Solitude, it turned out, was somewhat relative.

From the beach, Quarsh Panaka watched his charges frolic in the sun with an all-too-familiar expression on his face. He had argued to bring ten of his people down to the water's edge with him, and Padmé had conceded. Eventually. This give-and-take had once been his custom when it came to dealings with the queen—even if their relationship had grown colder and more formal of late. He was a professional, so he stood there and glowered, knowing that today of all days, his interference would not be welcomed.

"You let me do that," Saché said. The youngest handmaiden wore a swimming suit cut in the same style as the rest of them, but where the others bared skin to the sun, she bared a large collection of mottled scars that wrapped around her arms, legs, and neck. Yané paddled next to her and ran her fingers through Saché's hair.

"I couldn't have stopped you," Padmé said. She shook her head, shedding drops of water—and the last few blossoms. Waist-deep in the shining lake and speaking in her own voice, she might have been mistaken for a normal girl, but even now there was something about her bearing that hinted at more. "Though I could have cried out and got a mouthful of lake water for my trouble."

"And Captain Panaka would have felt honor bound to rescue you." Sabé said it in Amidala's voice, and Saché and Yané both straightened out of reflex before Yané sent a wave of water toward the older girl as repayment. Sabé merely swept a flower from her cheek as it landed on her, and continued to float, unbothered by the ruckus. "So really, you were preserving the dignity of many, not to mention a fine pair of boots."

Unbothered, but not unaware, Sabé spoke loudly enough to be heard by all those who were swimming, as well as several of the guards, who did little to conceal their amusement.

"You have aged me prematurely, my ladies," Panaka said. There was a hint of warmth in his tone, but the uncrossable distance remained. "My wife will hardly recognize me when I go home."

"Your wife has no such problem," said Mariek Panaka from her position three paces away from him. She was not in uniform, because she had been in swimming with the queen. She was wrapped in a bright orange sarong that made her brown skin glow in the late morning sun, and her dark hair dripped down her back while the rest of her dried.

"Well," said Padmé, wading toward the shore with Sabé, as always, in her wake. "Soon we will all be able to rest."

And there it was: the veermok in the room addressed at last. Because the end was coming, and neither the beauty of Naboo's lake country nor the best of company could stop it. When the election was over and the new ruler of Naboo was announced, Padmé Amidala would be in search of a new task or calling or profession, and so would most of those in her service. Some, like Panaka, looked forward to retirement, as much as anyone on Naboo ever retired. Padmé guessed

Panaka had received several job offers, but they were past the stage where they discussed such personal matters, now. The younger ones, like Eirtaé and Saché, sought the future on their own terms. Musicians, doctors, parents, farmers, and all combinations thereof—it was a time for dreams. Change was coming, and it was coming fast. No one, not even Sabé, had dared to ask the queen about her plans.

Rabé stood up and followed the queen. Eirtaé dove down one more time—a sort of farewell—and then joined the others as they gathered themselves and left the water, too. They didn't have to, not with so many guards and Sabé besides, but they would always choose the queen when they could, and soon, they would no longer be able to.

Away from the lake house, Naboo was voting. The gears of democracy were well oiled, and centuries of tradition made the biennial event run smoothly, even with the inclusion of Gungan voters for only the second time in the planet's history. Though few of them chose to vote, Padmé knew her efforts to include them were appreciated because Boss Nass had told her as much. Loudly. Naboo was not quite as united as she might have liked it to be at the end of her four years of service to it, but the people were happy with what she had done.

Almost too happy, it turned out. A faction had tried to amend the constitution so that Padmé could run again. This had been tried only once before, during a time of great upheaval in Naboo's past, and Padmé could see no reason to fight for something she neither wanted nor believed was right. She had given four years to Naboo, and now it was time for someone else's vision, someone else's hands, to select the course. That was the soul of Naboo's democratic body, that change and service in short stretches were better than stagnant rulership, and Padmé was happy to play all the parts her role included.

"You weren't even tempted?" Sabé had asked when the messenger had come with the amendment for Padmé to read and she had returned it unsigned after the barest of glances. It was the closest they had yet come to discussion of the future.

"Of course I was tempted," Padmé had replied. She settled back in her seat, and Sabé resumed brushing her hair. "I thought of at least ten more things I could do with another term while I was reading the proposal. But that's not how our legacies work. Not here. We serve and we allow others to serve."

Sabé had said nothing more.

Now, wrapped in vivid sarongs on the beach, they retrieved their sandals and followed the guards up toward the house. When they reached the grassy hill at the base of the wide stone stairs, Padmé stopped to brush off her feet. They all halted with her.

"Sand," she said, by way of explanation.

"I'm sure the housekeeping droids appreciate your efforts, Your Highness," Eirtaé said. Her face was handmaiden-straight, so only a few people got the joke.

The steps weren't very steep on this side of the house. The port—for water vessels in this case; there wasn't really a place to land an airship—was on the other side of the estate, and those steps were cut straight into the spur on which the house was set. This way had been purposely constructed as a path to the water, and therefore it was both more beautiful and more leisurely an ascent. Padmé and Mariek led the way up, with Panaka behind them and the rest of the handmaidens and guards strung along like so many ducklings.

Sabé had paused at the bottom to fasten her sandals. Padmé saw her grimace slightly when she realized that there was, in fact, still sand between her toes. Sabé shook her shoes as clear as she could and then began to climb at an almost leisurely pace. Sabé didn't often allow her mind to wander when she was with the queen, but here and now, with so little at stake and peaceful change rapidly approaching, Padmé was happy to see her relax as Sergeant Tonra fell into step beside her. He was somewhat taller than Panaka, with white skin that was usually pale, though two weeks in the sun had reddened his face significantly. He had come down the steps just as Padmé had decided to return to the house but was not the least bit winded by his exertions.

"There are several messages for Her Highness." He spoke quietly to Sabé, but Padmé still overheard him. "None of them are urgent, but one is official and will require the queen to open it herself."

"Thank you, Sergeant," Sabé replied, ever competent. "We'll get to them presently."

Tonra nodded but did not fall back. Padmé expected Sabé to bristle, as she usually did if she thought someone meant to guard her person, even though she granted more leniency to those who had fought in the Battle of Naboo, as Tonra had. Sabé was as protective of her own privacy as Padmé was of hers—albeit for different reasons. Perhaps, Padmé decided, Sabé was finally allowing herself to appreciate the view.

The lake spread out as they climbed, its water reflecting the sky with such perfection that, but for a few waves, it was possible to convince oneself that sky and water had been somehow reversed. The green hills that rose up from the shore also descended down into the depths, and what few puffy clouds skirted the blue above were mirrored exactly in the blue below. It was as though two bowls were pressed against each other, their rims forming the treed horizon. There was no sign of human habitation jutting out from between the trees, except for the house they were climbing toward, and the sky above them was never dotted with ships or flying recorder droids or anything else that might puncture the quiet with unwanted noise.

The house itself was made of yellow rock, and roofed in red, with copper-green domes. There were several sections, each with its own purpose ranging from habitation to cooking, all linked by a series of elaborate gardens. The property belonged to the government, and Padmé had used it as a retreat for much of her career, beginning back when she was first in the junior legislative program as a child. She didn't own any part of it, but she had influenced the layout and décor in subtle ways so that there was no doubting that it was a place she dearly loved. It was an oasis, a haven. Padmé had always come here to relax, and even though this was, in theory, the most relaxing visit she had ever taken here, it was obvious to all who saw her that she could not quite quiet her mind.

The queen had arrived two weeks earlier for the customary seclusion during the final campaign, and today was the election at last. Padmé was officially neutral with regard to her successor, though she had of course done her civic duty and cast a vote. A droid had departed with all of their ballots early in the day, but they hadn't spoken of politics more than absolutely necessary since their arrival, and not at all since that morning. Padmé had run unopposed in her second term, though there had been a few write-in candidates, as there always were. This was the first time she had been this uninvolved in her planet's politics since she began her studies. She liked it—and also found it deeply unsettling in a way she couldn't quite explain.

Padmé had hoped the exertion of swimming would help. The distance to the island was something she hadn't attempted in several months, though her handmaidens were always game to try. She'd thought the swim would at least tire her out too much to think. Instead, her thoughts had only reordered themselves. Even Saché's dunking hadn't helped.

She had a great deal to think about. Who was she, after all, when she was not Queen of Naboo? She had entered politics so early and with such zeal that she had no other identity. She had taken five handmaidens with her, and each of them had been shaped by their roles, as well, to the point where they had all taken names in her honor after she was elected. Who were they, when they were allowed to be themselves? Everyone knew that Rabé dreamed of music, while Yané dreamed of a house full of children that Saché would also call home, and so on and so on with each of the others, but it was more challenging for Padmé to see herself in any of their futures. Would they have room in their lives for Padmé when Amidala no longer held them as queen? And who would she be, even if they did?

"You're going to trip if you don't stop daydreaming," Mariek said beside the queen on the steps. "And won't that be just the way for you to end your reign, falling up the stairs because you were thinking too hard about things that are no longer yours to think about."

"I can't help it," Padmé admitted. She never could. "But you're right. I'll wait until I'm alone before I let myself drift that far."

"You'll never be alone, my lady," Mariek said. "And I don't mean all of this production, either." She gestured vaguely at the queen's retinue and smiled widely. "It will be different, but you will be different, too, and you're smart enough to figure it out."

"Thank you," Padmé said. "It's strange to want two things that are entirely different from one another. I am ready to stop, but I also feel like I could have done more."

"I know," Mariek said. "That's why I wrote you in, anyway."

"That's a spoiled ballot!" Padmé protested, stopping dead in her tracks. Everyone below them on the steps halted, too, and looked up to see what had caused the queen to stop walking. "And you're not supposed to tell me who you voted for."

Mariek began to laugh, and Quarsh stepped up to take his wife's arm.

"Don't tease the queen, love. I know from personal experience that she has her ways of making you pay for it, and even if she's pressed for time, I have absolute faith in her abilities." For just a moment, he was her captain again, the one who had trained them all so well before preparedness had turned to paranoia. Padmé missed him dreadfully.

Mariek laughed harder.

"My lady?" Panaka offered his other arm. "I know you don't need it, but I am happiest when I know you have my support."

"Of course, Captain," Padmé said rather formally. She took his arm and began to climb again. "Since I am so near the end of my term as queen, it behooves me to show measured judgment in all things."

"You have always done so, my lady, even when we disagreed," Panaka said. It was almost a peace offering. "That's why I wrote you in, too."

The Queen of Naboo laughed in the sunlight as she reached the house with her companions and her guards. The watergate stood thrown open, for this was a place of peace and reflection, and had never needed defending from a hostile force. Before them was the quiet courtyard and sun-drenched gardens where they would wait to hear the news, and behind them was the world that voted on the shape that news would take. Queen Amidala entered the house as the ruler of a planet, one last time.